Awakening

APHRODITE

Awakening

APHRODITE

CHRISTINE LISTER

Cover Image: Aphrodite by Emma Wiseman
www.emmawisephotography.com.au

Cover design and typesetting by Luke Harris
www.workingtype.com.au

Published in Australia by Australian Inspiration 2022
www.australianinspiration.com.au

ISBN: 978-0-6453926-0-9

Contents

CONTENTS

The woman who returns to the instinctual and creative nature will come back to life. She will want to play. She will still want to grow, both wide and deep. But first, there has to be a cleansing.
Clarissa Pinkola Estés, Women Who Run With the Wolves: Myths and stories of the wild woman archetype

What a woman desires above all else is the power of sovereignty, the right to exercise her own free will.
Ethel Johnson Phelps, Gawain and Lady Ragnell

PART ONE

SEASONS OF THE SOUL

The wound is the place where the light enters you.

Rumi

Preface

Aphrodite is still with me. I awake early and lie abed, lost in a reverie. Last night's magical night tour of the Louvre Museum is still indelibly etched in my mind, especially the highlight — a succession of the sublime. A series of paintings, frescoes, sculptures and statues of women — women embodying femininity, power and freedom. Women as goddesses.

I close my eyes, and I am there, once more. The *Venus de Milo*, in all her glory, rises up in front of me. Like gravity, the goddess pulls me towards her. I inhale deeply, drinking her in. With her delicate features and elegant curves, she gazes serenely ahead, her expression peaceful. Raised on her divine pedestal, this beautiful muse is a force of nature. I want to fall at her feet, to worship her.

This enchanting figure, representing the Greek goddess Aphrodite, touches my soul. The Goddess of Love Beauty and Desire, the essence of feminine beauty, grace, and sensual vitality, a symbol of personal power and freedom — freedom of the soul. The epitome of a woman. The kind of woman I want to be.

I gaze at this magnificent marble woman again, and I am enraptured. Then an epiphany. This divine goddess is calling me, inviting me into her temple of love. A priestess in the Temple of Aphrodite?

I open my eyes, smile and stretch languorously, and then a heartfelt, "Yes! Yes! Let the quest begin!"

1. Letting Go

SIX MONTHS EARLIER...

My eyes roam restlessly around Eirene's study searching for a sign. I look down and see that my fingers are drumming on my thighs, betraying the nervousness I feel.

"Be still my beating heart. Breathe," I command. "Trust in the Universe. William will be here. He always is." I clasp my hands together in my lap, close my eyes and take a deep breath.

"Good to see you again. How long is it since your last reading, Sweet?" asks Eirene, as she sits opposite me. My eyes open with a start. She looks so ordinary, yet she is anything but. *Spiritual medium and clairvoyant with over thirty years' experience* claims her card, with blue eyes imprinted on it. Those blue eyes now gaze at me from under pencilled brows.

"A year ago," I say, my voice quavering a little. Last spring. I come each year in spring. Eirene hands me the deck of cards.

"Shuffle the cards." Awkwardly I do as she asks, then hand them back. Eirene fans them across the table with the flair of a casino dealer.

"Choose five." I choose those hidden under layers, like those thoughts that lie hidden in me. I believe Tarot cards reveal the divine law of the Universe, that they contain the secrets of the human heart. As I hand them to her, she says, "There is a very strong emotional energy around you today, Sweet. Let's see why." She lays the cards out one by one, face up.

"He's showing me his grave. I can see red — red trees, red flowers. Do you know where this is?" asks Eirene in her husky smoker's voice. I nod.

As I stare out the window behind Eirene, I picture my garden. I can see red too. I am sitting on the window seat in the living room, my favorite place in the house. The big picture window frames three red Dogwood trees — silent sentinels. I planted them when William was diagnosed with melanoma. Underneath I'd scattered red Flanders poppy seeds, trusting in the secret language of color and the healing power of nature to overcome this threat to my world. Echoing his red hair, they were a symbol of our love, our passion and the color of our lives.

"Yes, it's in my garden."

"He's showing me something under the tree. He's disturbed by it," Eirene says as she turns over another card. My heart starts palpitating wildly. William is here again, and he has something he wants to say to me.

Both our wills had specified that our ashes be scattered in the garden. It seemed a natural thing to do. We'd married in the garden. Our home and our lives were embedded there. A month after William had died, I'd invited family and friends over to scatter the ashes, but I'd changed my mind.

"A woman's prerogative," his dear friend David had said, "and William is not here to argue with you."

"I beg to differ," I'd replied then and smiled, showing them his urn nestling at the foot of the Dogwood trees.

"It's the urn with William's ashes," I now say out loud to Eirene, "I couldn't spread them, I couldn't let go of him. I told William he would have to wait for me. When I died our ashes would be scattered together."

Tears gathered. Here I was, seven years later desperately hoping William would make his presence felt once more. My hands edged around the seat of the chair seeking something solid to hold on to.

⁂

Grieving takes time. It's a sacred rite of passage and as individual as a fingerprint. William and I were paradise ducks, mating for life. Our life was like a fairy story. Under his aegis, I flourished, my career flourished. So too the garden. We were healthy, energetic, engaged and totally immersed in living our happily ever after day after day. Until the cancer intervened.

Now that he was no longer here, the past loomed again, malevolent. I felt unsafe, riddled with inexplicable fears. Everything seemed uglier. I felt so utterly alone – bereft. The overwhelming sense of loss of my husband, lover, best friend and soulmate was compounded by my loss of identity.

Who was I? Who will I be now?

You don't think you can go on, and yet you do. Like walking, one foot after the other, one day after another, and somehow the focus moves from dying to living. I'd grounded myself in Mother Earth and nature, paying attention to the cycles of the moon and the seasons, the plants and animals in the garden, feeling the Earth's slow rhythms, honoring my own natural rhythms and inner voice and allowing the spirituality around me to seep into my soul.

॰॰

Now, here I was, with Eirene again. Another spring, hoping that being near William would bring some comfort.

"William's asking you to let him go. He can't wait for you," said Eirene rousing me from my reverie. "It's too long. You're going to be around for a long time, Sweet. He's saying, you have to let him go."

Tears welled. "I will, Sweetheart. Soon."

"Another card," says Eirene. I pick up another and hand it to her. *The Fool.*

"A new man is coming into your life. He is intelligent, learned, creative and kind. You will commit to him and you will move from where you are living, possibly overseas. Travel is coming back into your life."

My ears prick up. My hands massage one another nervously. Another man. My dream man. Could this be true? "How long before I meet him?"

"Within the next year. Another card." I hand it to her.

"I see a young man, Sweet. He cares for you. Do you know who this is?"

"Yes. My nephew. We are very close."

"I can see a bridge, a pond and water lilies. Do you know where this is?"

"No," I say, disappointed. Eirene holds her hand out for another card. I unearth one hidden from view.

"You will see it within the next year. A man is linked with this bridge. There is a lot of good energy coming into your life. Time to leave the sadness behind, Sweet."

2. Endings and Beginnings

Yesterday was spring. Today is summer. Endings and beginnings. Life inhales then exhales.

Looking out from the window seat, my window to the world, I sip coffee watching entranced as the wind dislodges the final Dogwood blossoms. They float off the branches like red snowflakes, falling softly to the ground below, settling like a mantle over the urn with William's ashes. A poignant reminder of what was, slowly being buried there, too. All that remains is an aching loneliness and a desperate longing to be held, to be touched, to be loved, which, all too often is assuaged by a pervading numbness and the feeling of living in a nether world.

As the breeze stirs, more blossoms drift off. The four petals of each blossom form a cross; the centre of each blossom like a crown of thorns. In their place, already forming, are tiny red berries. Life after death. I sigh. I know I have to let William go, but not just yet. First, I know I need to free the woman trapped there, too. I sit here day after day watching the world go by, but I no longer see, and am blind to my true nature. A woman living her life in the shadows, hiding beneath the layers of life. The real me is hidden from the world at large and, worse, hidden even from myself. The bird feeder sways gently in the breeze. A lone gold finch comes to visit. His feathers already bright yellow. A welcome sign that warmer weather is on the way.

∂

The front door bell rings. Kiki races to the door, her tail wagging expectantly. A familiar face peers through the frosted glass door as I open it.

"Cindy, my dear, welcome. How lovely to see you again!"

"Darling! Mwah. Mwah," she mouths loudly close to my face, but preserving her lipstick. "It's lovely to see you, too. Look at you!" We hug, then step back to look each other up and down. Still holding on to her hands, my eyes drink her in. She is like nectar. Big, brown smiling eyes are framed by long luscious, fake eye lashes. Her generous mouth, painted in the deep red she loves, smiles back at me, the laugh lines in evidence. Her hair is stylish and short: a brown bob with light layering. Although she seems a little fuller than the last time we met, she looks radiant and is as expensively dressed as always. Black patent leather heels and matching clutch, a black pencil skirt that hugs her gorgeous behind and a string of baroque pearls hanging over a shimmering silver-grey top. Fabulously dressed, leaving me in awe.

"You're looking as wonderful as ever, my dear," I tell her. Cindy looks me over briefly, without comment. In my shorts, old grey T-shirt and flats, hair down loose, I feel anything but wonderful beside her.

"Not as wonderful as I would like, Darling. I've added a few pounds since Brian died – bless his soul – but Fernando, my personal trainer is something of a god. He's sorting me out now. Giving my behind a real workout." She winks and shimmies through the kitchen, smart suitcase in tow.

"There's a nice bottle of Cab Sav open," I call after her.

"You know me too well, Darling," she replies. She helps herself to a drink, freshens up in the bathroom, then joins me in the conservatory.

"It's so good to have you here. We haven't lived on the same coast since we were toddlers. You do know that you are my favorite cousin," I say.

"I'm your only one, you cheeky thing," she says before becoming serious. "We've got a whole lot of talking to do before the others come."

"Let's start with you, Cindy, how are you doing?"

"Fine, I'm fine. Really, I am!" she says. "I've lost three husbands now. I loved them all. Sometimes I wonder if I am cursed." Cindy holds a hand to her throat, swallowing hard. "I didn't even know Brian had a heart condition. Just as well he didn't die on the job. I would have been mortified. Just as I am when I hear the vicious gossip suggesting I offed them all. The only consolation is I'm as rich as Cleopatra." A tear forms. She blinks it away, looks down and takes another large sip.

Not the only consolation. I look at Cindy with admiration. She's a very attractive, willowy brunette. Hard to believe she's sixty. Just a year older than me. Deep in thought, Cindy strokes her face unconsciously as she often does when her thoughts are far away. She looks up and smiles, a smile tinged with sadness, yet inviting my confidence, strong enough to bear my sadness too.

"It was seven years yesterday. William has asked me to let him go, Cindy. I think that was his way of saying it's time for me to move on. And it is. I've determined it's time to open up my world and stop living as if I'm looking in the rear vision mirror."

"Good on you. Merry widows, that's what we're going to be." Cindy reaches forward to chink my glass, her smile wide and radiant. I respond in kind. "You first, Eve. Let's find your new man. I need a break from husbanding. I'm not ready to start dating again yet. You'll be my special project. Why don't I look at planning a trip to Europe for us in the fall? And you should try online dating. Have a look at some dating sites? I met Brian online."

I listened as Cindy spoke, thinking maybe that the time has come. I saw an ad on TV the other day for such a site. A man and a woman looking pensive. At the end they were strolling on the beach hand in hand. A little laugh escapes. Maybe...

"Be prepared though," Cindy continues, waking me from my daydream. "You may have to kiss a few frogs before you meet your prince. A hundred maybe!"

"Frogs! Yuk! I hate frogs! I can't bear to touch them, or even worse have one touch me or kiss me. No way, could I kiss a hundred of the slimy creatures, but I'll have a look. And a trip to Europe sounds wonderful. I haven't been overseas since William died."

3. William and Eve

The doorbell rings again. Kiki leaps off the chair and runs to the door, with me in tow again. Our usual doorbell routine.

"Okay. Okay. Calm down so I can let them in." I open up the door to see two familiar red-heads. My beloved niece and nephew.

"She remembers us," says Rachel, giving Kiki a face rub.

"Of course, she remembers you. It's wonderful to have you here. I always forget how striking you both are. Come on in." Richard bends down and picks up Kiki who licks his face with gusto. He holds her out to Rachel who ruffles her face.

"I've missed you, Kiki," said Rachel. Twins, close in heart and mind, but apart from the red hair and green eyes, physically and emotionally you would never know. Richard towers over his sister. Ruggedly handsome with his curly hair cropped short and dimples almost always on show, he has a commanding presence. He looks up at me and smiles, his intelligent eyes taking me in, talking to me.

"Hello, Eve. It's good to see you again, and Kiki." Richard's deep voice undercuts the gentleness inside him.

I smile back. "And it's fabulous to see you. I'd say you've grown, but not likely. Outwards in the arms, maybe."

"Ah, you know. Always working out." He flexes a bicep and laughs.

My eyes turn to Rachel, a foot shorter. The figure hugging, low-cut burgundy dress shows off her curves to perfection. Long hair frames a face with a flawless ivory complexion. She senses me watching her. Her green eyes bore into me. Wearing precious little makeup, there is an ethereal beauty about her, the pale pink pouting lips, the only hint of the feisty, fiery temperament within.

"Come here," I say opening my arms." Rachel comes to me. We hug, holding each other close. "I've missed you," I say, choking up.

"And I've missed you. I miss Uncle William, too. I miss all the good times we had," says Rachel with a catch in her voice. Richard comes closer to us.

"Can I join in please, ladies?" Our arms reach out around Richard to form a tight knit circle. "Thanks for inviting us," says Richard.

"David and Susan are upstairs. They flew in from Spokane earlier. Cindy's in the kitchen. She's a dear. Our self-appointed chef has arranged dinner so I can just enjoy you being here with me again."

⁂

An hour later we're in the living room, nibbling on Cindy's offerings. Crab bites, prosciutto and melon and Charleston cheese dip. Kiki lies between the twins, her head resting on Rachel's lap, sensing where she is needed most. Rachel's hand strokes her gently, unconsciously. David stands up, reaches into the ice bucket and brings out a bottle of Veuve Clicquot. Opening it, he pours everyone a glass.

"Susan and I first tasted this at Eve and William's wedding. And it's the same toast I propose today — to Eve and William, a wonderful day and a wonderful couple."

"Cheers. To Eve and William." We chorus and chink glasses. I breathe in.

"Some other special guests are staying here, too," I say. "It's some time since you've seen them, but I'm sure you'll remember them. Come upstairs." I walk upstairs to my bedroom and throw open the window overlooking the pond. Everyone crowds around the window seat. Two red-throated loons are swimming in the water, side by side. Two loons flew out of the woodlands on the day William died. They'd never been seen in the area before, but they settled in and around the pond and stayed for four days. The day after William's funeral they flew away. Now, seven years later, they're back again.

"Oh my!" says Susan, sitting down on the bed, mouth agape, speechless. The loons call to each other.

"Doesn't their call have a special name, Eve?" asks Rachel.

"Yes," I reply, "the plesiosaur duet. It's magical, isn't it?"

David pushes through, "When did they arrive?"

"Yesterday, on the anniversary of Williams passing."

"How fitting. On the day you finally scattered the ashes," says David, smiling warmly.

I shrug my shoulders and grimace at Susan. "No, I changed my mind again." David looks at me shocked. "I'm just not ready yet."

"Seven years and you're still not ready," says David in amazement.

Richard places a protective arm around me, his giant hand gently strokes the middle of my back. "Maybe William is trying to tell you something, Eve."

"Yes, he is, isn't he? He sent his winged messengers this time. He's back to his curmudgeonly ways, trying to hurry me up. Hanging around makes him cranky." I feel the room swell with pressure like the vacuum in the jars on my back during cupping therapy. I shrug back the tears.

"More champagne methinks," interjects Cindy. "This way, please," she says, shepherding us back downstairs to the living room. Cindy refills our glasses, then offers around the canapés, before sitting down on the sofa between Rachel and me. The men remain standing.

"How's work, Richard?" asks David, steering the conversation elsewhere.

"Plenty of it," says Richard, his voice booming, picking up the cue. "The company is doing well, but Dad's starting to struggle. He's ageing."

"It happens to us all," says David, patting his balding head.

Richard continues, keen to say his piece, "Dad's out of his depth with the new technologies."

"That makes two of us," said David, "I'll have to retire soon."

"The biggest problem is he won't listen," said Richard exasperatedly.

"You can say that again," says Rachel, sitting back, crossing her slim legs.

"People won't put up with his style of management these days, no matter how rich and powerful you are," Cindy chimes in.

Richard leans forward, "We don't tell him all that is going on. It's easier that way."

"How's your practice going, Rachel?" asks Susan, keen to move away from the touchy topic.

"Really well! It's picked up this year, which is ironic given I'm a psychotherapist who specializes in relationship counselling and am newly divorced from a bastard, cheating husband." Cindy and Susan grimace. Another topic no one wanted to mention was raised by the one person we were tip-toeing around.

Richard cuts in to avoid embarrassment. "Eve, tell us how you and Uncle William met, including all the juicy bits. Sis and I are thirty-three, old enough to know about such things."

"They never told Susan and me the dirty details either," says David with a twinkle in his brown eyes, "and we are just past the age of consent." He winks at me. I look over at Susan and David, now in their mid-fifties. Still a good looking brunette, Susan's hardly aged. Her smile a warm embrace. David is balding, his waistline thickening but the grin on his face still speaks of youthful vitality. We've been friends for twenty-five years.

I take a sip of champagne, gaze longingly at Richard and Rachel, then at the Dogwood trees and start back in time. "I met William in London playing in a squash final. I was twenty-nine. He was thirty-three, the same age you twins are now. We were both working in Fleet Street and I was doing some guest lecturing in journalism at Goldsmiths, at the University of London as well.

William had never married. Rumour had it he left behind a trail of broken hearts wherever he worked. I had fled to London after my first marriage broke up, hating all men and with a steely resolve never to marry again."

"My sentiments exactly," interposes Rachel. I laugh.

"William and I were on opposing teams. My team was trounced. After the match, he asked if I'd like to play on his team." I close my eyes for a moment and I see the cheeky grin on his face.

"Perhaps you'd like to be part of a winning team for a change," he had said. And I did. I knew he liked me and liked playing with me, but he sensed my reserve and kept his distance. We often had a drink in the pub after a match, but he was always a proper gentleman. Can you believe that?"

"No," they all chorused.

"A year later when we both returned home, William to New York and me to New Jersey, we continued to play squash. One hot summer's night, after winning another championship, I invited the team home to celebrate. One by one they left. At four in the morning, William and I were sitting on the living room floor looking at each other, when William leant over and kissed me, gently at first, then passionately. It was the longest, most beautiful kiss ever. And the beginning of our passionate love affair."

I cupped the champagne with both hands and felt my wedding ring make a soft tinkle of on the glass. "For six months, William kept proposing and I kept saying no, thinking it safer to do so. But he became progressively more disheartened, sadder. I felt he was going to give up on me. That's when I realized I couldn't bear the thought of losing him, so, I proposed to him."

"I didn't know that," says Cindy surprised.

"Well, a girl's got to keep some secrets," I say. "You know what they say about forward women. Anyway, we married a month later. He didn't want to give me a chance to change my mind. All of you were here. And your mom, too, kids." I look over to Richard and Rachel. "You were nine."

"I remember, especially the food, my favorite treat, hot dogs, with onions and relish. I had four of them," said Richard, "and a big bellyache afterwards."

"William and food went hand in hand," said Susan. "And so did music. It didn't matter if you came here, went out to dinner, or went on a holiday, the planning for the day revolved around food and music."

"And such awful bloody music too," said Rachel, "mostly Country music. Boring." We all laugh.

"Time for dinner," announces Cindy. "Southern comfort food — barbeque pork ribs, potatoes in their jackets and coleslaw. Eve and I had the best ribs on a trip to Memphis and Nashville," said Cindy winking at me, with a knowing smile.

Cindy had been really down after her second husband died, so I suggested she come over. When she did, William decided a magical musical tour would be the cure. And it was. Blues in Beale Street and The Grand Ole Opry followed by ribs everywhere we went.

"Use your fingers. Be as messy as you like," says Cindy. "I have large napkins to tie around our necks and finger bowls. And because you won't be able to talk, I'm putting on some music." By the time Van Morrison's, *Brand New Day* is resounding through the dining room, our hands are sticky with sauce and I am deep in thought.

When all the dark clouds roll away
And the sun begins to shine
I see my freedom from across the way

Freedom. The word swirls around in my mind. The freedom to move on. Like the yellowing of the finch's feathers signals a new season, this could be a new chapter in my life. I just have to find the wherewithal to take the first step. I look up. Cindy's eyes meet mine. She mouths me a big kiss and I wink.

4. Frogs

The house is quiet. Everyone returned home yesterday, even the loons. I'm allowing myself the luxury of staying in bed a little longer this morning playing with my iPad, surfing dating sites on the internet. Sunlight streams through the window. I love the sun. It fills my heart and soul with warmth and lifts my spirits. They need a lift.

I'm nervous about entering the world of online dating, and with it the possibility of bringing men back into my life. Evocative conversations in cyber space designed to find the man of my dreams. Does this man of my dreams even exist? Maybe he's just a figment of Eirene's imagination.

I sigh. I miss William. I miss having him in my life. I miss the sense of belonging, of having someone to talk to, to do things with, to be close to, even to argue with. Most of all I miss the passion for life and living we shared. I felt alive. Sometimes I think part of me died when William did. I've been such a solitary soul for so long, a widow, the woman in me seemingly invisible. No one sees me anymore. My living is more in the mind, living my life through my garden or my words because that's a safer way to be. I talk to my dog. I talk to my journal. I write my life. I've forgotten the art of talking to people. To men. Up close and personal, I am often an elective mute.

Come on, Eve. You can do this. Time you emerged from your cosy cocoon and started to live again. I sit up straight, and settle on a dating site. I look at the online profile then down at Kiki, who is eyeing me expectantly. "Come on, girl, let's go for a walk. I'll tackle this later." Kiki's eyes light up and she races to the stairs. "It's easy enough. All I want is another William, but a William who can cook and dance."

໖

Ping! Ping! Ping! I jump as I enter the study. What's that? The heart is showing seven contacts. It's only an hour since I made my profile live and the computer is alive with the sound of men. "Woo hoo!"

Thomas sent you a kiss:

I'd like to get to know you, would you be interested?

He's 63, an attractive, intelligent, caring, sensitive male, single, honest and clean shaven with a good sense of humor. He is warm, affectionate, fit and fun loving, a very active person who works out at the gym regularly. That fits with the muscle-bound pose in his photo.

"Hmmmm. Not bad. The same age as William. Wonder what he's looking for?" I push my glasses back up my nose, my overly large, bright blue hipster glasses. I love the bold statement they make about me which is good because I can't see for shit without them.

> An honest, articulate, vibrant woman with a lively intellect and a good sense of humor, who is handling her past and present with style.

That's me!

> For fun and friendship initially and a longer-term relationship if that eventuates. Otherwise, friendship is fine.

Fine for me too. That gives me time to feel my way. I send a kiss in return, my first internet kiss. Thomas comes back quickly. Wow! He loves my profile, loves that I'm a kind and gentle soul plus he loves my long blonde hair and blue eyes. He thinks I look very beautiful. He'd love to talk and meet, but he's hopeless at emails. Although flattered by his comments, I'm still wary. Am I comfortable with giving him my number? I'm not so sure about that. I'd better sleep on it.

A week and two phone calls later, having been to the rest room half a dozen times in the last hour, I am anxiously scanning the people coming through the entrance to the local shopping mall. I'm meeting Thomas for coffee. A hunch-backed old man appears, shuffling around looking for someone. There is something familiar about him. Oh my god! It's him. He's ancient. He looks as old as Methuselah. I turn to move away and he waves to me.

"Eve?" By the time he arrives next to me, he is wheezing, struggling for breath. I hear a rattle in his lungs, but heaven help me, I start laughing. This is not online dating, it's carbon dating.

"What are you laughing at?"

"You're nothing like your photo," I say, trying unsuccessfully to stifle the laughter with my hand.

"Oh, it was taken a little while ago," he says offhandedly, dismissing it. "Shall we go and have a coffee?"

No way. Are there no rules in this shitty caper? That's a blast from the past. Anglo Saxon curse words coming to the fore. I am back in a foreign country. I sneak another look at Thomas and cringe. I want to run away but courtesy demands I follow. Besides, in his condition he may up and die if he starts chasing me. In the café, I keep my eyes averted and focus on drinking my coffee, desperate to escape, hoping the waiter knows how to give CPR.

The conversation is awkward and stilted. Me giving abrupt answers to Thomas's eager questions punctuated now by intermittent nervous giggles which involuntarily keep erupting from inside me, embarrassingly so. I nearly choke on one as I swallow the last of my coffee.

"Can I see you again, Eve?" he asks.

No way on God's green earth am I going to see you again. You won't last that long anyway. "No, I don't think so," I say politely. "Thank you for the coffee." I walk away quickly.

❧

A week later, I am walking up to L'Arte della Patisserie to meet Ronald. He's sixty. We've been corresponding regularly in between mutual bouts of dog walking, gardening, reading and listening to music. He had his own business for thirty years, is now retired, but spends time looking after his investments and playing double bass in the local Chamber Orchestra. We have lots in common and he's a Gemini, too.

I wonder if he's like me; there are two faces to this woman. Eve, the quieter, reflective personality with the bleeding heart. The upright citizen and the ethical journalist and teacher who dominated my working life, determined to right the wrongs of the world. The face that is mostly shown to the world. And the uninhibited Evie, with her wilder, underground nature, where the laughter and naughtiness resides. I like her. She was fun but she's been in hibernation since William died.

Ronald sees me coming and waves, then leans back nonchalantly on his car – a snazzy sports coupe. I've no idea what kind as vanity prevails today. I'm taking a risk and not wearing my glasses. As I near, I see he is immaculately dressed, knife like creases in his grey pants, a silk shirt and expensive loafers. Woo hoo! This one's a good 'un. I draw closer.

"Hello, Eve. Lovely to meet you." He extends a hand. Ughhh-hhh... I note with horror the age spots and pale, wafer-thin skin on his hand. I look up. In spite of his broad smile, all I see is the ill-fitting wig that fails to cover the crusted sores from recent hair transplant surgery. An antique Ken doll.

"Ummmmm... I feel sick." Without another word, I turn tail and run.

5. Cindy

The light on the answering machine is flashing. I listen.

"Hello, Eve, Darling. I've been very busy coming to grips with everything and everyone – setting up house, the admin for the foundation and the role of a trustee, but I'm really enjoying being here. It will take a while before I am settled. I'm just checking in to see if you have had any dates."

I call her up. "What's happening with the foundation?"

"Well, as you know, Brian set up *The Positive Ageing Institute* after his parents died of Alzheimer's. I want to expand it to include research into eastern medical practices and associated complementary therapies and interventions to offset the effects of aging."

"Sounds a huge undertaking and exciting."

"It is and it will require many more benefactors. Lots of networking needed. But enough of me. What's been happening with your online dating, Eve?"

"Two geriatric frogs who scared the life out of me. They understated their age by at least a decade or two."

Cindy laughs. "That's a hazard of online dating. Like I said, you may have to kiss a hundred of those. Were they really that bad, Eve?"

"One was like death warmed up and the other so frail, I could see him in his casket with his BMW car keys on his chest."

"Goodness," Cindy laughs.

"There's no way I'm having anyone else die on me," I say indignantly. "Maybe I'll become a cougar and date toy boys instead."

"Don't be ridiculous, Eve. Just kick back and enjoy it a little. Dating can be fun."

"Nah, Cindy. I've come off the site. It's too scary. I'm going to buy a couple of Ragdoll kittens and grow cabbages instead."

"A cat woman growing cabbages. Don't you dare, Eve," says Cindy raising her voice.

"Just kidding, Cindy. Keep your skirt on."

"Didn't you see anyone you liked?"

"A few, but they didn't kiss me or email me."

"Why on earth didn't you initiate contact, Eve?"

"In my day, it was polite for a woman to wait to be asked."

"Eve, my dear, you are hopeless. A dinosaur. Go back on. Lower the age range in your profile and, if you find someone you like, email them, don't kiss them. Make the first move. Be bold." I hang up wondering if Evie will come out of hiding to help me. But what is it I want?

～

The first day I go back online I see Peter. Go Evie. I email him straight away. He's thinking of going off the site as I'm coming back on. Maybe it's an omen. Smiling eyes, thick, dark hair, a scientist, handyman and gardener who is learning French, loves dancing, can cook, cycles daily and, best of all, he is fit and healthy. He looks good for sixty... or so the photos lead me to believe. If not, I'll be really annoyed. Many things about him resonate but the proof will be in the pudding.

I wake early and reach for my iPad. Another email from Peter. There's much about him that sounds good. How could anyone tick so many of my boxes, boxes I didn't even know I had? He even makes his own pizza dough. What kind of man makes his own pizza dough? Then the doubts creep in. Too good to be true? What isn't he telling me? Why isn't he taken?

What a strange time it is in my life. I used to fantasize about meeting strange men like Keanu Reeves, Daniel Craig, or better still, Mr. Darcy. His devastatingly sexy body clambering out of the lake after an early morning swim coming towards me. All our inhibitions forgotten. Now, instead, I'm looking at meeting strange men in cyber space, imagining new possibilities for my life from the comfort of my bed.

It's a crescent moon tomorrow – time to announce my intentions, hopes and wishes for the month. I email Peter asking him to have lunch with me. He's the first man who has any sort of appeal, but we're yet to meet. So, my hopes, my high hopes, need to be kept in check.

No word from Peter for two days. Maybe today. I open my email. My heart drops. Nope. Nothing. Maybe I've scared him off by asking to meet him. Too forward.

"Enough," I chastise myself, waking Kiki from her slumber

at the foot of the bed. "A week or so ago he didn't even exist." Now I'm weaving him into my future, sight unseen. Still I'm dreaming again. I'm wanting more. Maybe I'm wanting too much.

Ping! I jump. "Yippee, Kiki! It's Peter! He's agreed to meet me for lunch." Kiki puts her two front paws on the bed and bites the air happily at the news. Relief floods through me. "I must write to him and I must tell Cindy, too," I say as I stroke her back lovingly.

꙳

I spy Cindy sitting at a table outside Georgio's. Unusually, she's there before me. She looks as fabulous as ever, beautifully groomed and wearing very expensive, casual chic this morning – tailored taupe pants with matching shoes and Gucci clutch. A cream silk blouse and large drop pearl earrings.

"Couldn't sleep?" I ask cheekily.

"You saucy thing, Darling," she says, waving her hand at me, "I can't wait to hear more about Peter. A Harvard grad. And a wealthy one at that. I'm impressed."

I grin. "Me, too," I say. We order coffee, then get down to business.

"When are you meeting him?" Cindy asks leaning forward eagerly.

"This Wednesday. He says he's really looking forward to it. I wrote four emails to him yesterday. Stayed in bed until I finished them all. It took me two and a half hours." I babble on. "Kiki gave up on her walk, and had a sulk,"

"Four emails in one day! Too much, Eve. Way too much."

"I know, it's a bit over the top, but probably less than one long one," I say worried by Cindy's reaction. "I hope Peter doesn't think I'm too full on."

"So do I," says Cindy firmly. She sees my crestfallen face, pats my hand and softens her voice. "There, there, Darling. What was so important you had to write four emails, anyway?"

I gulp. "I separated out the thoughts, the things I wanted to talk about – the past and William; things we have in common; things I love to do but don't do often enough and about the hazards of online dating. I wonder what he'll think of me."

"Did he reply to any?" Cindy asks solicitously, turning to look at the waiter bringing our coffee. "Thank you."

I give a nod of thanks to the waiter, then turn to Cindy. "Yes, an hour later, giving me more of his background," I say, hurriedly taking a sip. "His life is very full. He has much more in it than mine. Four children, lots of clubs and activities. He sounds very self-sufficient."

"That's good. I dislike men who need to be molly-coddled," she says firmly.

"I'm wondering where and if I will fit in. In a way, that could be a bonus. I don't want all of my time taken, just some of it with companionable things to do. I don't want to live someone else's life." But I do need more in my life, I think, as I sip coffee. I need to open up my world. I look at Cindy inviting her comment.

"And, neither should you, Darling. What a horrid thought!"

వ

As I walk down Main Street to the restaurant dressed simply, in black pants and sandals, with a lovely peach silk top, I wonder if I've chosen the right color. Peach is friendly and opens you up to new possibilities. My tummy doesn't agree. It's turning hula hoops. I see Peter standing in front of the restaurant looking to and fro. He's much taller than I thought, his dark hair is greying but he looks younger than sixty. Thank heavens.

He strides up to me, "Eve," he says, then envelopes me in a gigantic bear hug for what seems an eternity. Something around my right kidney pops. He releases me. I can barely breathe. "You are lovely!" he says, glancing at me up and down. "Let's go in." If my ribs aren't cracked and I can still walk. I wasn't looking for that kind of vice. What the hell will he be like when he knows me better?

I remain quiet as Peter does most of the talking, watching him closely. His Adam's apple is bobbing up and down. He's nervous, too. Good. I give him a lead. "Tell me how you make pizza dough." Peter takes a deep breath then launches into a discourse. The waiter comes to the table requesting our orders, cutting him off. Just as well. I now know enough about pizza dough to last for a lifetime.

I ask about dancing next. He slows down, his nervousness abating. Our food arrives. We talk amiably in between mouthfuls of food and start to relax. After a pleasant lunch he walks me to the car. When I open the door, he grabs my arms and kisses me hard on the lips. Heaven help me. I stand there rooted to the spot, literally gobsmacked. Is moderation in his lexicon? Making love could be a health hazard.

"You're as lovely and comfortable to be with, as I'd imagined, Eve," he says earnestly. "I thoroughly enjoyed our preliminary skirmish. Can we do it again?"

Do I want to see him again? I look him over. He's a nice enough guy. A friend, maybe. None of the mucky complicated bits.

"Skirmish is definitely the right word for your hugs and kisses."

"I apologize, Eve. I just saw you as an attractive, sweet and gentle person that I wanted to hug. I haven't hugged someone like that for a long time." He salutes me. "I promise not to do it again. I'll wear my L plates next time."

"If it makes you feel any better Peter, I played squash with William for two years before I let him kiss me."

"So, what do I need to do, Eve? Wait two years, play squash or...?" He grins at me. "Can I see you again?" I smile and nod.

"Great." He goes to kiss me again. I draw back. "Oh, oh. Down boy."

I laugh. "On the cheek is fine, for now." He kisses me on both cheeks, closes the door after I hop in the car then walks away. I pull out my cell phone and check it.

Dream Man has sent you an email.

6. Richard

"It's Him!" I yell as I hurry inside the front door, startling Kiki. "Sorry Little Girl, I didn't mean to frighten you, but your mom's excited. Eirene's prediction is coming true! Cindy's away so you'll have to help me, but first, dinner for you."

Richard's car pulls up in the drive, here for our... I'm not sure what. He asked if he could see me in private a month ago, but has rescheduled three times. It must be something important for him to do that. Either that or Rachel is driving him mad and he wants to move in here. I love him, but no. No way. I open the door and stand there waiting. Kiki leaves her food and races out to greet him.

"Beer please, Eve. It's been a tough day," he moans, ignoring Kiki.

"Come in." As I say this, he's already halfway down the hallway to the kitchen loosening his tie and rolling up his shirtsleeves. Richard nods as I pass him his beer. "Cheers," he says. We tap drinks.

"Come, let's sit in the conservatory and talk there before dinner."

"Thanks, but I'm not hungry. A beer is fine." We sit on the

chairs facing one another. Kiki settles unobtrusively at Richard's feet.

"What's up?"

"A few things really, Eve. I have to make some major decisions soon and wanted to run some things past you." He looks at me whilst taking another sip of his beer. "Dad's a rough diamond. He's difficult to work with or even be around for too long. He trod on anyone he could to reach the top." He sighs and sips his beer again. "He's done well. Davis Constructions is now the largest builder in the state but he hasn't got many friends, though. I'm not sure he's even got one."

"No matter how tough he was with you and Rachel, he loved you. He believed by giving you everything, that you wouldn't have to do things the same way as him."

"Yeah, but he won't let go. He doesn't give us room to breathe and grow or do our own thing. It's Dad's way or the highway." He pauses, takes a deep breath, then goes on. "I've worked in his firm since I finished college. Rachel and I live in an apartment in a building he owns. Before that Rachel and her husband lived in an apartment he owns. Her practice operates from one of his premises. I love my work, I do, but he's got me in his pocket." Richard sighs heavily and takes a big swig of his beer, finishing it in another gulp. "Can I have another, please?" he asks.

"Of course, you can, Richie. Go for it." I encourage, inadvertently using the nickname I called him when he was younger. A Freudian slip? I'm not sure he's his own man yet. As he sits back down, I question him gently. "What kind of life do you want, Richard?"

"I live with my sister. I don't date. Apart from the gym and playing tennis with college buddies, I don't have time for myself. And now Dad wants me to take over the residential side of the business. He wants me to move back in with him." He groans. "If I do that, I'll have no life of my own."

"Tell me what's happening with Rachel," I ask. "What happens to her if you move back in with your dad?"

Richard strokes Kiki as he talks. "Oh, that's another thing. She's built a brick wall around herself. Whenever I try to talk to her, she closes up. Doesn't want to know and doesn't want to do anything to help me or herself. I'm worried about her."

"She's still hurting," I say. "Divorce is hard enough. Being left for another woman doesn't do much for the ego, but for a relationship counsellor, it must be humiliating."

"Could you talk to her please, Eve? Maybe she'll open up to you," he pleads.

"I'll try, but I doubt it. More of your dad's steely stubbornness in her. Some of his abrasiveness, too. She's apt to speak her mind without fear or favour. But I'll try."

"Thanks, Eve."

"What are *you* going to do, Richard? What do *you* want?"

Richard eyes his beer, examining the label. He pulls at one corner, continuing to look down as he answers. "I love the work we're in. And I'm good at it. Dad threw me into it after college, but I do it better than him. He's not in touch with business today."

"You are gifted at what you do."

"But I need more in my life than just work. It's not enough," he says emphatically.

I lean closer to him. "And neither should it be. What would you most like to do at the moment?"

"I need... I need time. Time for me," says Richard, "I haven't experienced the world. I don't think I've been in love with anyone. And, I'm thirty-three years old."

"It's never too late, Richard. You're the same age as William when we met," I say. "But you already know what to do, Richard. Just do it. Take some time out, time for you."

"How can I with Dad breathing down my neck? And Rachel is off the rails after getting screwed by that hopeless prick of a husband – ex-husband thank God." Anger rises in his voice for the first time since arriving.

"Just tell them and tell them why. Stand up to your dad. Don't let him beat you down. They'll understand. They love you. We all do."

Richard's large hands open and close with frustration on the knees of his trousers.

"Take six months off." I see the shocked look on his face. "Alright, three. Three months off, which includes some time in Europe and tracking down your mum in Berlin. I found a whole new way of looking at the world in Europe and I found the love of my life there, although it took me years to acknowledge it. Tell your dad you're looking for opportunities to expand the business internationally. If you're going to head up the residential business soon, start looking into an apartment block in London or the like."

"I guess. Maybe that'd help swing him around," he says, disbelievingly.

"I'm sure he has some good contacts you could tap into, Richard."

"I'm sure he has, but will he give them to me?"

"Forget about your dad. It's time for you. Go find your mom. Ella wasn't much older than you when she found the courage to leave Alan. It's time for her to be back in your life, Richard. Reach out to her."

Richard continues to inspect the label of his beer, rubbing and scratching at the corners. I'm worried about the boy. Yes, boy. All that macho working out cannot hide the fragility of the man in front of me. It's like he's still the teenager he was when his mom left. He clearly blames himself, just like Rachel does. My heart bleeds for him. As it did for Ella, a long time ago.

Richard finally nods, "Thanks, Eve. For everything. It *is* time for me." He necks his beer and stands. I can tell he's holding something back, but he's his father's son. The sensitive emotions don't come easily to him and his sister. I hug him as I can tell he won't hug me first.

"Take care, Richard. Let me know how it goes with your dad. I'll give you Ella's address when you're ready. Make contact before you go."

"I will. Thanks again, Eve."

7. Sven

"What are you smiling at, Eve?" I jump and nearly hose Cindy down as I turn around. I look at my watch, amazed. I've been out in the garden watering for an hour.

"When did you get back?" I ask, seeing uncharacteristic dark shadows under her eyes. Her face devoid of makeup.

"Yesterday. I'm exhausted, quanked, to use an old-fashioned word. So much rigmarole involved in expanding the research parameters underpinning the foundation. And I've got thrush again. It flares when I'm under stress. I see Dr. Lester tomorrow. What were you smiling at, Eve? You looked a million miles away."

"I was. Lost in space, with the moon, the stars and romantic far-off worlds," I say dreamily, waving the hose to and fro over the garden bed.

"Do tell," says Cindy eagerly, her face lighting up as she takes my arm in hers and leads me towards the house. I drop the hose and prise it away from her briefly to turn it off at the tap.

"Cindy, you'll find some cold glasses in the freezer and a bottle of Chardonnay in the fridge. The heat is awful, so bring it out to the porch, please. And then I'll tell you all about Sven," I say with a wicked grin, titillating her.

Cindy returns with the glasses of wine. She hands me one. "Cheers. Now, 'fess up, Darling. Who on earth is Sven? Last time we spoke you were delighting in the pleasures of Peter."

"Thanks. Cheers." We tap glasses. I feel a smile light up my face. "Well, I haven't actually met him yet, but we've been exchanging emails for the past ten days. He writes to me late at night, and I write back to him early in the morning."

"Good for you. What does he do?" she asks.

"He's a marine geophysicist and engineer, immigrated from Germany in his teens, often employed as a trouble shooter on big oil and gas rigs. He was involved in the clean-up of the big spill in the Gulf."

"Oh, no! You don't want to get involved with one of them," says Cindy worriedly, slamming down her glass. "Those *fly in fly out* guys are here one day, gone the next, for months at a time. You can't trust them, either."

"Relax. He's out of contract. He's had enough trouble shooting and wants to settle here in New Jersey or New York. He studied here eons ago and wants to come back. It's an omen!" I say, to calm her. "While he's doing that, he's indulging his other passions – he's an amateur astronomer, and a connoisseur of art. And... he's a romantic.

I've had the loveliest time. I write to him about gardens and nature and beauty and writing and he sends me photos of paintings. I was entranced by a particularly beautiful one of a naked woman lying in a field. A goddess really. In between talking about astronomy and art, he quotes Shakespeare. Cindy, he's delightful."

"Hmmmm... Sounds too good to be true, Eve." I ignore her pessimism and quote Shakespeare.

Shall I compare thee to a summer's day?
Thou art more lovely and more temperate.
Rough winds do shake the darling buds of May,
And summer's lease hath all too short a date.

I drift off into space and picture the supermoon that Sven pointed out to me three nights ago. That's the nickname for full moons when our celestial neighbour is closest to Earth, apparently. A lovely phenomenon where the moon appears exceptionally large. I blink as Cindy snaps her fingers, bringing me back into the garden.

"And you're dying to meet him, Eve. I can tell,' says Cindy with furrowed brow.

"I am. I really love the sound of this man on paper." Would that he is as good in the flesh."

"When? When are you going to meet?"

"I don't know. He hasn't asked. I think he's avoiding me. Maybe I'll invite him here for dinner. He says he loves the sound of my garden."

"I bet he does." I hear her low, barbed reply. "That's a lovely idea, Eve." Cindy drains her glass and stands up. "Got to go. No rest for the wicked. Stay there, Darling. Finish your drink." She bends over and kisses me twice. "Sven sounds wonderful. I'm pleased for you."

After she's gone, I sit back and rest the chilled wine on my chest, allowing cool droplets to run down between my breasts and onto my stomach. A slight breeze wafts over me. Rain is coming. I smile, raise my glass and talk to the moon. "Don't listen to her. I give in. I surrender. I'm hopelessly addicted to you, Sven. To your letters, to the images you conjure. An astronomer with a telescope studying the moon and stars each night, bringing in far off worlds of romance, destiny, timelessness, lives and places beyond imagining."

Back here on earth, I've been slaving in the garden, stripping it back, creating bare canvasses throughout for mini gardens within the garden, imagining a very different kind of future. My nether regions quiver. I do not fully understand why or how but I have these new sensations inside me. I'm aroused in every way imaginable, such heightened awareness and stimulation.

I sigh, a delicious sigh, and stretch. Time to turn in, where Sven will be with me once more in words and in my imaginings. For some yet elusive reason, he chooses to keep his bodily presence out of reach. I must change that. My overwhelming need, at the moment, dear Sven is for you, just you, to see you, to know you are real and not just a fabulous figment of my imagination.

I open my iPad.

Eve, I haven't heard from you for over a week. Are you OK?

Would you like to have dinner with me on Friday?

Peter

A week ago? It seems like forever. I'd forgotten all about Peter. I'll write in the morning. A 'Dear Peter' letter, a nice one. He's a nice man. I turn off the light and imagine a romantic rendezvous with Sven.

8. Imaginings

The garden is singing and sighing. It rained overnight. It's so long since it has rained. Rain sets my world to rights. Without that delicious dampness my soul starts to shrivel and sere in concert with the plants. I'm always hoping for rain, impatient for summer to end.

My mind turns to Sven. He's become entwined in my world, indelibly etched into my consciousness. The sensuality and eroticism, a delightful surprise. After nearly a decade of drought I thought that part of my garden had well and truly shrivelled up and died. All my instincts are telling me to trust him, to trust that he is not only a good man, but will be good for me. I feel good about myself, but need to bring some normality back into my life. I write to Sven and ask him if we can meet up this Friday. Unusually, he replies straight away.

What do you want to do to me?

Dear Sven,
What do I want to do to you? My basic instincts have taken over.
I keep imagining myself as that naked woman in the field, my
ripe body calling out for you.

I have not made love for nearly a decade and never felt the need to do so, but each time I summon you into my consciousness, a delicious stimulating jolt appears. Such a rare phenomenon.

I've decided I can't go on like this, that on this Friday I want you to make love to me. I can't believe what I'm saying to you. I thought desire had passed me by, but more than anything else, more than talking to you, I want to hold you, to have you near me.

I do not know if making love with you is possible, but I am willing to find out. I do know you will have to be oh so gentle with me, physically as well as emotionally.

Eve x

ॐ

I awaken just after 4.30 am thinking of Sven as has become my custom. This morning instead of turning on the light and reaching for my iPad to read his reply — the reply I know will be there, I lie in the dark, stretching slowly, languorously, thinking of him and the chain of events I have set in motion. My nether regions tweak a good morning, softer and more sensual than the spasms that rocked me insistently yesterday.

I think of him constantly and in return receive these delicious sensations — electrical charges, although always pleasant. Sometimes a feeling of warmth, at other times a contraction when my body lurches forward. It's all highly arousing, and so erotic. The need to touch myself, to pleasure myself to quell these stirrings is growing too. In a not too subtle way, I am being made aware that my sexual energy is reawakening. And who is the only person I can entrust with the sensitive and delicate task of confirming that, as well as everything else, I am a sexual being? Sven.

I finally turn on the light and read his tender reply. I know I am in safe hands. Sven will be my guide on the first part of our magical journey together. Outside the darkness is softening. The trees are still black silhouettes but sunrise will surely come. I have the same certainty that capturing such a precious moment is right for me. I am suddenly overcome with the enormity of what is happening, of what I am asking of Sven. The sky is lightening once more. Time to turn off the light and usher in the dawn.

Dearest Eve, as you have now become,

I read your letter and had to go downstairs for my period of unwinding, relaxation, problem solving and inspiration.

It would be a great honour to take you into this new sphere. It has to be done in a special way. I will need to relax with you, have some conversation, food and wine.

Are you happy for me to come to the garden of delights for a private meeting of mind, body and spirit? Your mind, emotions and feelings are complex. I will blend into your needs.

Tell me more of what revolutions are going on inside you. It is wonderful.

Love Sven

As I close my iPad, my room is suddenly aglow. The sun

pierces through the opened curtains, bringing light, where there was darkness.

9. The heat is on

Instead of lying in bed, I'm up early to water the garden. I stand there musing as the spray courses over the orchard dripping off the clusters of bright red apples ripening on the trees. The garden is a living thing, a giving thing. I nurture it and it nurtures me. I water to ensure a lush greenness abounds to welcome Sven this evening. Sven and Eve in the garden of my delights. Wonderful. Suddenly William springs to mind and the word *betrayal* is conjured up. A shiver runs up my spine, chilling me to the bone. I shrug the unwelcome thought away and focus on watering.

The forecast is for a hot windy day with a change coming overnight. At present it is warm, with a balmy breeze rippling through the flower beds, kissing the cheeks of the ripening fruit and ruffling the feathers of a pair of eastern bluebirds feasting on the red berries of the Dogwood trees. The male has a brilliant blue head and back, with a warm reddish-brown breast. The female colors are similar, but somewhat muted. I wonder if Sven will be my bluebird and I his muted female. I finish watering and head indoors.

I look around the house. Beauty abounds here, too. Large

palms, orchids and peace lilies everywhere. I love orchids with a passion but my orchid house is devoid of flowers. It's too early in the season. Yesterday, I bought several sprays of blue Singapore orchids, some peace lilies and a big bunch of oncidiums or dancing ladies with long flowering spikes of delicate yellow flowers that quiver when the wind blows. They are on the coffee table in the living room, near the open window, catching the breeze.

ॐ

Time for my horoscope. I open my iPad and read.

GEMINI: Key words: free spirit, protester. Mood: dazzling.

Life is about to get pretty interesting, so hold on to your hat. Of course, changes and uncertainty don't make you nervous; quite the opposite, in fact. Instead of letting the unusual conditions today bother you, you'll thrive under them.

Just be sure to stay witty, and keep an open schedule. Anything could come up -- an impromptu trip, an exciting invitation from a friend, even a brand-new, engaging acquaintance — and you want to be ready for it.

ॐ

"I will be!" Feeling my luck is in, I shuffle my Tarot cards and turn over the top one. *The Lovers.* Perfect. Such synchronicity. I wondered if I should share my spiritual side with any of my men, but Cindy counselled against it.

"Keep your spiritual quirks to yourself, Eve. You don't want to scare them off. Men aren't so open to the spiritual."

As I wander through the house checking all is in readiness, I feel a gentleness about me, a lightness of being. I walk into the bedroom and look at my perfumes all lined up across the dressing table.

"I wonder what perfume I should wear tonight, Kiki." I touch all the bottles, lightly. "*Sensuous Nude*, of course." I laugh. Evie's back in town.

Cindy glides through the doorway, breaking into my reverie. "My god, Eve, look at you." She eyes me with disgust. Grubby hands and feet, tattered singlet and shorts, tangled hair that hasn't been washed for three days and a dirt-streaked face with not a skerrick of make up on it. "You've got a hot date tonight and you look like something the cat dragged in."

I protest like a chastised child. "I've been out in the garden watering and checking on all the plants and flowers inside. I want the place to look wonderful."

"Sven won't be interested in plants and the garden. He'll be looking at you. Clothes, underwear, hair, makeup, jewellery, perfume? What have you decided?" Only the perfume, but I can't tell her that. I divert the conversation.

"I was thinking of my black Karen Millen capri pants with my cream silk blouse. It's going to be hot."

"Eve, I despair of you. Think feminine, romantic and color. Bright colors suit you. You're attractive, but you still need to make the most of your attributes, especially at your age." My age? Why is everything reduced to age as you grow older? I don't feel old. "Are you going to put your hair up?" I shake my head.

"Oh, it looks lovely when it's up, you can see your face." She's looking askance at me, hands clutched together in awkward concern. I grin and bear it. I know she's disappointed. She wants me to look my best for this first date but something from the eons of time tells me men prefer hair down rather than up. Then again so do I. I'll make it more presentable.

"I have to work. I'll ring later to see what you've decided."

As soon as she's gone, I race to my wardrobe. What to wear? What shoes? With what clutch? Do I even need a clutch in my own house? Of course not, Silly. I shower and scrub the garden off me, washing my hair twice, then turn on some mood music, Marvin Gaye's *Let's Get It On*. I try things on. A skirt with a flowery blouse. No, too prissy. Dresses, one, two, three – plain, floral, patterned, throwing them off as quickly as I throw them on. I'm getting stickier by the minute.

Finally, after much deliberating and much Marvin Gaye asking me *what's going on*, I settle on white capri pants and white sandals with a bright cobalt blue silk top. I'll wear the bluebird's colors tonight. Blue for the sea and the sky – the essence of Sven. And blue for me — the color of spirit, intuition, imagination and inspiration. The essence of me.

What next? Sexy underwear? I rattle through my three drawers. I haven't got any. Plain white underwire bra and hipsters it is. Definitely not my control panties. I must ask Rachel to come shopping next week to update my lingerie. Or then again, maybe not. Or, maybe not yet.

Clothing decided, I turn on (and get turned on) by Al Green, to help me with my makeup. I sigh. Too many wrinkles to count these days but dark circles, too. They've appeared from the lack of sleep and early morning emails. Concealer might melt in this heat, but I'll try it anyway.

"Why am I putting myself through all this, Kiki?" Kiki sits by my feet and wags her tail at the mention of her name. "Yes. You know something's up, don't you, girl?" My nerves get the better of me so I decide to shower again.

Hair? If I don't put it up, then I'll need to put some rollers in so it's not so messy. Then it will be lovely and fluffy hanging down. That means blow drying it and it's hot already. Goddamn! Makeup, while the rollers are in. It's been so long since I've worn makeup. My hand is shaking. The pencil slips over my eyelid into my eye.

"Noooooo!" My eyes start to water, I blink. Kiki moves back as I stagger around, mascara streaming down under my eyes. I can't see a thing. I turn and grab for a towel, but it falls to the floor. I bend down to get it. "Owwww!" I scream in agony as I bang my forehead on the side of the towel rail. "Rrrowww," Kiki responds with a girly howl. At least someone's enjoying the show. I find the towel and dab my eyes while rubbing my forehead.

I take a look at my work in the mirror. "Oh, Kiki. I look like a raccoon." Cleaning the pencil off my eyelids and the mascara from under my eyes, I start again. The mark on my forehead is not too red, so I go for the mascara. More mascara and more agony, giving myself an even bigger poke in the eye. This time my eyes are streaming.

"I give up. I give up. It's not going to happen, Kiki. No mascara until my hand stops shaking. Just as well I plucked my eyebrows yesterday, otherwise I might need bloody eye surgery." At the last moment I change my mind about the perfume.

"Screw *Sensuous Nude*, I need *Youth Dew*."

Hours later, I am ready. My hair is shiny, full of body and bounce. It swings when I walk and I even managed some makeup, including lipstick for a change. I've added my dangling lapis lazuli earrings and matching bracelet, to match my top. Highly spiritual, celestial blue crystals that reveal truth and wisdom and empower the senses. Not bad, Eve. Not bad at all.

10. A New Dawn

The doorbell rings. Kiki barks and races to the door. I steel myself, before heading to the door. I take a deep breath and open it. The heat hits me like a furnace. My gaze travels upward, from the shoes (casual — scuffed), to the jeans (denim – ill-fitting, yet well-worn), tan buckled belt, black shirt (sleeves rolled up — unironed), to the tanned, weather-beaten face and brown eyes. Sven in the flesh. Not that he has gone to as much trouble with his appearance as I did.

"So, we meet at last," he says, making no move to kiss me.

"Come in out of the heat. It's oppressive out there." Sven picks up his large hold all. I hear bottles clinking as he follows me to the kitchen. Kiki retreats to the far end of the hallway.

"Come and say hello to our guest, Kiki." She refuses, instead taking up her immutable Buddha stance, staring at Sven. "Oh, Kiki. Come on."

"Don't worry. Dogs don't seem to like me much," he says warily, lifting his heavy bag onto the bench. Surreptitiously, I study him. With a few days' stubble growth, his face looks craggy and is crowned by a mop of red unruly hair. He has a rugged outdoor look, certainly not a dream man.

"Look at me, you can't tell me I'm your dream man," he says, bluntly, as if reading my thoughts.

I pause, sensing his nervousness, maybe even embarrassment. "What's on the inside is more important. You know that. Besides how can you appreciate art without understanding what real beauty is about."

Somewhat mollified, he responds, "That's what Arthur Clarke says we're here for. *The pursuit of knowledge and the creation of beauty.*"

"Wise man. Would you like something to drink?"

"I've brought champagne." Sven unearths a bottle from his bag, plus two bottles of red wine and a six pack of beer. "Want me to open it?"

"I already have one open. Sorry, I couldn't wait. I'll pour you a glass." I put the champagne and beer in the fridge, remove the opened bottle, pour a glass for Sven and top up mine.

"Cheers, to a wonderful night." We chink glasses.

"Cheers, to a wonderful night," he echoes and takes a large draught.

"I want to show you the garden, before it gets too dark. Bring your drink, as it is still very hot outside." He swallows the rest of the champagne, then goes to the fridge and pulls out a beer.

Daylight is fading as I take him on a tour of the garden. As we wander around, I stop and point out garden features like the orchid house, the pond, the bluestone paving or the Dogwoods. Sven admires and talks knowledgeably about plant species, but remains distant and formal, no hint of proximity. Kiki follows but maintains her distance, too. Nothing is going as planned, I opine. It's like he's a different person, unreachable.

"Beyond the fence is an orchard – apples, apricots, pears and cherries and some herbs and vegetables." I pause, "but we're going to eat here." I lead him into the conservatory. A table is laid out with a selection of dips, cheeses and a large antipasto platter I thought would satisfy the hunger of a man his size. Plus, a bottle of Cuvaison 2017 Estate Pinot Noir, a lovely light red from the Napa Valley.

"What a lovely setting you have here, Eve. No wonder you call it the garden of delights. I'll just go and get some more beer."

As night falls, the stars come into view, but the setting seems more and more surreal. We eat slowly and chat desultorily about anything and everything except us and why he is here. I had switched to water a while ago, but Sven drinks steadily. After finishing the beer, he started on the red wine. He pours the last of the second bottle into his glass and polishes it off. I look at Sven and wonder what's coming next. This man is like a stranger to me, nothing like the intimate, romantic Romeo of his emails.

I stand. "It's late." Sven struggles to his feet, then lurches towards me, smiling for the first time all night. Smirking more like. He is drunk, so gloriously drunk he can barely stand.

"I'll put you in the spare room." He wraps his arms around me, and presses his face into my neck, the first time he has touched me all night. I should be seeing stars. Instead, the body odour and the booze emanating from his pores, clouds my eyes and senses.

Out of the blue, I ask, "Have you another contract?" He shakes his head drunkenly. A deep sense of unease settles over me. "I can't imagine living on a rig or even a life lived half on land and half on the sea."

"You get used to it. To not putting down roots. To living in the moment." He kisses me on the nape of the neck, his breath hot against my skin. "I want to be close to you," he whispers. I relent.

"Fool," I say to myself. Nevertheless, operating on a wing and a prayer, I turn off the lights and lead Sven upstairs, steadying him as we go.

࿔

When I emerge naked from the bathroom, Sven lifts the sheet to welcome me into bed. I lie beside him, hands by my side, my heart racing. He draws me close, skin on skin, then mouth on mouth, kissing me slowly, tenderly. I ignore the bodily smells. His mouth moves to my neck, nibbling it gently, then to my breasts, stroking them one by one, then suckling my nipples. My body melts. A lightning bolt surges through me.

Sven talks as he touches me, his words mostly a comforting hum. I only catch snatches of what he is saying as his mouth nuzzles into my body. No matter. Although the language is foreign, I understand every word. His magic touch unearths pleasure zones in my body I never knew existed. What exquisite language he uses –caressing, stroking, kissing, suckling.

And my body talks back, sometimes openly, invitingly, sometimes softly, sensuously, crooning, keening, rocking and shocking me to the core until it no longer seems mine. I cry out to him, drawing him ever closer, desperate to have him inside me. This is what I want, the connection I crave.

Sven tries to enter me several times, but his penis remains flaccid. Despite rubbing valiantly to rouse it, it stubbornly refuses to maintain an erection. Disgusted, he returns to using his fingers and mouth to talk to me. Soon my body is talking back again. Caught up in a vortex of swirling emotions and sensations, I grunt, I groan, I sigh, I moan, I laugh, I cry, but mostly I hum, a harmony emanating from the very core of me until finally I cry out. I spasm over and over until I am spent and think that I can take no more. Then his fingers start talking to me, again, coaxing me back to life again and again – sometimes insistent, sometimes pleading, but always tenderly, lovingly, showing me the way.

I am a woman again. My sexual awakening belongs in the real world and not in my imaginings. Suddenly overnight, a life force pulses through me and my heart expands. I'm in love with life, and in love with the possibility, that love and beauty are not behind me. I want to dance and shout *Hallelujah!* I love everybody, but most of all I love the precious gift bestowed on me at this time in my life.

Outside I hear the rain. Rain, rain glorious rain! Welcome to my paradise Sven. The drought is broken. The rivers are running. Magically, in one sweet night, new life has returned.

A lush moistness abounds. A smile comes over me spreading into every nook and cranny of the garden of my delights which quivers in response. I pay homage to the welcoming rain.

I awaken in his arms in the predawn light. Sven is here. He's spent the whole night holding me, enfolding me, never letting me go. He is spent. He senses that I'm awake, finally releases me and turns over. I creep to the bathroom, then return to bed. I touch his body invitingly, my fingers tracing over his belly and around his genitals, but he is dead to the world. I snuggle into his back, to sleep, perchance to dream. A new dawn has come.

11. Summer Reckoning

Thump! My eyes jerk open. Kiki is standing on the bed staring at me, defiantly, challenging me to tell her to get off. She knows she's not allowed on the bed.

"What's up, Little Girl?"

"Rrrrrrr, rrrrrrrr," comes the soft nasally groan in reply. I look over at the other side of the bed. I can see the imprint on the pillow where he was, but Sven has disappeared.

"What have you done with him?" Kiki doesn't move, just continues to stand and stare. He must be downstairs making me coffee. I wait.

A breeze wafts through the window accompanied by a smell of freshness. With the change in temperature and overnight rain, Nature reminds me of how our rhythms are in tune with hers. She's breathed new life, new energy into me, my body and mind no longer leaden, stifled by the heat. I stretch slowly, sensuously, my arms like petals unfolding tenderly. Seeds held deep underground for too long have burst into life as delicate flowers. I peel back the bed cover and head to the bathroom.

I peer into the mirror. I examine my reflection minutely, as I did when I lost my virginity. Can you tell I made love? No answer there. Instead, all I see are lines, wrinkles and sunspots, the curse of growing older. Will Sven see them too, I wonder as I head downstairs?

No Sven. No coffee brewing. Just dirty dishes and wine glasses. My heart drops. He's gone. He didn't even say goodbye. I see a note on the bench, grab it.

Thanks for a wonderful evening. Sorry for letting you down. S

Yes, he did, but he made up for it. The phone rings. I pick it up, not looking.

"It's okay. Can I see you again?"

"Mrs. Jardine?" says a strange male voice.

"Sorry, I thought it was someone else. This is Eve Jardine."

"It's Jack, from the Flora Garden Centre here. Your orchid potting mix is in."

I swallow. "Thanks, Jack. I'll be down later today to pick it up."

I slowly put down the phone, my mind reeling. Who is Sven really? Alarm bells start to ring. I know virtually nothing about him, not where he lives, his surname, not even his cell phone number. How ridiculous. I email him.

Tell me you will be with me again soon, please.

The reply comes almost instantaneously.

Sorry Eve, I can't. I am off in a few days, to Australia this time, a nine- month contract with Kimberley Gas. Maybe catch up when I return?

❧

I slam the lid of the iPad down, startling Kiki. He knew. He damn well knew! He played me. I stand there running my hands over my body, slowly, sensuously until I feel the heat at my core rising again. The anger dissipates and a smile slowly washes over me. It wouldn't have mattered if I'd known. I was like a moth to the flame. I grin. And it was worth it. But, there is no love lost, only lust, spilt and overflowing.

The cage door is open but I don't recognize the woman in there, this overtly sexual and sensual being filled with such passion and desire. My hands press against my womb. Has she been hiding deep inside me, waiting for the right time to emerge into the world? I take a deep breath, awestruck. At fifty-nine, have I found another wondrous part of me still needing to be realized?

"Come on Kiki, let's go out into the garden." As I step out fresh aromas fill my nostrils. It is gloriously damp underfoot but leaf and tree litter are strewn everywhere, courtesy of yesterday's fierce heat and gusty cool change overnight. Apart from a few scorched leaves, the garden is relatively unscathed. Thank heavens. I head to the rear of the house, to the orchard.

As I near the apple trees, I see bruises on the ripening apples. On the side of the apples exposed to the sun are yellow and brown patches – sunburn. I sigh. The apple trees won't die, but the apples are spoilt, a delicious season gone begging. Just like Sven.

12. Rachel

"Good evening, Eve, Lovely to see you again. You're looking as beautiful as ever," says Alex, the owner of *Mezza*,
kissing me on both cheeks.

"Thank you. It is wonderful to be here, Alex." I've taken some
care to look good – slim fitting purple sheath dress, strappy
black sandals and my hair tied fashionably to one side with a
purple ribbon. Purple for sensitivity, compassion and understanding, all of which I will need in spades tonight. "My niece
Rachel is joining me, tonight. Do you have a quiet table for us,
please?"

"Of course. We always have a table for you. Come this way."
Alex leads me to an intimate little nook near the front window.

"Perfect." Alex pulls out a chair for me, then pushes it back in
when I sit. "Thank you. William and I loved dining here. You
made us feel like family."

"You are part of our family, Eve."

"Eve's part of my family, too." With impeccable timing as
always, Rachel appears from behind Alex's back. "I'm Rachel,
Eve's niece," says Rachel extending her hand to Alex. He holds
her hand, kisses it, and then pulls out a chair for her.

"Welcome, Rachel. Beauty indeed runs deep in the family."
Rachel smiles radiantly, unused to such charm and attention.
She looks stunning in tight fitting black suit – short skirt,
tailored waist length jacket with an emerald green camisole
and staggeringly high black crocodile skin heels. Her hair is
tied back with a black barrette, in working mode.

"I need a drink badly, Eve. A difficult client. Is Pinot Grigio
and some sparkling water alright with you?"

"Yes, thank you. And some dips and appetisers to start with
please, Alex. You'll know what to bring." Alex bows as he leaves,
quickly returning with wine and water.

"Here's to beauty," I toast.

"Yes, indeed," says Rachel. We drink.

"How's Richard's plans for the trip going?" I ask.

"Really great. He's off in two weeks' time – Italy, the UK,
Germany and France. He's made contact with mom and is
meeting up with her and her new man, Max, in Berlin. I'm so
envious. I wish I was going with him, but I realize he wants to
take time for himself. Even Dad's stopped griping about him
being on holiday for so long and has made him network with
some bigwigs in Europe."

"Impressive. Your turn next, Rachel. Time to spread your
wings."

"Not yet." She runs her fingers down the stem of her wine
glass and looks up. "What's been happening in your life, Eve?"

"You won't believe it. Cindy said I should try online dating,
and I have been."

"Really? No, I don't believe it," said Rachel looking at me in amazement. "Have you had any dates?"

"Yes, four." I gulp silently, "All frogs though, no princes. It's a bit scary starting over at my age. I'm not even sure what I'm looking for, apart from another William, but I doubt any man exists who could fill his shoes."

"That doesn't mean you shouldn't try. Good on you, Eve."

"What about you, Rachel, are you dating?"

"No way," she says, her green eyes flashing.

"Not all men are like Raymond, Rachel."

"Maybe not, but I'm not willing to find out," says Rachel angrily.

Alex brings a large tray of appetisers. We tuck in. I take a deep breath.

"Rachel, you're only thirty-three. Don't waste precious time living with anger and regrets. What about children?"

"Don't you start on my biological clock ticking, Eve. I get that nearly every day. *Don't you want kids? Is your career more important to you? Aren't you maternal? Is there something wrong with you?* Busy bodies and so rude. No, I don't want kids. I'm going to get cats instead." Rachel's face is flushed and her hands are balled into tight fists.

I remember that same anger. I couldn't have children but it took two years to find out. I felt under siege from a constant barrage of questions. *Are you pregnant? Are you trying? Have you tried?* Intruding on such an intensely private, painful and intimate matter. I hated it, angry that other people felt they had the right to have some input into my life. It was suffocating.

"Whatever progress women think we've made, we still live in a culture of assumed motherhood, where little girls are expected from birth to go on to have children of their own."

"There's nothing like being told you're a ticking time bomb, with your womb set to reach its expiration date any time now," said Rachel angrily.

"I felt a failure when I couldn't have kids. My first marriage to John broke up because of it."

"You aren't a failure, Eve," says Rachel now holding my hands in hers.

"I know that now, Rachel." I felt I'd failed William, too, in a way. He said he didn't mind, but I did. I wanted a part of him to be left behind. Instead, all I have are his ashes," I say, tears welling.

Rachel dabs tears from her eyes. "Look at us. What a hopeless pair we are."

"Feeling makes you vulnerable, but at least you know you're alive." Rachel nods. "When we sublimate our passion in our homes and gardens, in our children or our pets, or in our career, our existence becomes robotic and we lose touch with our essential nature."

"So true," says Rachel.

"The real problem is, instead of healing our wounds or our injured instinct, we become inured to the pain or pretend it doesn't exist."

"You would've made a great psychotherapist, Eve."

I laugh. "Much easier said than done, as you well know, Rach."

"I agree, Eve. We become pseudo women, saturated with an infernal busyness that stops us reflecting on who we really are, what we are really feeling and what it is we really want."

"I've been living in a nether world since William died, seeing myself as a widow for life. It's easier than taking a chance on life again." I grab her hand. "I don't want you to make the same mistake."

"I won't. Let's eat. Alex may worry we're crying over the food being so bad."

13. Swimming with a shark

I've lost my cherry. I'm no longer an internet virgin. I log on for a bit of virtual kissing, back to life in the dating slipstream. Looking. Always looking. A smorgasbord of suitable or, all too often, unsuitable men are but a fingertip away.

Ping! Someone's sent me a kiss! My heart leaps, that familiar excitement, in spite of all the heartache and disappointment.

I'd like to get to know you, would you be interested?

I check Mark's profile.

Yes, thank you.

"Beep. Beep." A strange beeping is coming from my computer. What is going on? The beeping stops. About five minutes later the noise appears again. I search the screen and see the green light. I hit the *allow chat* button. It's Mark.

"Hello Mark," I say. No answer. Oops. I realize it's a written chat.

MARK SAID

Hi

Nice to "see" you

EVE SAID

Hello to you, but haven't seen you yet.

Too true 😊

I am very happy to email a current pic

Many thanks.

Will sign off for now with a smile to my face.

Will you hang on here for a few minutes whilst I transmit it?

I don't want another tall, dark + debonair man to sweep you off your feet in the interim.

Laughing again.

You are after all, extremely attractive.

Even more so on the inside.

OMG! I must have been a good boy in my past life.

Not in this life?

Subject to conjecture.

What else do you do when you're not chatting up women?

Let me tell you...

I don't smoke, and I drink very little alcohol.

I have no experience with or interest in drugs.

I don't smoke or do drugs either but I do indulge in wine.

Ok ... are we close enough friends to talk about some mildly intimate specifics?

Yes.

I do not have any STDs

I am a condom user, unless in a long-term monogamous relationship.

I don't either.

Health and well-being are crucial in my life.

I love the touch of a woman, her closeness

and smell, the pheromones and intimacies.

Touch is the most important sense to me,

touching and being touched. It is coming

back into my life after many years without it.

Yes. It's a beautiful thing. I am a middle-aged man,

not as virile as I once was, but my penis (small/medium)

still functions, and I love sex. I was well into adulthood

when I began to experience that intimacy is as important as

orgasm.

I think you have just been censored.

I agree about intimacy.

Younger people don't understand that.

(😊 @ the "censored" comment)

Just pushing boundaries here. I am rather naughty, you know.

I know. So am I, my own boundaries.

I'm sure you are!

And I respect that you are pushing your own too.

Do you do this often?

Well, I have been explicit … your turn now.

No, I don't do this often.

In fact, not for years. I promise.

I made love for the first time in many

years recently and it was beautiful.

Good on you!

Do you still see the person?

Not being judgmental.

        No. He jumped ship and ran away to sea.

        Once was enough.

I am happy to take his place. The only limit

I have is that I am strictly hetero.

Everything else is on the table; no limits.

        What a strange conversation we are having.

It's not strange. We would have it in due course anyhow.

I'm sure that you have some fantasies that you may never have

disclosed.

You can feel safe with me.

        I am going where I have never gone before.

        Feeling safe is really important.

Where would you like to go?

You can say it. I won't be shocked.

        I'm a neophyte in this sexual world.

        I am shocking myself. I come from the era

        where women were either Madonnas or Whores.

A nice place to be coming from, not going to.

Okay, let me lead ... do you fantasize about for example,

about being tied up and/or having your bottom spanked?

        Never. Anything that impinges on my

        freedom is an anathema. No domination.

Okay ... walking through the forest and

making love with others watching?

        No way.

Love walking through forests though.

🙂 Funny!

That's a change.

So, sex is on a bed one on one?

Thanks! 🤍

One on one, but venue can vary.

Okay ... another shocking question? Ready?

Yes

Pubic hair: shaved, waxed, or trimmed?

No

Au natural?

The doorbell rings. Saved by the bell. I've been swimming with a shark.

No. Blue rinsed and body permed.

Have to go. Bye!

I slam the iPad cover down on Mark and his wayward charms. "Come in, Cindy. Thank heavens you're here."

PART 2

SOWING SEEDS

Out beyond ideas of rightdoing and wrongdoing,
there is a field.
I will meet you there. When that soul lies down in the grass,
the world is too full to talk about.

Rumi

14. Autumn

C ool, crisp, shorter days have ushered in fall and a changing palette of colors in the foliage. Vibrant hues of copper,
orange and deep crimson are appearing in the woodlands. The
deep green leaves on the Dogwoods are turning burgundy red.
But, all too soon the remaining ripe red fruit, the leaves and the
colors will be gone. Winter is coming.

I am trying hard to live in the present, and to keep believing
in a future – a future where the sense of connection is created
anew and imbued with new meaning. My body is no longer
numb. It is a thinking, feeling entity, filled with longing. Longing for closeness, for intimacy. My body is crying out to be
touched, to be loved, to let me know I'm still alive.

When Sven awoke it from hibernation I felt connected to life
and living again. But he is no longer here. There is no one here.
No one near. No one even on the horizon. Do I skip back into
my safe cocoon, numb my mind and body? Or do I continue
the search? I'm getting older. There's not much time left. Is this
the autumn of my life?"

&

The doorbell rings. Kiki doesn't move. She stays with me. I'm not expecting anyone. It's 5.30 pm. I open the door. It's Cindy, looking divine in tailored black trouser suit and diamond studs. Her face is full of concern as she looks at me. I look and feel like something the cat dragged in. "Come in, Cindy." She follows me in and closes the door behind her.

Once we are in the kitchen, she finally speaks. "I hadn't heard from you. I felt something was wrong." She looks closely at me. "Are you alright, Eve?"

It's a week since I'd had a rant. I'd told her I hate online dating. I hate men ignoring me, or overlooking me or telling me I'm too old or taking off overseas without telling me. I'm sick of it. I give up. I told her I would ring.

"I'm okay, Cindy, just feeling down. I didn't want to dump on you again. You've got more than enough on your plate."

"Has something happened, Eve? Did you make your profile more appealing as I suggested?"

"No, I've left my run too late. I'm past this, Cindy. It really is time for cats."

"Don't you dare give up, Eve. I won't let you. It's never too late to live a little." She gives me a bear hug. I choke up. "Come on, time for a drink. We'll go over what I'm thinking about for our trip."

Three hours, two bottles of wine and one takeout pizza later, my mood has mellowed, like fine fall foliage. As I drift off to sleep, I know I have to let go of the past and keep searching, keep hoping, keep trusting that the Universe will guide me to the person who is right for me. Cindy, exhausted from her labors exhorting me onwards, is sleeping in the bedroom next door, with an early wakeup call set. I love her.

15. Evie

Up early, I'm walking through the copper-colored woodlands, setting a cracking pace. Kiki, animated for the first time in a while, woofs at the chipmunks and squirrels darting about the leaf-strewn forest floor. The air is fresh and invigorating. My mind is crystal clear. I'm going to start researching about sexuality. Naïveté at this juncture in my life is problematic. I don't know enough about my anatomy and how it functions let alone begin to understand the depth of my reaction with Sven.

Sex education in school was purely about reproduction and menstruation. Sex was never spoken about by mom or dad — a taboo topic; dirty and hidden. I never really talked about sex with William, either. The abusive past was left behind. In its stead, sex was safe, pleasurable and passionate, although not very adventurous. I preferred it that way. I was happier cuddling. Not at all like *Lady Chatterley's Lover* which I'm going to revisit for starters. Time to get down and dirty.

And, I'm not going to revise my profile. I'm going to create a new one – Evie, in upper case. EVIE is going to be younger and bolder, with a new photo showing some cleavage, and looking for younger men.

Headline:

Warm, wise, nurturing and sensual soul.

Describe yourself:

Imbued with a curious, adventurous spirit, I am gentle and generous, loving and lovable, and passionate about life and living,
orchids and gardening, books and writing. Longing to chase
white rabbits.

My ideal partner:

A romantic. Someone to make my heart sing, my spirit soar, my
body quiver and my garden grow, is my kind of wonderful.

I make my profile live and head for a much-needed shower.
Evie's going shopping for new clothes and shoes. Then a visit to
the beauty salon for a massage, a manicure, and a hair and makeup
makeover. And, most important, to take Cindy for dinner at a
swish new Italian restaurant, Florentine, as a thank you.

ॐ

By the time I return, my inbox is awash with emails and kisses.
The computer is pinging thick and fast with men. Men of all
ages, many much younger. Fantastic, Evie, you've hit the hot
button. A roller coaster of hope, anticipation and desire dances
deliciously before my eyes. My new profile seems to be seen as
an open invitation for naughtiness. The erotic as an antidote
to numbness and dying. Whacky doo! And then, whack! What
the hell are you doing, Evie? William comes flooding into my

consciousness and I quickly become invisible again.

"Tea, Kiki. I need a calming cup of Chamomile tea while I work out what to do." Later, in a chastened state, I discard the kisses and scan through the dozens and dozens of emails, many heartfelt, which brings William to mind again. We had a physical, emotional and spiritual connection. That's what I'm looking for. That's what I want, again. And, if I'm being honest with myself, intimacy and sexuality are part of the equation. I'll sleep on it. Tomorrow...

ॐ

I wake at 5.00 am. William is standing at the foot of the bed looking at me. I gasp, "What are you doing here? Why are you here?" My voice is soft, hesitant. He just stands there and smiles at me, that beautiful, crooked, knowing smile. He hasn't aged. Damn him.

"I'm looking, Sweetheart. I'm trying. I really am. But you'll have to wait a bit. I'm late starting over. I haven't learnt the lingo, yet. I'm doing some research, but I think I'm going to need some lessons. It's not safe out there without you to protect me." William smiles. The smile warms me. He lingers a while longer, then disappears. I blink. Tears fill my eyes. Is he worried about me? Angry for not spreading his ashes? Or just bemused with my recalcitrance and intrepid nature as he often was? I don't know. Why now?

I turn on the light, reach for my Tarot cards, shuffle and

turn the top card over. *Death — endings, beginnings, change, transformation, transition.* I pick up the phone.

"Hello, Eve. What's up?" asks Rachel, concerned by my early morning call. She's a sensitive too. It's our shared secret. There's a spiritual side to her nature which, in her profession, she needs to keep well hidden.

"William appeared to me early this morning. He's never made his presence felt in person before. And I'm not sure why." Between sniffs, I tell her the story.

"He loves you, Eve. He always will," she says.

"But why now?" I ask, voice choking up.

"You've started dating, Eve. He's telling you it's okay to date. He's telling you it's okay to let him go."

"Do you really think so, Rachel?" I ask, wishing it were so.

"Of course, I do. He's happy for you, Eve. Trust me, I feel it. And I am, too."

I sob again, relieved by her reassurance. "I'm hopeless."

"No, you're not. You're very special, Eve. That's why William loved you."

"Thanks, Rachel. Thanks so much. Time for a walk. We'll catch up soon and you can fill me in on how Richard is going overseas. And about what's happening with you. Love you."

"Love you, too," Rachel replies and hangs up.

"It's time," I tell myself as I look out the study window. It's a beautiful day out there, very still. Soft autumn sunshine filtering through the trees, my favorite season. It's time, Eve. Time to open up a window into your carefully ordered and cloistered world. Time to listen to your heart. Your intuition is telling you something is lost. The echo to a long-lost consciousness that your heart heard when you were with Sven. I turn to the computer. Time to let EVIE take flight. The screensaver morphs into a butterfly unfolding its wings.

16. More Frogs

I'm sitting in the spa pool of the local swimming centre, my eyes closed. Thoughts swirl around in my mind as the jets buffet my body. My body is fluid. I succumb to the rocking movement allowing my mind to roam freely whilst the water caresses my body. Just as music caresses my soul. Music and water move me – my two great releases at the moment. Symphonies and piano concertos and swirling water. Lullabies for a woman in the lushness of creation.

Over the past ten days I've been assiduously culling, looking for men who most appeal. Yes. No. Yes. No. No. No!!! Starting tomorrow, I've arranged to meet two different men, three days apart. Max and Charles.

Max, short for Maximillian, swirls around in my mind. He's 52, a South African business man with his own helicopter. He loves dining out, opening nights at the opera and has a remote, romantic cabin with a wood fire overlooking the ocean. He says he'd love to fly me there, and that he'd love to make love to me on the rug in front of the fire. He sounds strong, confident, in charge of his world and the women in it. He also sounds smooth and sexy, just like the water swirling sensuously around my thighs. I can't wait to meet him.

The jets turn off. All is quiet. As the water stills Charles comes to mind. 50, a committed environmentalist, a psychologist with a flourishing practice, and a passion for Jung. I tell him about my two differing personalities – the introverted, understated Eve, who likes to play it safe and the bolder Evie, venturing where she has never been before. Charles seems to understand me better than I understand myself. He's counselling me, encouraging me to let go. He woos me with music and his beautiful writing, caressing me, calming me, and more often, challenging me. It's like a breath of fresh air or perhaps more like the kiss of life, awakening me from a deep, deep sleep. He sounds so right for me but if he turns out to be a frog or a fraud, I've told him I will stomp on him and squash him to bits.

The spa jets kick on once again. The sound blasting through my mind like a symphony. Charles loves classical music as I do. A special favorite is Russian composer, Mussorgsky's ten-part suite — *Pictures at an Exhibition*. The music depicts an imaginary tour of an art collection, reaching its majestic climax at the tenth and final picture, a proposed sketch of the Great Gate of Kiev. My mind goes wild with the water, the anticipation building up to a crescendo. But first, Max.

❧

I'm walking downtown to meet Max at Urbane, an apt place to meet a suave, sophisticated South African. I know he is a player, but probably, for the first time in my life, I want to play. I'm dressed to the nines in bright red, walking a little unsteadily, unused to the high heels and wearing *Sensuous Nude*.

I recognize Max waiting for me outside the restaurant. He sees me approaching, walks up to me and takes my hands, his hazel eyes looking at me lasciviously. He's tall, well built; his sandy colored hair falls across his forehead; smartly dressed in taupe trousers, navy blue blazer and pale blue open necked shirt. I smile at him and say, "Hello."

"You're even lovelier than your photo." He kisses me, shocking me by firmly tongue kissing me and rubbing my breasts at the same time. He pulls back, looks at me, his hands still holding my breasts. "Are you sure you want to eat?"

"Yes," I say and pull away as he starts to fondle my breasts again, moving towards the restaurant. "I'm hungry." Am I hungry for this, I wonder?

Inside Max asks for a quiet table away from others. "Let's order quickly so we can get out of here." We do. Risotto for Max and a chicken salad for me. When he won't stop talking, hardly pauses to draw breath, I understand why.

"You're so sexy, I can't wait to fuck you. Good on you for putting in a wide age range. Younger men are more virile. They can come three to four times a night and sustain the effort longer, but they're often not as considerate of women though." He pauses to draw breath. "They're like racing cars without brakes, but I'm a kind, considerate and caring lover. I'm getting hard just sitting here talking to you. Do you want to feel me?" He opens his mouth again. The waiter arrives with our meals.

I put my hand up. "Stop talking and eat."

"Whatever you want me to do I will do it. There are no limits. No orifice is sacred." I put down my head, ignoring him and start eating. For once it is a relief the restaurant is so noisy. I can't hear a lot of what Max is saying, although his animated manner and the way he is salivating over me, rather than his food, conveys it adequately enough. He's so open and pragmatic about what he wants and wants to do to me. Wordlessly, in between mouthfuls of food and sips of wine, I look at him fascinated, this creature from another planet, but a strangely benign one. I feel no threat, but I feel no connection, no desire either.

"Let's get out of here," he says, "you can follow me home." As soon as we are outside, he fondles my breasts and tongue kisses me again. I extricate myself a little more expertly. Amused, intrigued even, I hop in my car and follow his Mercedes wondering what is in store. At the next intersection the lights are red. As I pull up behind him, the old Eve hops in the car.

"What the hell are you playing at, Evie?" When the lights change to green, Max drives on. I turn right and head home.

ॐ

Last chance. Charles texts to say he is waiting out the front of my house. Despite Cindy's warnings, I gave this one my address. Call it a hunch; I felt no danger. Taking a deep breath, I pick up my bag and walk outside. I'm surprised to see a Winnebago parked there. Standing beside it is a tall, thin man with dark shoulder-length hair pulled back in a pony tail. Dressed all in black, he looks very reminiscent of a Renaissance priest. He smiles as I walk towards him.

"Evie?"

My insides hollow out. Then a laugh erupts. "Is this your home?"

"And my office. Solar powered, too."

Heaven help me, not a fucking frog, a goddamn hermit crab. I laugh, a wry laugh. "Sucked in, Evie," I say, sotto voce.

The smile vanishes. "I didn't suck you in."

"No, it's my fault. I'm still on training wheels. It's not safe to be playing outside on the streets." I turn and walk back inside.

I'm out! Out of online dating forever! Out of men! I head to the fridge for some wine. I'm awash with emotion. I gulp. I can't do this anymore. It's like being on a gigantic roller coaster. I pour myself a glass and head into the study. I'm coming off this site.

Ping!

Romanza has sent you an email. I read.

This online experience is demanding and addictive, often disappointing and cruel. In my imagination, you are perfect. Then we meet, and no matter how beautiful you are, it's like waking up from a dream. Then we go back on the internet looking for another fantasy as real as a dream. Meet me tomorrow. Show me you are real.

Matias

My finger hovers over the delete button, but I can't help myself. Matias looks like an exotic movie star. 56. Divorced. An Argentinian business man. Dark, artistic, passionate about realism and economics, romanticism and beauty. Addicted to the tango and poetry. He is looking for a gentle person, sensitive, intelligent and feminine. Someone who likes to read, talk, walk and is comfortable with silence. Someone to dance the tango with.

"How can you not meet him?" I ask myself, deep in thought. Be brave, Evie. This is a leap of faith.

Ping! I jump.

So Darling,

It was you who turned out to be the frog. Unlike you, I do not need to stomp on you, for I know you are suffering enough already for your foolishness, although I do have some more tough love.

If it helps, from my point of view, it was the heroine EVIE who was writing to me, and the reactionary EVE who did not find the courage to cleave from her own shadow when we came together.

EVE, I forgive you what you did to me, but that you did it to yourself. How could I forgive that?

Love and hugs,

Charles

I laugh out loud, a belly laugh. I'll email Matias to tell him I'll meet him tomorrow.

17. Pregnant with potential

I walk into the jungle that is my orchid house. The orchids are spiking. In the rear corner, I spy an orchid with three long pendulous spikes spilling over its basket. It is slowly starting to open. I gaze at it, awestruck by its beauty, and the promise of more to come. I tenderly fondle around each of the orchids to check if more budding babies are to be found. The deliciously seductive orchid flowering season has begun. Precious blooms, pregnant with potential, will emerge through hooded helmets like bears coming out of hibernation.

I'm ready to come out of hibernation soon too I muse as I stand there admiring my precious beauties. My research has led me to Tantra. The essence of Tantra is liberation – to expand, be free and to be liberated. I want to explore and express my sensual self more fully. To embrace the divine feminine within. I yearn for the kind of sex I read about. Sex that is beautiful, transformative and deeply connecting — sacred sexuality. A more spiritual yet intensely passionate way of expressing sexual love. But I need more guidance. I've discovered that the Goddess Shaney is running a workshop a month after we return from Europe – to encourage sexual confidence and explore the broad spectrum of what sexuality is. I hope Cindy will come with me.

My eyes alight on another possible spike. I gently run my fingers over it. Ah, yes. My face breaks out in a smile at the promise this lush juicy shoot holds. As I stroke the emerging spike sensuously, my smile widens at the thought of another promising lush juicy shoot my research has unearthed –*Aphrodisiac Male Escorts*. An escort agency run by women for women. I giggle. Evie, you wicked, wicked woman. No way can I tell anyone about this yet. Anyway, I doubt I'll have the courage to find out any more myself. A personal sex trainer. That's too far out of the ball park, even for you, Evie.

18. Matias

It's raining hard. The wind is blowing a gale, threatening to turn my umbrella inside out. My heart is beating fast as I turn the corner. I see Matias outside the café, under the canopy, pacing back and forth, trying to catch a glimpse of me. His dark wavy hair is slicked back. As I move into view, he rushes to meet me and brings my umbrella under control. Not nearly as tall as I'd expected.

"Eve." He lifts my hand to his lips and leaves his lips there while his dark flashing eyes bore into me. What a handsome looking devil he is. Clean shaven, swarthy complexion, olive skin. His lean, muscular build encased in fitted long-sleeved bright green shirt, black jeans, a tan leather belt with a striking silver buckle and tan leather boots with stacked heels giving him a little more height. Antonio Banderas springs to mind.

He kisses my hand again, keeps holding onto it as if magnetically attached, then leads me into the café. Feeling a little overawed, but curious nonetheless, I sit down. Matias sits beside me, so close he is almost on top of me. I can't move, and I can scarcely breathe. A waitress comes over.

"What would you like to drink?" I order a café latte and look at Matias.

"No, I don't want anything." A hand gesture dismisses her. He moves closer, looking at me intensely, our faces almost touching. "You are beautiful," he says, stroking the hair around my face. I quiver at his touch, beyond words. My coffee arrives. I take sips in between bouts of getting my hand delicately stroked. The more I look at him, the more I see he's incredibly handsome. Short, dark and handsome. Well two out of three ain't bad. I finish my coffee.

"Come let's go," Matias says leaving $10 on the table. "Let me walk you to your car." Hand on my back, he guides me out of the café. He puts my umbrella up, then places his arm around my waist drawing me close. Our bodies touch as we walk, oblivious of the wind and rain whipping around us. When we reach the car, Matias turns to face me, handing me the umbrella. His fingers find my lips, tracing gently around them before moving around my hairline, the sensations exquisite. He puts both hands around my face, draws me towards him, kisses me tenderly, then draws back to look at me.

"You are beautiful. I love your blue eyes. Your skin is so soft," he says before kissing me again.

This time I return the kiss. "Thank you," I say, dumbfounded.

"Get in the car." I do as I am told, Matias hops in. I turn and offer my face to him. The exquisite tracery on my lips is extended to my cheeks, forehead and then my hair. I shiver. He alternates his lips with his fingers, tender kisses as light as a feather dancing across my lips and my face. I close my eyes. He stops, and I can hardly bear it. I open my eyes to see his brown eyes looking at me with such smoldering intensity I feel I will ignite.

"I have to go. I have a business meeting. Can I see you tomorrow evening?"

"Yes."

"Will you dance the tango with me?"

"Yes, but you'll have to teach me."

~

Lying in bed the morning after, with a large mug of coffee, I'm looking out. The weather is wild. The rain coming in horizontally, smashing against the window. Such extreme autumn weather. I do hope the weather in Europe will be kinder. Cindy and I are leaving in three weeks. We'll be away for a month. It will be wonderful.

I've been dreaming about Matias all night, ridiculously over the top happy dreams with fairy tale endings. We have the most amazing connection, but there's a touch of unreality about what happened. When I'm near him, I feel I have no will of my own. Now I feel the need to take things more slowly, to let us evolve rather than force the pace. Dreaming is fine, but the real world is more complicated. I write to tell him so. He replies.

I was worried the suddenness of my approach might have scared you away. Tomorrow night. Your reserve and reticence are giving me time to wake up as well, to fully understand it. It felt like coming down from outer space, entering this reality that almost does not belong to anything.

6.30pm at Tango Tambien Dance Studio in Hoboken. I'll meet you there. I have a client to meet beforehand. We will have half an hour to ourselves.

El tango te espera (the tango waits for you). Anibal Troila

Matias

Okay.

Hope is faith holding out its hand in the dark. George Iles

Eve

❧

Matias is waiting out the front of the dance studio, his eyes flitting, deep in thought. Tonight, he's all in black — tight V neck T shirt, showing off his buffed body. Shiny pants, fitted at the waist and hips and flared at the ankles, showing off his trim body, together with patent leather dancing shoes. His hair is slicked down and tied back in a ponytail. Even in black he has real flair. I'm wearing a bright red dress and red shoes — the only shoes I have with heels and a strap that look remotely like dancing shoes — yet I feel like a pea hen beside him.

"Eve. You look lovely." He takes my hand and kisses it again.

"Thank you. It's good to see you again, Matias. Do you dance here often?"

Matias ushers me into the studio. "Yes, I do. I teach Argentinian tango, but more often I come here to practise. I dance in competitions. It's an addiction."

"I know all about addictions. I'm addicted to making dreams come true. Learning to dance the tango is one of mine," I say.

"Sit here." We sit, facing each other, knees touching, Matias taking my hands in his. I'll tell you a little about the tango before I show you how to dance. "Tango dance steps are hot, passionate and precise." His proximity is overpowering.

"The Argentine Tango originated in the streets of Buenos Aires. Originally the dance was about acting out the relationship between a prostitute and her pimp and was considered obscene by polite society. This form of tango spread throughout the underworld for many years before being picked up in Paris and becoming fashionable in Europe." He pauses to see if I'm following. I nod and smile.

"Because of its popularity overseas, Argentinian high society welcomed it into their own lives. It's now the most popular dance in Argentina." Matias stands up, turns on the music, then opens his arms. I walk into them, eager to learn this dance.

"Tango starts with embracing. It's the first connection into the dance. The man must hold the woman securely but with freedom to move. He must lead, not force. Move your arm up higher, around my neck." He pulls me close, our heads nearly touching, positioning my body slightly to the left of his, my belly close to his, my chest upright. His exoticism is captivating.

"Music is another point of connection. Don't just listen to

the music, feel it. In tango we dance to what we feel, there are no counts. We'll walk to the music. Walking is the foundation of tango." He moves forward and I take slow even steps backwards. Matias brings his feet together and stops. We're in a close embrace. I can hardly breathe. He steps back with longer strides. I stumble towards him. Eve, you klutz. His arm gathers me in.

"Just follow, don't think." We continue the pattern of walking, bringing our feet together, then reversing. Sometimes short steps, sometimes long.

"Look to my chest. Feel the music." We are close, chests touching.

He switches to a pattern — slow, slow, quick, quick, slow. A sultry last step, his left foot arcing towards his right to close, the pattern ready to begin again. I move.

"No! Wait for my lead. Don't think. Feel, feel my lead." He guides me around so beautifully, I am swept away by the music, by his nearness. He pauses, our arms and bodies still connected, "Be still with me." He moves his head back so his eyes are looking into mine. "Every time I dance with you, you are my woman," he says and kisses me passionately. I am blown away by this dance, by this man.

"Matias, I love dancing, but nothing compares to this."

"Because of you Eve, *I wheeled with the stars. My heart broke loose on the wind.* That's Pablo Neruda talking for me." I kiss him on the cheek. We arrange another rendezvous. This time at *La Luna* for dinner the following evening.

ào

Matias is waiting for me outside the restaurant dressed in a dark blue silk shirt, navy blue trousers, with a dark tan snake skin boots and leather belt. I have chosen dark blue, too, but in contrast to his attire, I feel like a washed-out rag. I shouldn't have come. A storm is brewing in my stomach, a bug of some sort.

Matias lifts my hand theatrically again, presses his lips to it while staring into my eyes. My insides melt. He ushers me in proprietorially. Once inside he dictates to the waiting staff where we are to sit, what wine to bring, what food we're to eat. Really rich food. I sit quietly and listen, uncomfortable. Beads of sweats keep appearing. I excuse myself to go the bathroom. I want to throw up but can't. All I want is to go home but Matias is fussing so.

"Matias, I feel unwell. I think I should go home."

"No, don't go, Eve." He grabs my hand and rubs it. "Please eat something." He places a selection of food on my plate. "Please." I push the food around on my plate, nibbling a little for half an hour. A waiter comes over.

"Is there a problem with the food, Madame?"

"No," I say feeling embarrassed. "I am unwell. Matias, I must go." Reluctantly he agrees to let me go, but not before I agree to another rendezvous in two days, a drive to the beach.

19. Dreaming

I'm still feeling tired this morning, but I'm hoping the bug is sweated out of my system. Once this humid, stormy weather is over, I'll feel better too. It's depleting on mind, body and soul. The garden has been neglected these past few days. Matias keeps ringing and texting virtually on the hour checking how I am, what I'm doing, wanting to be with me. And spouting poetry.

Don't go far off...

Don't go far off, not even for a day, because --

A day will seem like an eternity waiting for you.

🐦

I've had so little love in my life for too long, I've learned to live without it. Although I yearn for it, this is too much, too soon. I need to recover my equilibrium. We're going for a drive to the beach today. I'll have to ease back a little. The doorbell rings, breaking into my thoughts. I open the door.

"Hello Matias, welcome to my paradise." He kisses me tenderly on the cheek, then looks at me with concern.

"How are you, Eve?"

"I'm feeling better, thanks Matias, but still not quite right."

"What a beautiful place you have here, Eve."

"Yes, it is. I love it. It's my haven."

"Are you ready, Eve?"

"Yes, I am," I say, picking up my bag. Kiki moves forward. "Stay, Kiki."

"Kiki can come, too. I haven't met her yet." Matias fetches a rug from the boot for the back seat. I put Kiki on it. By the time we clamber into the front of his BMW, Kiki has her front paws on the console inserting herself between Matias and me.

"Hello, Kiki," he says. Kiki licks his nose. Matias pulls back as if bitten, then wipes his nose.

"That's just Kiki saying hello," I say. She settles into the confines of the back seat. As we drive down the coast, Matias is calm and quiet for a change. The silence is comforting. I relax and start to nod off. He adjusts the seat back for me. The momentum soon puts me to sleep. The car stops and I wake. Matias is looking at me, stroking my forehead tenderly.

"Would you and Kiki like to come for a walk on the beach?"

"We'd love to." I fix her lead and we walk along the beach slowly and companionably, arm in arm. We near a park with a small group of shops.

"Would you like a drink, Eve?"

"Yes, please, sparkling water." Kiki and I sit on the grass and wait for Matias to return. He brings water for Kiki, too. Afterwards we lie on the grass, my head on his chest, Kiki lying next to me. We talk — a different kind of talking – a kind, gentle sharing of our intimate lives. Matias strokes me.

"I find you beautiful, Eve, a goddess. I've not been with another woman since my divorce." I find that wonderful. I talk of William, feeling freer to be me, more comfortable with him than before. Matias listens for a change. Lying here with him is wonderful. Thank heavens he's come into my life.

I peer into the mirror. My eyes have dark circles underneath from the lack of sleep. I'm no longer a beautiful goddess. Matias knows I'm going overseas soon. He comes over to kiss me in the morning before he goes to work and then calls in most evenings. In between he rings, texts and emails. I've no time or energy for the rest of my life. When he's with me he cannot keep his hands and mouth off me. He wants me just because I'm here. And when I'm not, he purloins poetry.

> Don't leave me, even for an hour, because
>
> each minute will seem like a lifetime,
>
> and my bleeding heart will stop beating.

Yesterday afternoon Matias drove me to the nursery to pick up some plants. We spent several hours together. Then later, just before I went out with an old colleague for dinner, Matias rang to ask if he could call in to say goodnight. He had to see me before going to sleep. He is a romantic of the highest order, hopelessly smitten as never before in his life he says. I rather believe him.

In a quiet moment of reflection, and there are not too many of those at the moment, I think perhaps that this man could look after me. It's strange how quickly the possibilities for our lives change. I love that Matias loves me so much and finds me beautiful. I must admit, my initial reticence which kept him at bay, is almost gone. I'm hungry for him, for his love. He loves me and wants me with a passion which has taken me by surprise.

༄

The doorbell rings. Kiki and I both jump. We've been dozing on the divan waiting for Matias. I check my watch. It is 11.30 pm. I open the door. "Hello."

Matias embraces me. "It's been so long since I've seen you."

"It's only been a few hours," I say, laughingly. "Come in. I'll pour you a glass of red wine."

"No wine yet please, Eve. I've something to ask you. Let's sit." We sit on the divan and Kiki jumps in between us, her face close to Matias', eyeballing him. He pushes her down.

"Ugh! Her breath stinks." Kiki goes to jump back up.

I can see Matias is disturbed. "No, Kiki. Come, sit here," I say firmly and pat the seat on the other side of me. She looks at me, but stays put. "Come on, Little Girl," I say more softly. Kiki refuses to budge and stares at Matias defiantly, whose face is looking like thunder. I pick her up and place her beside me.

"She needs training. Why don't you send her away to one of those training schools?" says Matias.

"No, Kiki doesn't need training. She's just taking some time to get used to you being in my life. Up until now, it's just been the two of us." I say conciliatorily.

"Well, she'd better hurry up. Now, where was I?" My hand reaches out almost involuntarily to stroke Kiki. Matias retrieves it. He looks into my eyes and kisses me, a breathtakingly beautiful kiss, then says, "You are my everything. I look at you, even when you are not present, and I wonder if everything around me is made of you. I cannot hear anything but you."

"Oh, Matias." My finger grazes his lips as he speaks. His eyes are liquid.

"Eve, I cannot function when I'm not with you. I want to be with you, to give you the world the way you want it. I wish to be the air you breathe, so I can be around you. I love you. I want to marry you." I draw his face to mine and kiss him.

"Eve, will you come to my place this weekend so we can be together as husband and wife?"

I inhale sharply. So much. So soon. And yet so right. Yes. I want to be with him. As I exhale slowly, my body softens, the reply comes easily. "Yes, Matias, I will." I throw my arms around his neck and hug him tightly, joy in my heart. Yes, yes. I will. I'm dreaming, dreams with happy endings, all the more exquisite because they're based on the wonderful reality of Matias.

"Thank you, Eve. The feeling is unreal; a dream. The impossible becoming possible. I'll leave you to sleep now." He kisses my forehead, my nose and my mouth with exquisite gentleness, then stands up. We walk hand in hand to the door. I feel like I'm walking on air.

༂

I am home again, exhausted from missing you. But not for much longer.

Don't leave me for a second, my dearest,

because in that moment I will wonder if you have gone so far, you have disappeared from me forever.

20. We wonderful women

Rachel and I are seated around the kitchen bench, drinking champagne, chatting desultorily, and waiting for Cindy again. Punctuality is not her strong suit. Kiki licks Rachel's legs. She reaches down, pats her affectionately and looks up at me.

"Would you like me to mind Kiki when you and Cindy go away?" Rachel asks. "I could stay here and look after her. I'm at a bit of a loose end with Richard away."

"Would you? That would be wonderful, Rachel. She'd be happier with you than being in kennels. Are you sure it's not too much?"

"Not at all. She'll be good company," Rachel says. The doorbell rings. Kiki charges to the door. I follow and open the door. "Welcome, Cindy."

Unusually, she's wearing her glasses, and looks a little flustered. She heads into the kitchen. "Hello, Darlings. I need something to drink."

Rachel pours her a glass of champagne. "What's up, Cindy?" The bubbles fizzle up and over the side of the glass.

"That's what's happening inside of me. I'm fizzing," she says disgustedly.

"What do you mean fizzing, Cindy?" asks Rachel.

"Getting old is mortifying. I can't see properly without my glasses anymore," she says, outraged.

"Calm down, Old Girl," I say, soothingly.

"Don't call me that. I'm not old," she retorts.

"I'm just teasing, Cindy. Tell us what has happened."

Cindy sits down on a stool, takes a sip of her champagne, and gulps. "Setting up the foundation is so stressful. I've had a backache for three days and my thrush has flared again. Dr. Lester prescribed vaginal pessaries again, one each day for three days. Today was the last day," she says, lowering her voice. She pauses, hesitating. She rubs her throat, then takes a bigger sip of champagne. I nod at her to go on. Rachel and I lean forward to hear her better. "I came home, but was running late to come here. I couldn't find my glasses but I managed to peel off the foil. Then the goddamn pessary wouldn't fit in the goddamn applicator." She pauses again, wringing her hands.

"Go on, Cindy," says Rachel encouragingly.

"So, I pushed it up inside me," she says, her face looking pained. "And then I started fizzing." Rachel and I look at each other trying in vain not to smile. "There's nothing to smile about getting old," she says, looking at each of us sternly in turn.

"You are not old, Cindy," I say trying to mollify her. "Tell us what happened."

"Well, I knew something was wrong. So, I fetched the foil wrapper out of the garbage and found my glasses." Cindy pauses again, for effect, sure of her audience now. Rachel and I look at her pleadingly, begging her to tell the rest of the story.

"And it was a suppository, one of Brian's with a painkiller in it," she says standing up, hands on her hips, daring us to say something. Rachel and I titter.

"Well, that must have been a shock to your system," says Rachel trying to be serious. "Perhaps, you've discovered a new cure for thrush." We cover our mouths with our hands, but the tittering continues.

Cindy looks at us, smiles and then starts to giggle. "I do hope so, Darlings. It cured my backache and, apart from fizzing, I'm feeling good." We all burst out laughing. Laughing until tears stream from our eyes and we are doubling up in pain.

Half an hour later, the champagne is flowing freely. So too the fun and laughter. This time because I'm regaling them with my dating tales. Just before I serve dinner, I show them Matias' photo and a print out of his profile.

"Oh my god, Eve, he looks like Antonio Banderas,' says Cindy excitedly.

Rachel's eyes light up. "Let me read his profile." Cindy and Rachel huddle together, giggling excitedly as they read. "Ooh! He sounds amazing. What happened with him, Eve? Have you met him yet?"

"Tell you after we've eaten," I say teasing them. They look at me horrified as I place the lasagne and salad on the bench. I wave a bottle of Pinot Noir tantalizingly as a white flag. "And, Rachel, after you tell me what's happening with you and Richard," I laugh, a wicked laugh. They're hooked. Now I have to reel them in.

"Bitch," they chorus loudly before tucking into the food.

"Where's Richard at the moment, Rachel? asks Cindy. "Eve and I meet him in London in a fortnight and, hopefully, again in Paris before we all head home."

"I feel so envious of you all," says Rachel with a moue. Between mouthfuls, Rachel talks of Richard. Her face softens when she talks of him. They are so close.

"Richard's having the time of his life. He's in Italy at the moment. Next to Germany to meet up with Mom, then England and finally, France. He's never travelled on his own before and is loving the freedom. Best of all, he's dating."

"Do tell, Darling," asks Cindy eagerly.

"Yes, do tell," I echo, excited by the news.

"Well, he doesn't give me names or details, just says it's good to feel normal at long last."

"That's marvellous, Rachel." I say feeling relieved. "And what about you?"

She sighs, shoulders sagging a little. "Nothing much happening in my world. But I'm checking out some therapists. Some internal work first, I think. Perhaps while I'm living here with Kiki. At least she loves me."

"Good on you," I say, patting her hand fondly. "Your turn will come."

"I'm not sure I want to get involved again," says Rachel, her sadness seeping through. I feel for her. She's been burned, but the anger is subsiding. Thankfully.

Cindy holds up her glass. "To men. Where would we be

without them?" Rachel pulls a face. "And to us, we wonderful women," Cindy adds sagely, ever the diplomat.

"To men. And to us, we wonderful women," we echo loudly, tapping glasses.

※

After dinner we adjourn to the conservatory. "Who do you want to hear about next?"

"Matias!" they scream.

"Matias is a romantic of the highest order." My voices softens as I talk about him. I've been keeping him a secret, not believing what was happening to me.

"What does he do?" asks Cindy, eager to establish his financial pedigree first.

"He's rich. Comes from one of the wealthiest families in Argentina. He has mining and real estate investments, but his main business is designing high level IT security systems for banks and large companies."

"Okay. He passes Cindy's first criteria," says Rachel grinning.

I tell them of our first meeting, our night at Tango Tambien and going to the beach.

"You really like him, Eve. Your face is all dreamy," says Cindy.

"He says he is hopelessly smitten, as never before in his life." The girls lean forward, eager to hear more. "A gentleman too. He opens doors, carries things for me, buys me gifts, quotes poetry, says he cherishes me."

"How long have you known him?" queries Rachel, doubtingly.

"Ten days. He calls in before work to kiss me good morning and after work, to kiss me goodnight." It feels good opening up to them.

"And then goes home?" asks Cindy in disbelief.

I nod. "Such a gentle man too, he touches me, strokes me and kisses me like I'm precious at every opportunity." Rachel and Cindy are mesmerised.

"Is that all?" asks Cindy archly.

"Last night he invited me to stay at his place," I say, omitting the marriage proposal.

"Woo hoo! When, when, when?" Cindy screams.

"Tomorrow night." I watch as a big smile creases Rachel's face. She is pleased for me. So is Cindy.

Later in bed that night I remember the happiness and laughter; talking about the possibility of naughtiness and advice, lots of advice, some crude, but the best, from Rachel. *"Never say never, Eve."* It was the most wonderful evening. I opened up my world to them and they loved it; loved that I was exploring, letting go in this way, because they love me. Loved it because they could see I was enjoying telling the story. I feel our lovemaking has been given the seal of approval. I'll ring Matias and tell him in the morning. I smile and turn off the light.

಄

I dare not think of your phone call this morning, Eve. You came close to me to telling me you loved me, that you are in love, feel loved, and are living it deeply. After this, what else should I want, ever? Death can come and what I feel now will last forever.

Matias

಄

Forever. The word resonates in my mind. I look down at my left hand. I twist my ring around. It's time.

A few minutes ago, I took off my wedding ring. It's been on my finger for 24 years. I'm no longer looking at what was, but what could be, with love all around me and hope in my heart. Matias, I am entrusting me with you.

Eve

You're *killing me softly* Eve, with your love and trust. You turning toward me, your elegance, your fragrant beauty, your mind, your natural femininity, your words of engagement, your decision to leave the past where it belongs.

All this is more than I ever expected to happen in my life. I'm so grateful that you exist and feel so privileged to be with you. I will cherish your time with me

Matias

21. An empress

I pull up in the driveway of Matias's house at 7.00 pm. According to my Tarot card I am an *Empress*. I look and feel like an empress — *the archetype of feminine power. Mysterious, fertile, and sexual, she augurs a need for us to be in touch with our feminine side, to listen to our intuition, and to give priority to our emotions and passions. The Empress can signify coming abundance.* I do hope so.

The wind has eased. No rain, although dark clouds hover. Matias is waiting at the front door, an ancient oak door with beautiful iron work. The house is huge, like a castle with four turrets set on an acre of manicured lawn and landscaped gardens. Matias opens the car door and holds out his hand. He looks gorgeous and sexy in black leather trousers, belt, boots and a bright red silk shirt, his dark hair slicked down. The stacked Cuban heels add a couple of inches to his height. I step from the car. He kisses my hand then moves his lips slowly up my arm, all the while looking into my eyes, before kissing me on the lips hard. I draw back in surprise.

"I want you, Eve. It is so long since I've been with a woman." I move my body into his, and smile at him. Our eyes meet.

"Time to change that."

"Let's go inside. Welcome to my home, Eve. You look especially beautiful tonight." I'm wearing the new rose pink dress,
with matching shoes, underwear and lipstick I bought today,
plus my dangly gold gypsy earrings and gold clutch. My hair
is down and bouncy, my face lightly made up and I'm wearing
Opium, a heavy, sensuous, all-pervading perfume; an addiction
of mine. I look around, awestruck.

"Thank you. What a fabulous place you have here, Matias."

"Come, I'll show you." The inside is as palatial as outside.
Large leadlight windows and high ceilings increase the sense of
space. Heavy oak beams span the huge living areas. The slate
floors are covered with large Persian rugs. Antique oak furni-
ture everywhere. Paintings, mostly old landscapes adorn the
walls. Ornate iron light fittings hang from the beams. Heavy
damask drapes are tied back with cords. Two arched stained-
glass windows, reminiscent of the Renaissance period, dominate
the living room, giving it a sense of timelessness.

"It is magnificent, Matias." We come to the stairs.

"This way, I'll show you upstairs." He holds my hand and
leads me up a giant oak staircase, showing me the study, the
guest bedrooms and bathrooms. "And this is my bedroom." The
same tasteful furnishings again, complemented by a deep, red
carpet. A huge oak four poster with white broderie anglaise
bedspread and large pillows, faces a large leadlight window overlooking the garden. A beech tree is framed there, silhouetted by
a garden light. Beauty everywhere. It is breathtaking. As I look

outside, Matias comes up behind me. He wraps his arms around me, squeezes me tight, then nibbles the back of my neck. His teeth graze across my shoulder. I shudder. A sharp pain in my neck. He bit me. I turn around in surprise. Matias's dark eyes are smouldering.

"I love you, Eve." He kisses me hard, his tongue probing deeply for the first time. Our bodies meld together. I feel his arousal. A spasm rocks me.

"And I love you." I finally say it and I mean it. The first time since William.

❧

My eyes are closed. I don't want to open them. Matias is lying beside me, his fingers tracing delicate patterns around the sockets. He stops. I sense him willing me to wake. I force my eyes open and blink. Daylight. Matias is looking at me. Concern in his eyes. I'm curled up in a fetal ball trying to assuage the pain.

There's a deep, gnawing ache in my belly. My nether regions are sore and swollen. My insides are either stinging or burning or both. Oh, heavens. What's that smell? It's me. Yuk! I smell something awful. Dried sweat is caked all over my body. I run my hands through my damp hair. It's tangled and matted. I rub under my eyes. Dark pencil and bits of mascara on my fingers showing my makeup is askew. I must look a fright. I feel a fright.

"You hurt me," I blurt out accusingly, wrapping my arms around my body protectively.

"I'm sorry, Eve. How could things go so wrong? I got carried away."

"I understand, but you still hurt me, Matias." Tears fill my eyes. I'm no longer sure of this man. If I ever was, comes a voice from deep inside. My body tenses up.

"It's been so long since I've been with a woman, Eve, I forgot my manners. Please forgive me. I didn't mean to hurt you. Please don't leave me." The tears start to fall. Matias picks up a tissue, gently dabs at my tears, and then cleans away the dark smudges. "There," he says, "that looks better." He kisses me gently on each cheek, then lightly on the lips, before drawing back to look at me, adoringly, like a sad puppy. In spite of everything, I feel sorry for him.

"I'm not going to leave you. We're still learning about each other, Matias."

"Thank you for being so understanding," says Matias, his eyes downcast.

"But making love comfortably is important," I say, touching his face, tenderly.

"I'll kiss you and make it better," he says, pulling down the satin sheet and exposing my naked body. I shiver. My mind and body are screaming. I want to crawl home, like a wounded animal back to its lair. I don't want to make love ever again. No, it wasn't making love. It was sex with a vengeance.

Matias uncurls my arms and lies me flat. I stiffen. He kisses me on the mouth, the neck, the breasts. His mouth moving inexorably downwards. I whimper.

"Please, please be gentle with me this time," I pray. His lips alight on the entrance to my sex, kissing me softly, round and round. His tongue moves in tandem, caressing my clitoris which flutters briefly in response. Matias takes this as a signal to mount me. My body contracts, wanting to repel the invader. Sensing this, he pushes harder. A knife-like pain shoots through me. I scream, shocking us both. I sob. Tears roll down my cheeks. Matias rolls off then leans over me on one elbow, licking my tears away.

"We'll go away for a year. Just be on our own, the two of us. Switzerland. I want to go to Switzerland. We'll marry there. Of course, we'll need a pre-nup agreement. And…" I put my fingers to his lips.

"Matias, I need time to adjust to all of this." Dark thoughts intrude. He tells me, never asks, just assumes I'll do whatever he wants, that I'm his for the taking, especially in his castle. "I need to go home and feed Kiki. To take her for a walk."

Matias draws back as if scalded. "You would leave me for a dog?" His anger is palpable. He stands, body rigid, fists balled. Another side of him is being revealed, a dark side.

"I'm not leaving you," I say quietly, trying to console him. "I need to go home. Why don't you come with me?" Then just as suddenly, the anger disappears, as if it were never there.

"I adore you, Eve. I love you. I will look after you. If you're sick, I'll wipe your face. If you're messy down below, I'll clean you up." I touch his lips. What preciousness. I am beguiled by him. "I do not seek to own you, or possess you, Eve. And I won't hurry you anymore. I'll give you a year to make up your mind."

Relief floods through me. It will work out. We will work out. And then the thought strikes me. Cindy and I leave for Europe next weekend. I'm looking forward to that. Old and new horizons. I wonder how he'll manage me being away for a month.

22. Old wounds

Sunlight is streaming through the window. I feel good. I look over at Matias. He's still asleep, with Kiki snuggled up close. She's calmer about him. So am I. The phone rings. Matias and Kiki stir. I pick it up. It's Cindy. I slide out of bed.

"Hello, Cindy. Hang on a minute, while I put on a robe. Matias is still asleep."

"Oooh, you wanton woman," says Cindy. "I'm dying to know all about it."

"Back again, Cindy. Look, Matias will be getting up for work soon. If you like, come over for a coffee? You can meet him, and we can talk after he's gone."

"I'll be there with bells on, Darling. Forty-five minutes. Can't wait to meet him."

༞

I show Cindy into the kitchen. Heaven knows how she manages to look so good at such short notice. Matias is sitting at the kitchen bench drinking coffee. He stands.

I introduce them formally, "Cindy, meet Matias. Matias,

117

Cindy." Matias takes her hand, places it theatrically to his mouth, looks into her eyes, then kisses it.

"Pleased to meet you, Cindy. You're a beautiful woman, too." Stunned by the early morning chivalry, Cindy is a little lost for words, but not for long.

"Lovely to meet you at last. Eve has told me all about you." Matias looks askance at me. "Well, not everything," adds Cindy hastily.

"I must be off," says Matias. "Duty calls. Pleased to meet you, Cindy. I'll leave you and Eve to talk. And I wish you an enjoyable trip," he says formally and bows. Turning to me, he says, "I'll see you tonight, Eve," and gives me a lingering kiss. "Stay there with Cindy. I'll see myself out."

"Unbelievable, Darling," says Cindy open mouthed. "He's like a knight of old. Now, tell me all about your dirty weekend," she asks rubbing her hands together with glee. I laugh. Her enthusiasm is infectious. As I describe his house, she drinks it in.

"It sounds like a fairy tale castle. What about the bedroom?"

"I could barely stand up straight the morning after. He was over enthusiastic, to say the least," I say wanting to confide. "He apologized saying he hadn't been with a woman for so long he forgot his manners."

"What a quaint turn of phrase he has," says Cindy.

"It will take a while for me to get used to sex again. Matias brought back the nightmares of my first marriage." My body holds memories. Those memories rise up to meet me. I ran into John's arms as a young teenager fleeing from home. He was eight years older. Like many abused children, my instincts were wounded. I'd never learned to negotiate the jungle safely on my own, unable to discern who the predators were. John assumed territorial rights over me and my body and I acceded, not knowing any different.

When I couldn't have kids, he impregnated someone else. Ashamed and humiliated I ran away to England. There were occasional lovers, but sex wasn't important. Until William. I felt safe for the first time in my life. He was so tender and loving, so caring and so protective. He would never do anything to hurt me. But Matias might... The memories fade as reality kicks back in. My tummy winces. He has already hurt me.

"Maybe I'm too old for this hanky panky."

"What rubbish! Are you alright now?" she asks, her face full of concern.

"Just. Anyway, sex is off the menu until after we go away. Thank heavens. Matias is much calmer when he's just cuddling."

"A holiday is what you need. What we need. And, lots of fun, and, lots and lots of shopping," says Cindy with a grin on her face. She's a compulsive shopper.

"My world's been so limited since William died; this will be the dawning of a new era. I can't wait."

"Neither can I. Must rush. Mwah! Mwah!" she says heading to the front door. As I close the door behind her, I wince again, this time as the embarrassing memory of my visit to Dr Daniels earlier in the day floods back.

&

"Hello, Eve," I jump. I've been deep in thought. "Sorry. Did I give you a start?" asks Jeffrey Daniels, as he enters the room, a concerned look in his alert, all-seeing eyes hiding behind thick tortoiseshell glasses. Oh, so reassuring, but not today.

"Hello, Eve. It's been a while. What can I do for you?"

I squirm nervously. What will he think of me? A wave of heat colors my face. I put my hands to my face. "Oh dear, I'm blushing. I don't know how to start, Jeffrey." I want to crawl into the corner and hide.

"It's alright, Eve. Take your time. You can talk to me about anything. No need to be embarrassed. We've known each other for a long time." He smiles reassuringly at me.

Yes, and William, too. I think. What will William think of me? I take a deep breath and will myself to speak. "I had sex on the weekend," I blurt out. "I haven't had sex since before William died," I hasten to explain. I omit any mention of my one-night stand with Sven. He is an inconvenient truth. But where, I wonder, did I learn to lie so glibly? I continue, "It was really painful. I still hurt."

Jeffrey eyes me encouragingly. "Do you like this person?" I nod. "Is he someone you want to continue seeing?" I nod again. Words temporarily denied me. "That's good, Eve. I'm pleased for you. Pleased you are moving on. You've been on your own for a long time. Too long." I smile hesitantly. "Your body will need time to adjust. As you are aware, approaching menopause causes significant changes to the body, including the vagina. Are you still using the Vagifem pessaries?" I nod, still mute. "How often?"

"Twice a week," I say, voice cracking.

"Well, I'd like you to use them every day for two weeks, then go back to twice a week. That will moisten the vagina." I nod again. "Did you use a lubricant?"

I shake my head. "No," I say, feeling like a naïve schoolgirl.

"Well, lubricants can reduce the friction and pain during intercourse. A water-based lubricant is best. Condoms do not usually break with water-based lubricants. You did use a condom?" Jeffrey asks, his voice firmer.

I shake my head. "No." I blush again, feeling foolish as well as guilty this time.

"Safe sex is very important, Eve. STDs are rife. When you are feeling a bit better, I'd like you to come in for an STD check – just to be safe." My heart drops. I have never had to have a test before. Now I am a whore in need of a medical examination? When did I become so reckless?

"Okay." I nod.

"Until you know this man better, please make sure you are protected," he says kindly. "The other thing to realize is that your mind may need time to adjust too, to be able to relax. If you are not relaxed, sex can be very painful. Take the time to get to know each other, to explore each other's bodies so you are comfortable with each other." I nod again. Words still eluding me. But not thoughts. Why was I so comfortable with Sven?

"Eve," Jeffrey breaks into my thinking, "if this doesn't resolve the problem, you may need surgical intervention, but I doubt that."

"Oh, I hope not."

"I think it is best to refrain from sex until after you have healed, probably at least a week. I'll give you an ointment to apply which will relieve the pain. And I have some literature, which may help."

I breathe a sigh of relief. "Thank you, Jeffrey. Thank you so much." I stand, readying to make my escape. He comes around to my side of the desk and pats my shoulder.

"I'm pleased for you, Eve. William would be too."

I'm not so sure of that.

23. On the road again

"Take the second exit," says Cindy, reinforcing the directions from the GPS. After a few days sightseeing and shopping in London, we're coming off the M3 motorway onto the A303 heading for Stonehenge and the historic town of Bath but taking a detour on the way. William and I loved England, especially this part of the countryside. "About another forty-five minutes to Salisbury Cathedral, according to Grace," she adds, turning to me with a smile. We nicknamed our GPS Grace, after she saved us coming out of the London traffic. There, but for the grace of Grace, we would've been hopelessly lost.

"Thanks, Cindy. With you and Grace to guide me, I'm really enjoying driving." It's been eight years or more since I've driven in England."

"And I'm enjoying seeing the beauty of the English countryside, Eve. I rarely venture out of London." We watch entranced as the idyllic countryside, with its unique blend of rolling hills, wide valleys with lush green meadows interspersed with bustling market towns and unspoilt villages with thatched cottages, unfolds before us.

My cell phone rings, disturbing the peace and harmony.

Cindy looks at me with a grimace. "Heavens above! You only spoke to him a couple of hours ago." Matias gave me a cashed-up cell to travel with. And he's using it at every opportunity, no matter the time of day or how inconvenient, to find out where I am and what I'm doing, in spite of having a detailed daily itinerary.

"I know. He's missing me. He's not coping, and is feeling left out. He says he feels like a stray dog following us from a distance," I say apologetically.

"The Third Man, I call him. He's shadowing us. Do you want me to answer?" I nod. "It's Cindy here, Matias. Eve is driving and cannot speak with you," she says politely. Cindy listens, nods her head a couple of times, looks at me with raised eyebrows, and finally says, "I'll tell Eve it's important to ring you when we get to Salisbury." She ends the call. "And he thanked me for looking after you, because you are so precious to him." I smile and shake my head. I don't know what else to say.

My cell phone rings again. "Oh, this is ridiculous," says Cindy looking at me, questioningly. I nod and she reaches to pick it up. "Oh, it's Rachel," she says with a relieved look on her face. "Hello, Darling. Eve is driving. I'll switch the speaker on so she can hear. What are you and Kiki up to?"

"Kiki and I are having the loveliest time," says Rachel.

"That's wonderful," I say. "I'm so relieved she's with you, Rachel."

"By the sound of your emails, Eve, you two are having a wonderful time too."

"Yes, we are. What have you and Kiki been up to?" I ask, eager to know.

"Well, we walk every morning. We have breakfast and dinner together, and…"

"And what, Rachel?" I ask.

"We're even sleeping together. It's wonderful to have someone to sleep with for a change," says Rachel with a wry laugh. "And, I'm even looking at men again."

"You're spoiling her. Kiki's having a holiday too. Thanks so much for looking after her. And I'm pleased she's sparked some interest in a love life, again," I say. Such a special dog. I rescued her but then she rescued me. Taught me to love again. Perhaps she can do the same for Rachel.

"My pleasure. Enjoy the rest of your holiday, ladies," says Rachel.

"We will," Cindy and I say smiling at each other. "We will."

"What a magnificent building," Cindy says as we walk through the entrance. Our eyes are inevitably drawn upwards, over-awed by the towering columns, the stained-glass windows and the vaulted ceiling. Salisbury Cathedral is the epitome of the English Gothic style. After the crowded throngs at Westminster Abbey, it is a privilege to be here walking slowly amidst the peace and quiet of this sanctuary.

A bell sounds. People stop moving and look up to the pulpit.

A priest begins to pray. "They've been saying prayers here every day for nearly eight hundred years," Cindy says, reading to me from the booklet. A ray of light comes through a nearby stained-glass window and shines directly on Cindy, like a halo, highlighting her whole body. She turns to me, astounded.

"Okay. I'm listening, Lord. I'm all ears," she whispers, gives herself a light tap on the hand for being naughty, then turns back to look at the priest. I laugh softly. She is an indomitable personality, the best travelling buddy, and such fun to be with.

"Take the first exit, the A360 to Stonehenge," says Cindy, back in her navigator role. "Grace says we'll be there in seventeen minutes. It's only nine miles from Salisbury. We won't be able to enter the stone circle itself, but the mighty monoliths are almost as impressive from the outside."

I know. William and I once came early one morning, just before sunrise. I tremble as the memory flashes into my consciousness. It was a balmy summer's night, a full moon, a harvest moon. The surrounding corn fields were lit up as we'd traipsed through the field towards the mighty Sarsen rocks towering ahead of us, all the more mysterious by being bathed in moonlight.

Suddenly William had squeezed my hand and started leading me into the cornfields. "Let's take a gloriously pagan detour first," he'd said, grinning at me, He'd spread the blanket over the ground. After we'd made love, we'd lain there in each other's arms in a timeless wonderland watching the sunrise over the stone circle. I tremble again remembering such a magical visceral experience.

Cindy's voice shatters my reverie. "And Bath is thirty-three miles further on from Stonehenge. An hour there, another hour travelling. We'll be there at wine o'clock."

I smile. Wine o'clock can conveniently be at any hour of the day or night. "Cindy, perhaps I could entice you to a wine in the spa at the Roman Baths." Another joyfully illicit experience with William as we journeyed this part of the earth, so long ago.

24. London

Cindy and I are sitting in the American Bar at the Savoy, feeling very laid back. We've ordered Manhattan cocktails. "Our last night in England," Cindy muses thoughtfully. The waiter returns with our drinks. "A toast to us," she says and raises her glass.

"To us," I say. "To a fabulous time in England, Cindy." We touch glasses.

"To us," says Cindy, "And, tonight another treat is in store."

"I know, I can hardly wait." Richard is taking us to dinner at the Savoy Grill.

"Oh, look who's here, and he's brought someone with him," says Cindy excitedly. Richard strides across the room, his face beaming. He looks so well.

"James, meet Eve and Cindy," he says pointing to each of us in turn. "Two of the most beautiful women on earth. Our dinner companions this evening. Eve and Cindy, meet James, a colleague of mine." Our eyes turn upwards to James. He's several inches taller than Richard, but much leaner and drop dead gorgeous. Talk about tall, dark and handsome. Eirene's prediction springs to mind. No, too young, I think to myself.

"Pleased to meet you two lovely ladies," a cultured English accent. "Richard's been telling me about you. How are you finding London?" My cell rings. Cindy rolls her eyes at Richard. Richard looks at me, questioningly.

"Excuse me, I'll be back in a moment." I am so angry. I told him I was having dinner and would ring him after it finished. I take a deep breath. "Matias, I'm at the Savoy. Richard and James have just arrived."

"I miss you, Eve. I need you."

"Matias, I can't talk now. It is rude to the others. I'll ring you after dinner."

"Eve, emptiness is filling my space wider with every minute you are gone."

"Matias, I understand you are hurting, but I can't talk now. I must go." He ignores me and keeps on talking. I listen without responding for a few minutes, then say, "I have to go." Not waiting for a reply, I hang up and mute the phone before re-joining the others. There is a sinking feeling in my stomach.

Richard stands and gives me a cuddle when I return. "Great to see you, Eve. And in London of all places. Eve is my second Mom, James." I snuggle into his giant arms. He looks so happy. He also looks like Cindy has filled him in. Good. I don't want to talk about Matias. I sit down.

The waiter comes over, "Mr Davis, your booking is for eight. Would you like to order some cocktails, first?"

"Would you ladies like another Manhattan?" asks Richard.

"Yes, please." we say in unison, look at each other and laugh.

"And a G&T for you, James?"

"Of course," James replies, beaming at Richard.

"Two Manhattans and two gin and tonics," Richard says to the waiter. "And pray tell, what have you two lovelies been up to in England?" he says turning to us.

"Since I 'saw the light', Darling, I let Eve take charge and immerse us in English history and culture," says Cindy waving her hand royally at Richard.

"What do you mean, you saw the light?" asks James, leaning forward.

"Heaven shone its light on me in Salisbury Cathedral. I was lit up like a Christmas tree, Darlings," says Cindy, standing theatrically and stretching out both her hands like branches. Richard and James are bemused, and look at me queryingly. I explain the epiphany. They laugh.

"Cindy rarely ventures beyond shops when travelling. I wanted to show her more of England. I love it here. I lived here for two years. In a way I feel I belong here," I tell James.

Cindy stays standing, but picks up her glass, waving it in the air. "We saw the Magna Carta at Salisbury Cathedral — one of the world's most potent symbols of liberty. We drove through the beautiful Cotswold countryside to worship with the druids of old at the megalithic monuments of Stonehenge. We immersed ourselves in the healing waters at historic Bath, wine in hand." She waves her wine glass again. "And we visited the Oxford Botanic Garden, the oldest Botanic Garden in Britain, before returning to London."

She takes a sip of her drink, checks to see we are all listening, then continues. "We watched the changing of the guards at Buckingham Palace, the Horse Guards' parade at Whitehall and even visited Churchill's underground War Rooms." Cindy pauses while she sits down, "And, I loved being a tourist. Thanks, Eve." I smile and lift my glass to her.

"But did you visit a British pub? To see the real Britain?" asks James.

"Eve said I had to," said Cindy making a face. "At the Assembly Inn, in Bath."

I smile, Cindy didn't enjoy the rustic charm of the pub as much as William and I had. I can still see us sitting on a big leather couch talking with Farmer Brown and his best mate, an Airedale terrier named Lewis, named after Lewis Carroll. We supped on Bellringer Ale, and their speciality pie and mash. The pie was made of Marshfield beef, Bath blue cheese and Bellringer Ale. "Pity about the warm beer, though," William had said." We'd all laughed as Lewis barked agreement.

"But, today was the highlight of the trip," Cindy says, back on her soap box. "Today I saw *the* most potent symbol of liberty in action." Cindy pauses for effect again. "A woman with her credit card. I shopped at Harrods and Kensington High Street while Eve visited Kew Gardens." We all laugh, hopelessly at her. A waiter comes over.

"Mr. Davis, your table is ready."

"Thank you. Let's go through," says Richard showing us the way. When we're seated, he asks if everyone would like champagne.

We all nod. He signals for the waiter to come over and orders a bottle of Mumm. While we're waiting, he talks of Gordon Ramsay and the restaurant and the best dishes here, telling us that James and he dine here often.

"A working lunch to die for is the Scottish lobster bisque, followed by grilled Dover Sole." Richard puts his thumb and forefinger to his lips and blows a kiss. "Delicious." I watch him closely. There is a new found confidence about him. He's standing taller, walking taller. His giant hands are relaxed and expansive as he talks excitedly about how he and James are negotiating planning laws to bring their London project into being.

There is a camaraderie between them that I like. The waiter shows Richard the bottle of champagne. He nods. The waiter pours a little into Richard's flute. He tastes it, swirling it around his mouth like a connoisseur and indicates to the waiter to continue serving.

I meet Cindy's eyes and smile. My little boy Richie has grown up, I think proudly. We eat, drink and are merry. Very merry. The conversation flows like the wine. It is a wonderful evening. I want it to go on forever but Cindy is giving me a nudge.

"Okay," I mouth.

Cindy stands up and says, "Gentlemen, I've had the most wonderful evening. You've been superb hosts. But we have to be off early in the morning."

"Thank you, James," I say, standing up and offering my hand. "It was lovely to meet you. I hope we meet again. I stand up and move closer to Richard. Thank you so much, Richard. I loved it. We'll see you in Paris?" I ask looking up at him, lovingly.

"You bet," he says bending down to kiss me on the cheek. Cindy and I leave them there and hurry back to our hotel. It's nearly midnight. As she opens the door,

I say, "You go to bed, Cindy. I'll stay out here and ring Matias." She frowns but doesn't say anything. I take out my cell and look at it. Eight missed calls. I feel sick.

&

The alarm rings. I turn over, look at the clock and groan. 5.00 am. Cindy and I have to be ready by 6.00 am. Cindy's already in the shower. I'm tired, desperately tired. I sat on the floor in the corridor outside of our room talking to Matias so Cindy could get some sleep. It was 1.00 am before he'd calmed enough to finally let me go. I'm like a drug to him, an addiction that he craves, that he can't get enough of. Jealous of Cindy. Even jealous of us meeting with Richard and his friend last night.

How do I know which men you are meeting?

Wearily, I turn the cell back on. It pings wildly. I pick it up and look at it astounded. Twelve emails and twelve texts. Crazy stuff. The main tenor of them was,

Why did you turn your cell off? I called you back straight away and you had turned it off.

When something doesn't go according to his plan, the shock

waves are cataclysmic. This has got to stop. I pick up my cell and call Matias. My insides are reeling, but I steady my voice.

"Matias, Cindy and I are leaving for Paris early this morning. I turned it off so we could get some sleep. We spoke for an hour last night. Please be reasonable."

"You cut me out. You only show me you do not need me," he says angrily and hangs up. Stunned, I look at the phone. My hands are shaking. I can't believe how quickly he's turned. He's like a Jekyll and Hyde. Such hard work. And he's spoiling our holiday. I'll leave him to cool off and will ring him from Paris.

A resolute inner voice pipes up, "No. I won't! I'm not putting up with this kind of shit anymore!" I turn my travel cell off again and look at it wonderingly.

Cindy emerges from the bathroom, freshly made up, glowing with vitality and a big smile on her face. "Your turn, Darling. Momentous day. We're off to the City of Light." I look at the phone in my hand again. My hands have stopped shaking.

"And leaving the darkness behind," I say to myself. I throw my cell into the waste paper basket and head into the bathroom singing, *"I love Paris in the fall."*

25. I love Paris

Paris. I love Paris. Springtime or fall. Anytime at all. In the early morning light, as I gaze out our hotel window overlooking the Tuileries Gardens and the magnificent tree-lined pathways and boulevards, I feel my life force returning. Cindy and I have been in Paris for four days now. I look at the people bustling to and fro on the street below. A man is standing looking up at the hotel.

I shiver, inhale sharply and draw back from the window. Matias? He knows where I'm staying. Has he followed me here? I slip behind the curtains and peer through the side of the window. No, it's not Matias. It's my mind playing tricks. I start to breathe, again. Matias was slowly squeezing the life out of me, I realize now, but I was scared of him, and too scared to admit I had it wrong again. I open my travel diary to today's date and smile. I will!

Today I give myself the gift of freedom from the past. I move with joy into the now.

꿈

Cindy loves Paris as much as I do. Walking the streets of Paris each day is a favorite pastime of ours. The walks become serendipitous wanderings carrying us through the Paris of centuries, where discoveries are made, adventures abound, and bargains are to be had, as we cross through the boundaries of sight-seeing into the daily routines of Parisians. Paris is made for wandering. The French have coined a lovely word for a person who wanders the streets: *le flâneur*, one who strolls or loiters, usually without a destination.

The streets beckon us, leading us past monuments, down narrow alleyways, through arches, and into hidden squares. We are attuned to the city's rhythm and, no matter how aimlessly we stroll, we always end up somewhere magical – the banks of the Seine; the poetic streets of St-Germain; the tangled lanes around the Bastille and Canal St-Martin. Or losing ourselves in the steep, cobbled streets of Montmartre, one of the most historic and interesting neighborhoods in Paris. Until we remember that the Basilica of Sacre-Coeur sits on the crest of the hill, and if we continue heading uphill, there is little possibility of us being lost for long.

Making our mouths water wherever we wander is the woodsy scent of roasting chestnuts. Fall is the best season for food in Paris. Fresh croissants and café au lait for breakfast. Baguettes with sausages, hams, pâtés, terrines, foie gras, duck confit and delicious cheeses for lunch. And the Salon du Chocolat for a pick me up when we tire. As was needed yesterday after spending several hours at the fabulous Musée d'Orsay looking at Impressionist paintings. After overdosing on Renoir, Monet, Manet,

Degas, Van Gogh and others, Cindy and I overdosed on chocolate. Food and culture – the essence of Paris, of France. I could live here I muse joyfully, as I look out the window, and there's still more to come.

A river cruise tomorrow. Eight days following the winding Seine from Paris, through Northern France to the beaches of Normandy, and back. We'll travel through the landscapes that inspired great artists, and see Monet's Garden. A dream come true. We're back in Paris for two days, meeting up with Richard for dinner again, the night before we fly back home. I dance a little two step in delight at the thought. Tonight, we're splitting up. Cindy, cultured out, will go shopping at the Champs Élysées, while I'm going on a night tour of the Louvre. I sway in time to the music that fills my soul as Edith Piaf and I head into the bathroom.

The falling leaves drift by my window. The autumn leaves of red and gold...

26. Aphrodite calls

My cab drops me at the entrance to the Louvre at 6.20 pm. After paying and thanking the driver with my best *'merci beaucoup'*, I turn to the spectacle that is the famous glass pyramid. I've only seen it in the movie version of *The Da Vinci Code*. It wasn't built when William and I were last in Paris. Here, in the flesh and with dusk falling, it has a magical glow, reflecting the image and colors from the nearby Louvre building itself.

After staring in awe for a while, I go in. I've pre-booked a night tour, so I make my way over to the desk to get my guide book. Camille, the tour guide looks very Parisian. She wears a colorful silk scarf wrapped tightly but elegantly around her neck, black pencil skirt and smart white shirt. She has airs and graces you wouldn't find in a guide anywhere but Paris.

Night falls and suddenly this huge palace becomes an almost intimate place. As we discover small rooms filled with countless treasures, the quietness and darkness outside makes me feel like I am walking into a very impressive private art collection. Which is exactly what it used to be, the residence and art collection of French Kings and Queens! I'd imagined we'd only see the major works but we are seeing so much more and learning about less frequented pieces.

"I find the way the curators choose to intermingle old and new, and the well-known with the less well-known, inspiring," says the woman beside me.

"Ah, oui, but it is the images of women I find most inspiring. Goddesses all of them," says Camille. "I will show you Botticelli's broken-hearted virgins and Venuses — the most affecting in a room full of frescoes relocated from Florence; Luini's *Portrait of a Venetian Lady;* Ingres naked and erotic beauty — *Angelique* and..." she pauses as her eyes scope the group, "Rembrandt's greatest nude painting — the sensual but troubled, *Bathsheba at her Bath,* the object of King David's lust who also inspired Leonard Cohen's song *Hallelujah.*" We follow in her footsteps, listening to her commentary and admiring each female beauty in turn.

Finally, we arrive at the Grande Galerie. My heart stops. Up above, at the top of the Daru Staircase, stands a woman. A magnificent, marble woman. What she lacks in arms and head is made up for in a staggering pair of wings. I walk slowly up the stairs towards her, captivated, enthralled. *The Winged Victory of Samothrace* is her name, an artistic representation of Nike, the Greek Goddess of Speed, Strength and Victory.

At any moment I feel she could beat her wings and fly. The delicate folds of material that wrap around her add to her life and vitality. Here is woman. Complete and free, showing what is possible for womankind and for every woman: to be free and alive.

The tour moves on. Unwillingly, I follow. I don't want to

leave her. As we head into the Galerie des Antiques, the Gallery of Greek Antiquities, I am distracted, a new sense of vitality pulsing through me. *Victory* has taken my heart. The group pauses. As I glance around to take my bearings, the *Venus de Milo* rises up in front of me. Standing in stark contrast to *Victory* but with an equally powerful effect.

Like gravity, this magical figure representing the Greek goddess Aphrodite, pulls me towards her. I soak her in. No arms, but at least she has her head. She is more delicate. Her face, breasts and body are perfection. She bares herself, but has such a commanding presence that I want to fall at her feet, to worship her.

This divine goddess calls to me. She touches my soul. Aphrodite, in all her glory. Sensuality and sexuality exude from her. The Goddess of Love, Beauty and Desire, the most beautiful among goddesses. The epitome of a woman. The kind of woman I want to be. I shake my head at the thought, then look at Aphrodite anew, entranced.

"Could I become a goddess of love and beauty?" I ask silently.

As the tour group moves on, I make my way to the exit. I feel like I'm walking on air. My mind as free as a breeze. "Yes, yes, I can!" I say out loud as I walk down the steps from the Louvre. People nearby look at me, surprised. I smile at them and walk back to the hotel. The cruise along the Seine beckons tomorrow.

Time to immerse myself in history and the landscape and, time to listen to my soul talking. To Aphrodite.

27. Monet's garden

"We are in Monet's home in his beloved village of Giverny." My earphones talk to me as I wind my way around the garden. "There are two parts in Monet's garden: a flower garden called *Clos Normand* in front of the house and a Japanese inspired water garden on the other side of the road." I orientate myself, looking over to the flower garden, then back at the house with its signature green on the windows, shutters, steps, seats, even on the arches throughout the garden. As I walk around, the commentary continues.

"When Monet and his family settled in Giverny in 1883 he set about transforming the garden. He didn't like organized or constrained gardens. He married flowers according to their colors and left them to grow rather freely and naturally." I look about the wild profusion of flower beds, and climbers on the green arches, heartened by the warm, deep colors of autumn, the last flames of color burning before the garden falls asleep for the winter.

Sated, I leave *Clos Normand* and walk towards the path connecting the two gardens, listening, fascinated. "In 1893, ten years after his arrival at Giverny, Monet bought the land neighbouring his property. It was crossed by a small brook." Water laps at the side of the path as it winds around. I sit down on a green bench, wanting to hear the rest of the tape first. "Monet had the first small pond dug. Later on, the pond would be enlarged to its present-day size. In this water garden you will find the famous Japanese bridge covered with wisterias, other smaller bridges, weeping willows, a bamboo wood and above all the famous nympheas which bloom all summer long. Never before had a painter so shaped his subjects in nature before painting them. And so he created his works twice. Monet would find his inspiration in this water garden for more than twenty years."

I start walking again. As I round the corner the water garden opens up before me. I stand still, mesmerised. I feel like I've stepped straight into an Impressionist painting – a serene pool offering a mirror view of the world around. On the banks of the water garden, the islands of leaves of the water lilies with the few remaining let the trees bordering the pond reflect in the soft autumn sunlight. The black lines of the trunks and branches contrast with the opulence of the reds and golds. Every now and then, a puff of air dislodges some leaves. They drop, silently dancing in space before landing on the surface of the water.

My eyes are inexorably drawn to the end of the garden where there are two green Japanese bridges – an inverted one on the surface of the water, the other across it. The scene is breathtakingly beautiful and timeless. I gasp. I take out my camera and look through the viewfinder. As I focus the camera, Eirene's prediction comes back to me. This is the bridge she saw. Then a link to another bridge flashes into my consciousness. A bridge between the past and the present, from what was, to what can be. The Eve of old reincarnating as a goddess, but with someone to lead the way. A guide, and I know where to find him. The Aphrodisiac Male Escort Agency. A wave of gratitude washes over me. Instead of whispering, the Universe is shouting at me, and in a language I understand, urging me to give life to all I am seeing. And I will. I will.

୬

"The last night of our cruise. What a fabulous week it's been, Eve." Dusk is falling. Cindy and I are just sitting on the top deck of the boat, watching the countryside go by; at peace with the world and each other. Watching the wake of the water as we speed back to Paris is mesmerising.

"Fabulous," I say. In the past week, we have walked in the footsteps of Vincent Van Gogh; toured the harbor town of Honfleur the inspiration for many painters and paintings; walked through the medieval town of Rouen to see where Joan of Arc was burnt at the stake; seen the history of the Battle of Hastings told in tapestry in Bayeux; walked along Omaha Beach to the Allied landing sites before visiting a haunting reminder of the Allied forces' hard fight for freedom — the American Cemetery – and laying a rose at an unknown grave. But today was the highlight. I close my eyes. The movement of the river cradles me and suddenly I am back in Giverny, in Monet's water garden once more.

"Where are you?" asks Cindy bringing me back to the present.

I look at her and smile. "In Monet's Garden, again, walking over the Japanese bridge, looking at the water lilies – the nympheas," I say dreamily, "and, do you know what? I'm going to extend my pond and have a bridge built over it."

"My goodness, you have been inspired," says Cindy with a laugh. "What a wonderful idea. But that's a big project."

"I know," I say, still seeing the bridge in my mind.

Who will you get to help do that?" asks Cindy.

"The local garden center. It'll be my birthday present to myself. The big Six O is coming up in spring. I'm not looking forward to that."

"Why not, Darling? Sixty is the new forty," says Cindy standing up and sashaying around in front of me. "Just look at me." I giggle. Her unquenchable optimism is infectious.

"Yes, just look at you. What a magnificent specimen of womanhood you are."

"I know," she says feigning modesty, rotating her hips like a belly dancer as she waltzes around the deck. I laugh.

"Time to go downstairs and dress for our farewell dinner," says Cindy. "Let's knock their socks off, Darling. Last chance. We're back in Paris tomorrow."

I laugh again. "I'm so glad you brought me back to Europe again, Cindy. These past few weeks have been so inspiring. I've all these wonderful ideas running around in my head. I can't wait to get home, and start bringing them into being."

"Hang on, we've still got two days to go. I'm going to show you the heart of Paris, the real Paris, Eve. We're going shopping. You've got enough ideas in that fluffy little head of yours for the time being." I laugh again. We're so different and yet we get on so well. I love her and love being with her. I wonder what she has in store. It'll be something special. Of that, I am sure.

28. Bold steps

Cindy and I are waiting for the elevator. Unusually, we're both elegantly and expensively dressed in black, figure-hugging sheaths, luxury Jimmy Choo shoes with matching bags, nails varnished, hair coiffed, mine up in a French roll, revealing a face with a layer of expertly applied makeup. We spent our last two days in Paris shopping and being pampered, all to Cindy's instructions.

I did what I was told without question, much to Cindy's delight and mine. Even to buying Rachel's present for minding Kiki — a Japanese designer hand painted silk scarf and a hair comb. I look and feel fabulous, a new woman. When the door opens, I stand back to let Cindy enter before me. It's the private elevator to Le Jules Verne restaurant at the Eiffel Tower. I press the button.

Riding up in the elevator is like being inside a giant Meccano set structure — huge archways, giant beams, thousands of rivets and open to the elements. Dusk is falling. Slithers of Paris come into view as we ride up. The Trocadéro is lit up. The area is made up of a large square and incorporates a number of museums. It is dominated by the Palais de Chaillot, a neo-Classical building designed in two wings with a gap between to frame views of the Eiffel Tower across the river.

The views are perfect — from above and below. I look down. Long queues of people winding around the forecourt and under the arches look like trails of black ants. On another elevator going down, I spy two lovers locked in an embrace. I smile wistfully. Paris is made for lovers. My mind turns to William once more. On our last trip here William and I rode up to the top at midnight. Susan took a photograph of us as we kissed. I love that photo. Maybe one day again...

When the elevator door opens, we step out into time and space – one hundred and twenty-five metres above ground level overlooking the lights of Paris. The sky is a deep pink and purple. Notre Dame is in the distance, magnificent, breathtaking.

"Eve, Cindy." Richard's deep booming voice greets us. We look over to a table by the window where two men are seated. Richard stands up and walks over to us. "My goodness. What a glamorous pair you are," he says, looking at us with admiration. "Good to see you, Eve." He kisses me on both cheeks, European style. "And you too, Cindy," kissing her on both cheeks as well. I look at him and see a changed man.

"So good to see you too, Richard," I say, giving him a hug before he can escape. Europe has worked its magic once more. Confident, commanding presence, standing there in a tailored navy blue suit, pink shirt with navy blue and pink striped tie, and continental shoes, he looks like a sophisticated man about town.

"Come and meet, Edouard," he says ushering us to our table.

Edouard is standing, waiting for us. "Edouard, meet Cindy, and my aunt, Eve." Edouard bows. Mid-fifties, short, slim, dark complexion, wild curly hair, flashing eyes and flashy clothes, with the wildness of the gypsy about him. Matias springs to mind. I push him away, quickly.

"Mesdames, it's a great honor to meet you. Richard has told me so much about you, but not how beautiful you both are." I smile and extend my hand. Edouard picks it up and kisses it. I shake my head. Another knight of old.

"Edouard's an investment banker, helping source finance for our European project. It looks like it'll go ahead. Dad will be pleased," says Richard with a grin, his dimples on show. He is, too I see. "Let's sit down." We sit down, Richard and I closest to the window, facing each other. Cindy next to Richard, facing Edouard who's doing his best to charm both of us. Instead, my eyes are magnetically drawn to the panorama of Paris at night, unfolding before me. What better place to spend our last night?

I look around, taking in the restaurant's contemporary décor, the carbon fibre and leather chairs and the fabric covered walls. Our window is strategically placed to emphasize the imposing gears and iron framework of the Eiffel Tower. I'm in heaven, dining in one of the most iconic structures in the world. I wonder what culinary delights are in store.

Richard's voice calls me back. A waiter is standing nearby.

"Champagne, ladies?"

We smile and both say yes.

"And you, too, Edouard?" Richard asks.

"Of course, mon ami. We are in Paris."

Richard orders Mumm Rosé and adds, "I've taken the liberty of pre-ordering the six course *Menu Experience* for us. Check your menus." We read.

Duck foie gras terrine, black fig jelly, toasted brioche
Delicate watercress velouté, pan seared scallops, gold caviar
Truffled macaroni au gratin, pearl jus
Seared sea bass, two ways cep mushrooms and artichokes
Roasted saddle of lamb, garden vegetables, cooking jus
Preserved lemon basil sorbet

"Sounds absolutely mouth-watering, Richard," I say. Edouard nods.

"A great way to end our trip," says Cindy. "We've had the most fabulous time, Darlings," starts off Cindy, fluttering her eyes ostentatiously at Edouard. The waiter arrives with the champagne. Richard signals to him to pour, then lifts his glass and we follow.

"A la santé!" he says.

"A la santé!" we all say, and chink glasses one after the other. Cindy leads the conversation, telling all about our trip, but with eyes only for Edouard, who is listening intently, now only eyes for her. I smile at Richard and touch his hand.

"Tell me about your mom, Ella," I say quietly.

His green eyes light up. "It was wonderful seeing her again. I didn't think I would recognize her, but I did straight away. And she recognized me."

"How is she?" I ask, relieved to see the happiness on his face.

"Really happy. She and Max are both academics, working at the Free University of Berlin. Mom is now an Assistant Professor in the Department of Art History," he says proudly. "Do you believe that?" I nod. Yes, I do, feeling the same pride rising in me. I miss my big sister. We have so much in common. I realize, too late, I should have planned a visit, too.

"She wanted to hear all about what Rachel and I were doing. She seemed genuinely pleased to see me, to hear about us."

"Of course, she would be."

"Why does she stay away, Eve?"

"Running away is a family trait, Richard. We're lovers, not fighters. When we can't take any more, we flee. But we still feel guilty, believing people will think the worst of us. We shut ourselves off and then beat ourselves up. We're our own worst critics. Look at Rachel. She's the same."

"And me, too. I was almost to the same point, until you convinced me to come to Europe, Eve. I'm so glad I did. It's been a turning point in my life."

"I can see that, just looking at you," I say fondly, patting his hand.

"And, guess what, Eve?" he says excitedly, a twinkle in his eyes.

"Pray tell," I say eagerly, bringing my hands together in prayer.

"I've rented an apartment in Greenwich Village. I'm moving in soon after I return home." I look at him in amazement, joy in my heart. He's finally stepping out on his own. "That's absolutely the best news I've had for ages," I say proudly. "What about Rachel?"

"We both need our own space. She's dating again, too, believe it or not. A fellow called Scott she's raving about."

"How wonderful." I look at the stunning panorama of the City of Light below and the golden reflection of the Eiffel Tower in the Seine. Some momentous things are happening in our lives. Bold steps towards the future. We are all coming out of hiding and moving on with our lives. We're healing. Ella, too. I raise my glass.

"To us, Richard. To a golden new era. A la santé!"

29. Winter

The phone rings. The display reads *Private Number*. I wonder who it is.

"Hello, Eve."

"Matias?" My heart starts pounding.

"I want to meet with you, Eve."

I can hardly breathe. "Why? Why now?" is all I manage.

"I'm calling because I managed to get over the need to call you. I want to meet you because now I feel I can meet with you," Matias says quietly.

"I can't go through all that again, Matias." I say, shaking all over.

"I still want to see you, Eve, so I can talk to you, now that I can. It's not about what happened. That's not relevant. I have something I wish to say to you."

"I'll think about it, Matias. I'll seek some guidance as to whether it's right for me to meet you."

"I wait to hear from you, Eve. If you want to see me as well and listen to what I say, please do so." I hang up and throw the phone on the couch. What on earth could he have to say to me? I'm angry with him. No, I'm angry with myself. I'm still hurting.

I was too needy, much too needy. After years of being on my own, Matias was a romantic dream come true, or so I desperately wanted to believe. All my inner guidance was telling me he was wrong for me, but I ignored it. I kept telling myself he was my happy ending. I let myself down, yet again.

I go to the bedroom to get my Tarot cards. I sit down on the bed and shuffle, asking about the outcome of meeting with Matias. I turn up a card for me. *The Sun.* I shuffle for Matias. *The Sun: success, radiance and abundance. A rebirth.* Amazing, some kind of reconciliation? I look out the window and see just the faintest sliver of light. The moon is returning to darkness — a balsamic moon, the phase when we turn our attention inward, to the deepest parts of ourselves. And, if we're not in touch with those aspects of ourselves, then perhaps it's the time to search for it. I sigh. I must meet with Matias, to listen to what he has to say.

ॐ

Winter is here. Rain and now sun is spilling over the treetops onto the garden. It is beautiful. It is cold. There is very little warmth in the sun but it is warming to see. I look around. The garden is quieter, its sensual pleasures subdued. The water lilies lie dormant under the pond. Bulbs and seeds are still hidden underground. The tentacles of the wisteria that wind around my new Japanese bridge are bare. So, too the fruit trees and the Dogwoods, but tiny buds are appearing on the silver birches, the goddess trees that form an arbor around the mudstone seat on the other side of the bridge. Mother Nature's future beauty and bounty lies in waiting before me, in a myriad of shapes and ways.

I drive to the park. Matias is already there, standing beside his car. I park, take a deep breath, and walk towards him. I stop in front of him, about a metre away. He looks sad, solemn.

"Thank you for coming, Eve." I nod. "I see you the same way, but I am changed." The tears come unbidden spilling down my cheeks. I stand there, listening. "Maybe we can grow together again, making it as beautiful as it should have been in the first place," he continues. I continue standing there wordlessly, hands by my side, tears streaming down my face washing away the hurt and grief I didn't know was locked away inside.

Matias steps closer towards me. His fingers find my lips and caress them. They tenderly trace the tears down my face. Experiencing the gentleness of his touch again is an exquisite agony. A deep yearning pervades my being.

"Let me hold you. You are my meaning, my life. I still see you as beautiful as a goddess and as wonderful as a poem of love. I love you dearly and truly. I wish to see you again," he says, tears filling his eyes.

I find my voice. "No, Matias," I say, calmly but firmly. "You can't see me again." Matias' fingers drop away from my face. He looks at me, stunned.

"Let's walk somewhere, or drive somewhere. Or just let me hold you, if only for a time," he says, pleadingly, desperation in his eyes.

"No, Matias. The time for us is past. You'll have to live with the knowledge that once upon a time I loved you. Goodbye." I say, walking away.

"Please stop this obscenity, Eve. You did not love me," he shouts after me. I keep walking. "You're too cold, unfeeling. You're incapable of loving. Do you not see how ridiculous and exposed you are?" The cultured patina is gone. The predator is baring his teeth at last but the cruel barbs bounce off me. I am no longer his prey. No longer in his sway. The fear is gone. So too the power I'd handed over to him. He can't hurt me ever again.

I blow my nose and dry my tears. I hop in the car and turn on the ignition. As I look out over the steering wheel, the sun comes out from behind a cloud. It's time now to assume sovereignty over my kingdom and to find my prince. Matias is not the right man for me. He never was.

30. New moon

"Why did you see Matias, again?" asks Cindy, concern in her face. "I can't believe you did that." We're sitting in *The Coffee House*, three days later, waiting for our orders to arrive. It's cold and windy outside. I invited Cindy to coffee because I want to discuss the Tantra workshop with her.

"It was unfinished business," I say calmly. The darkness inhabiting my psyche is gone. The forbidden door is open, the light flooding inside.

"What could possibly be unfinished, Eve?" she says, not understanding.

"I was paralysed by the fear and shame of getting it so wrong once more. It was all my fault, Cindy. Matias was a predator, yet I fell for his charms. He was my first husband, John reincarnated, but in a more sophisticated guise. I ran away again, rather than dealing with the real issues. My self-preservation instincts are not yet honed. William kept the bad things at bay."

Cindy pats my hand willing me to go on. "My naïveté makes me easy prey. I'm still a novice, too long denied love. I was so needy, so filled with longing that I didn't understand what it was I was looking for. I created fantasies instead, romantic dreams which did not survive the light of day." The waiter comes with our coffees.

"Thank you," we say, then sip our coffee.

"You're too kind and too gentle, Eve. Much too loving for the likes of Matias."

"I agree. I have to stop acting nice and sweet just for civility's sake. Being good and compliant, especially when my soul is in peril, is downright dangerous."

"You haven't got a mean bone in your body, Eve, but it's high time you did. So, what now?" asks Cindy, arching an eyebrow.

"Become a bitch." I laugh. "No. I need to accept that my quest for happy endings and finding love again, are noble and worthwhile pursuits," I say looking at her, hoping she will understand.

"Of course, they are, Darling. You still believe in the tooth fairy, too," she says. No, I don't. But I do believe in goddesses and kingdoms and fairy tale endings.

I continue, "I need to listen to my intuition and inner guidance and to have the confidence to open up my world once more, Cindy."

"Women can be too hard on themselves. Not me, Darling. I realize how important my needs are. You need to, as well. When one door shuts, another door opens. And if it doesn't, sometimes you have to kick it down," says Cindy, with a grin, her eyes lighting up. I'm learning to I think as I look at her.

My soul needs nature and creativity to thrive. Most of all I need to get back in touch with the wild woman who lives inside me, the woman who has been excised from my consciousness. I had a rare glimpse of her when I was with Sven, but I need greater awareness and understanding of who she is and how I can bring her into being.

"Cindy, will you come to a Tantra workshop with me, this coming weekend?"

"A Tantra workshop?" she asks, surprised. "What do you know about Tantra?"

"Very little, Cindy, except that the essence of Tantra is liberation. And if we are to be free, our sexuality shouldn't be repressed. It's a door I need to open, wide."

"So true, Darling. I've been to Tantra sessions ages ago. Of course, I'll come. It should be fun. What's the course?"

"Fantastic. We are off to an Orgasmic Hearts Workshop," I say grinning.

છ

I hear Rachel's car pull up in the driveway. I walk to the front door and open it. Rachel rang earlier. She said she had something to tell me, but needed to do so in person. It must be important. I hope everything is alright. She's wearing her workday black again, but it's offset by the lovely lime green silk scarf I bought her. Kiki races out to greet her.

"Hello, Kiki," she says, leaning down to pat her. "And hello, Eve," she says, her smile not reaching her eyes. "Sorry to give you so little warning."

"I don't need warning. You can drop in on me anytime, Rachel," I say.

"Doesn't my scarf look fabulous, Eve?"

"Fabulous," I agree, walking back into the kitchen. Rachel and Kiki following.

"Would you like a glass of wine, Rachel?"

Her face clouds over. "Not yet thanks, Eve. I want to talk with you first."

She looks troubled. "Here or in the living room?" I ask.

"The living room please, Eve. Near the Dogwood trees." The silent sentinels I'd planted when William was diagnosed with melanoma. I switch on the garden lighting outside. The Dogwoods take on an ethereal look. We sit down on the couch and turn to face each other.

"What's up, Rach?" I ask.

"Uncle William appeared last night," she says, voice cracking, looking out the window at the trees highlighted there to stop me seeing her tears. I move closer to her and start rubbing her back, trying to soothe her.

"Go on, Precious," I say softly, using the nickname William gave her.

"I'd just ended a horrible phone call with Scott. We broke up. I walked out onto the balcony and there was Uncle William, just standing there, looking at me. I started crying, just like I am now. *'Why are you here?'* I asked." Rachel dabs at her tears.

"What happened then?" I ask, gently, continuing to rub her back.

"Oh, Eve, he walked over to me, put his arms around me, and said, *Of all the family, Rachel, you're the one I worry about.* He held me for a little while and then he disappeared," Rachel says through her tears. "Why, Eve?"

"Come here." I open my arms and hold her close while she sobs quietly. "He loves you, Rachel. He still worries about you and wants to protect you."

"I don't need protecting. I need a drink," says Rachel sitting up with a start, drying her eyes. Weakness always worries her.

"Me, too. And then you can tell me all about Scott," I say meaningfully.

"Let's sit on the window seat," I say when she returns from the bathroom. Her hair is combed. Her eyes are dry, although still red rimmed. I hand her a glass of Pinot Grigio. I turn off the lamp. We sit in the dark, either end of the seat facing each other, the highlighted Dogwood trees our backdrop. We touch glasses. "To William," I say.

"To William," Rachel replies. "One day I hope to find a William of my own."

"I hope you do, too, Precious. Now give over about Scott. And remember, William is listening in, too," I say with a grin.

Giving a wan smile in return, Rachel starts, "Daniel Anderson called me last week, asking, *Where's Scott? He hasn't turned up. He's missed his last three sessions.* Daniel knew I'd been seeing Scott. He's a psychologist, part of the group I practice with in my building. That's how I met Scott. I bumped into him as he came out of Daniel's office one day. *I don't know where he is.* I told him. *He tells me he's been coming to see you.* I felt such a fool, Eve."

"Go on," I say, stroking her leg. What's new? Feeling foolish is an occupational hazard for the women in our family. We care more about others than ourselves. Our self-preservation instincts are put in abeyance to our personal detriment.

"Well, I cancelled the next patient, said I was taken ill, which was so unprofessional. I felt dreadful," she says, pulling a face, "but I just had to find him." She takes a sip of her wine. "I found him in O'Reilly's pub. I knew where to look." She pauses, then swallows, "Scott has a drinking problem. He spends a lot of time there. He looked at me and said, *"What are you doing here?"* I looked at him, looked at myself and thought, *"What am I doing here? This guy's a jerk and I'm a fool for thinking I can make something of him."* Rachel looks at me, as if seeking censure. There is none. I've been there, too. Repeating the same mistakes and beating ourselves up for them. "I need to stop saving people, Eve. To accept there are some things I can't change or control; and some things I ought not change or control."

"Amen!" I say and lift my glass.

"And, I need to put some pleasure back in my life," says Rachel with feeling.

"Amen to that, too! Believe it or not, Rachel, I have the perfect solution," I say firmly. She looks at me.

"You're going to buy me a pair of Siamese cats," she says excitedly.

161

"No. Of course not. It's an Orgasmic Hearts Workshop," I say with a giggle.

"A what?" asks Rachel, mouth agape.

"A Tantra Orgasmic Hearts Workshop, with the Goddess Shaney, this weekend. Come along. Cindy is. You'll feel better about yourself. It'll be a distraction. And, it'll be fun." Rachel's eyes light up. "That's what we need, some fun in our lives." She looks out at the Dogwood trees.

"My God, Eve. What will you dream up next? And what will William think?" Rachel asks, interested in spite of herself.

"William will be delighted for us," I say, knowing deep in my heart, he will be.

Lying in the dark that evening, I look out at the stars and the moon above. It is a new moon, the opportunity to start anew. All the more reason to move forward into a brave new world. Ideas are swirling through my mind. New dreams, new desires and new ways of making them come true. I want to explore and learn about my sexuality.

This quest is not only about letting go of the past and the darkness that still lingers, but also about a sexual awakening, unleashing the wild woman trapped inside. New loves, new pleasures, new passions, new ways of relating, new ways of making love. And new guides, starting with the Goddess Shaney. I clasp my hands over my heart, take a deep breath and close my eyes. I am at peace. Sleep claims me.

A tall, dark and handsome man and I are sitting on the

granite seat in the garden, drinking champagne, suspended in time, and stark naked. Smiling, I awaken from my dream. My new man is coming. In summer. And this goddess will be ready for him.

31. Orgasmic hearts

"Welcome to Orgasmic Hearts, a workshop inspired by Western contemporary Tantra sexuality. My name is Shaney and I'm a Tantra Goddess," she says, smiling. "My intention is to create a day of flowing sensuality, one that is fun and transformational. To take the awkwardness out of sexuality. To encourage sexual confidence and explore the broad spectrum of what sexuality is." Shaney pauses and looks around at her audience. Eight of us — eight women, all in comfortable, casual wear as requested except Cindy, who feels more comfortable in a Joseph burgundy, stretch crepe jumpsuit.

We are seated on soft chairs in a circle listening and watching the goddess standing in bare feet before us. The soft fabric of her full length emerald green dress clings to her voluptuous body. Long brown hair cascades over bare shoulders, the ends curling amongst the subtly exposed cleavage. Pert nose, perfectly formed eyebrows, and a mouth painted deep red, as voluptuous as her body. The Goddess Shaney seems not of this world, her beauty ageless. Poetry in motion. Her hazel eyes meet mine and smile. A smile that radiates from deep within. I am entranced. I glance around the circle and see the rest of the group are too.

"Tantra is a philosophy that goes back more than 2000 years. The Tantrics revered sexuality as a path to enlightenment. I've been teaching about the sacredness of sexuality for four years. My mission is to liberate sexuality on the planet with a more conscious and loving connection to the foundation of being human." Shaney smiles. This time at Cindy who whispers to me,

"This is going to be fabulous, Darling," and pats my hand reassuringly.

"Self-nurture is critical to our sense of wellbeing. We all need to maintain our self-care tanks, our pleasure tanks. Often, we overlook our own needs to put others and important 'to do's' before our own nourishment," says Shaney, scanning the group again. "When we give to everyone else and do not turn our awareness inside to nurture our essence, we then have less to offer the world we live in." Rachel nods. I pat her knee fondly. "Today, what percentage is your pleasure tank at? Take a few minutes to talk to the people near you about what you could do to fill up your pleasure tank."

"Have a long, leisurely bubble bath," says Rachel drawing out her words.

"Put on some sexy lingerie," says Cindy, pouting sexily.

"I love sexy underwear, too," says Rachel, but I haven't bought any for ages."

"I haven't got any," I bemoan. "Anyone want to help me buy some?"

"I will, Eve," says Rachel. "That will be fun."

"I love massages, but I haven't had one for ages," I say.

"You should try Fernando. He is wonderful, Darling," says Cindy adding, "fortnightly facials, manicures and pedicures are essential to my wellbeing. As is shopping." Rachel and I laugh at her exuberance.

"My soul expands when I am in nature," I say hugging myself. "I love being in the garden and communing with my orchids."

"I prefer to love and commune with men, Darling," says Cindy grinning.

"Rich men," says Rachel, sighing. "I'm starting to realize how little I do to treat myself. My pleasure tank is running on empty." Shaney stands and interrupts.

"Let's leave it there, ladies. Complete your self-care list when you get home and make a commitment to do at least two things a day on your list. You deserve it! Now, shoes off and let's go over to the mat and seat ourselves in a circle again."

We move to the mat, Shaney sitting between Cindy and me. Shaney places her hands on her sex and her heart, "People can transform when they discover their conscious connection with their sex and their hearts. If everyone connected their sexual and heart energy with more awareness, the world would change. Place your right hand on your sex and your left hand on your heart. Close your eyes." We follow suit.

"Breathe deeply. Feel the sexuality in your body." I sit there, eyes closed, oblivious to all but Shaney's voice, feeling the warmth exuding from my sex. "By breathing and channelling energy from the sex into the heart, we connect more deeply with all that is around us and we are able to self-heal. The energy that comes from sex is potent and passionate." I nod knowingly.

" When it is transferred into the heart, there is an alchemy effect and it transforms into a loving energy that can fill the whole body with a higher frequency of love." A softness pervades my body. I feel like I am floating.

"Open your eyes, but leave your hands where they are. We are going to introduce ourselves. I want you to tell each other your name, where you are from and how your sexuality feels in your body."

Feeling a little uncomfortable, I look around. Rachel is doing the same. Whilst coming from a wide spectrum of backgrounds, mostly the other participants look thirtyish. Cindy and I, the elders of the tribe. Angel and Jasmine from New York City, Madison from Maryland, Hannah and Samantha, friends from Newark, introduce themselves and talk easily about their feelings.

Rachel is next. She takes a deep breath and looks at Shaney. "I'm Rachel, from Manhattan. I ask my clients to open up about their feelings and their relationships all the time. I'm just realizing how hard that is."

"Today may push some boundaries, Rachel," says Shaney. Her voice soft and mellifluous. "I really encourage you to feel them and whatever comes up. Take a little risk, go into your resistance and push your boundaries, but ensure it is emotionally safe to do so."

Rachel nods. "I'll pass on this one. It's so long since I have been in touch with my heart and my sex, it will take time to reconnect." No words are exchanged, just understanding murmurs and nods.

"Eve, your turn." Shaney taps me lightly on the knee. I jump. "You're last." I've been so deep in thought I missed what Cindy said.

The words come tumbling out. "I feel like Sleeping Beauty awakening from a hundred-year sleep. I'm no longer numb, I am a thinking, feeling woman. Not only is my heart and sex connected, but my spirit is too." I pause. "And it is beautiful. Oh, and by the way, I'm Eve from Edison." Shyly, I look around. Only smiles, even Rachel. I exhale, relieved. Shaney gives me a hug.

"Thanks, Eve. Thanks everyone. Today we'll be experiencing a variety of techniques. Give yourself permission to feel, to follow your desires, to get naked. Be authentic with your emotions. Let the body release if it wants to. We're sisters, here to support each other." I look over at Rachel and see she is still uneasy. Shaney continues, "If you feel any sexual energy today, feel it, embrace it. It's a natural energy... honor it! You may be confronted with practices that will challenge your comfort zone. Trust yourself and give it a go, but if something is too confronting, it's okay to sit out. Take responsibility for yourself." We nod agreement.

"Alright, some fundamentals," Shaney goes on, confidently, "Connection and Communication. Move forward, make the circle a little smaller so you can touch the person next to you." We all move forward, shuffling on our butts. "We are now Orgasmic Hearts," says Shaney smiling. "Connect to your breath. Let it flow down through the heart into your sex and back up to exit through the mouth."

We breathe in and out for a few minutes in silence. I hear the sound of my breathing. "I want you to access ways to light your own fire. To fill your tank. To learn to say, *yes*. But first, I want us to say a prayer, to honor the sacredness as a prayer to self and to focus the energy it manifests. Say it after me." Her voice flows as smoothly as her body.

I worship the sacredness of my sexuality. I honor my heart and my pleasure. I am an open vessel for love to flow through me. I am sacred. We intone after her.

"Now find a partner, someone you don't know and sit Yab Yum style." Shaney demonstrates sitting facing Rachel, with legs outstretched either side. Soon I'm sitting comfortably, legs straddled, Yab Yum style, with Madison from Maryland, a blonde. She looks like a younger version of me.

"Rub your palms together and let them hover over your partner," Shaney instructs. "Become aware of the energy." Madison and I rub our palms together then hesitantly hold them near our chests. I close my eyes and feel a subtle shift. I open my eyes and see Madison smiling at me.

"Did you feel that?" she asks. "My heart was talking to you." I smile and nod.

"This time," says Shaney, "place your left hand on your partner's heart and send energy through your hands. Practice sending and receiving." Madison and I shuffle closer together and reach out our hands to touch each other's heart.

"You send energy to me first, Eve," she says, closing her eyes. I close mine and concentrate. I can feel her heart beating. I feel her goodness. She opens her eyes. "Thanks, Eve. Now it's your turn to receive." We communicate without words.

"This time," says Shaney, breaking our concentration, "palms together, moving arms outward, building energy and opening the heart. Draw in a deep breath, meditate. Then rest your foreheads together. And repeat." Madison and I follow suit, ending up with our foreheads touching. An intimacy. Yet it feels comfortable. I feel I know her. We repeat the process.

"Everything you are receiving from your partner is a mirror. It's the perfect partner," Shaney explains. I look at her and reflect. Here she is, late twenties maybe, and yet she is the teacher, wiser in the ways of the world than I am. I am a learner, learning how to communicate anew, how to feel anew, tapping into a whole new way of being a woman.

ə♥

Four hours later, we're seated in a circle on our soft chairs again, weary yet still listening and watching the Goddess Shaney, intently. Her heartfelt way of talking, the natural way sexuality and sensuality exude from her, draws us in, like a magnet. It is beautiful to behold. Such confidence. Such knowing. The doubts disappear. The resolve strengthens. I want to be a goddess, too.

"Today, we learnt about our yoni — our *sacred temple* and about yoni worship. About the masculine and feminine qualities and energies that each of us have. About the chakras – the energy centres. About the Kundalini, the serpent energy in the body that rises when the body becomes aroused." Shaney's hands move as she talks, flowing like her words. "We have learnt about the importance of breath, erotic breath. The importance of touch — of sacred touch and self-love. How to communicate, to ask for what we desire, to be able to say yes and no. But most of all we have learned that orgasmic energy has the potential to transform." She looks around and smiles. "When we bring orgasmic energy into our bodies, we bring life force. Do you feel more alive?" Shaney is glowing. We are basking in her light.

"Yes," we all say loudly. Yes. Yes. Yes, I echo to myself.

"Before we finish, there are a couple of other things that may further develop your sexuality. This is a jade egg," says Shaney holding up a green egg, about the size of a quail's egg. A few eyes in the group nod in recognition. Cindy's eyes are fixated on the egg. I look at Rachel queryingly. She shrugs her shoulders.

"The stone egg practice emerged in ancient China. These practices were used to improve the physical and spiritual health of a woman and to strengthen the vagina, to make it more succulent and juicier." Rachel and I look at each other, amused. Rachel leans over to Cindy and says quietly,

"More succulent than a suppository, do you suppose?" We both laugh.

Cindy slaps me on the thigh, glares at Rachel and says, sotto voce. "Don't you dare embarrass me here, Bitches." Shaney, ignores us and goes on.

"The Jade Egg practice is really one of the most beautiful self-love exercises you can do, and will open you up to even deeper delight and pleasure. I encourage you to buy one." She looks around. "Would you like one, Eve?"

"Yes. I'll have one," I say, not having a clue, but willing to try.

"Me too," says Rachel, then lowers her voice, "a juicy pussy."

"What about you, Cindy?" asks Shaney, unsuspecting.

"There's no way a jade egg or any other unnatural object will be entering my inner sanctum, ever again," says Cindy, striding off in the direction of the rest room. Shaney looks at us, but Rachel and I just feign ignorance.

"A second, very sensual experience is a yoni massage. Now I can give you one of these, but if you prefer a man to massage you, there are some cards here for Francis," she says, passing the cards around. "I can recommend him. Go to his website and find out more about him and his philosophy." I already have his details. I got them some time ago. I giggle. He's next on my erotic education program. How fortunate Shaney mentioned him.

Shaney stands up. "Everyone stand and we will finish with a prayer. Hands on your heart and your sex again." We follow her lead. "I worship the sacredness of my sexuality." We all intone after her.

"I honor my heart and my pleasure." We repeat. "I am an open vessel for love to flow through me. I am sacred." The words resonate inside me.

"I am an open vessel for love to flow through me. I am sacred." I intone to myself. I am.

Thirty minutes later, after saying our goodbyes to Shaney and the other members of the group, we're having a wine in Rosetta's just down the road. It's been a long day, a good day, for me. I lean forward. "How did you find that, ladies? Rachel?"

She is thoughtful. "To be honest, Eve, I thought Shaney was going to be a charlatan. I had my guard up and was very sceptical. But as the day progressed, I saw we are on similar wavelengths, even though we come from very different backgrounds. I liked her. I liked a lot of what she had to say, especially about self-care and pleasure tanks and about breath and energy."

"Too much touchy-feely stuff for my liking," says Cindy, screwing up her nose in distaste. "Women taking turns undressing and massaging each other's breasts. Yuk! That was too much. Men are more my scene, Darlings."

"I'm pleased you sat that exercise out, Cindy," I say, "I got to work with Shaney taking turns worshipping the goddess within and being worshipped."

"And I got to keep the secrets of the armor-plated underwear beneath this gorgeous jumpsuit," says Cindy, wiggling her body around in the chair. We laugh. Appearance is so important to her, especially outward appearance.

I think back, watching Shaney reveal her beautiful body was fascinating. She is divine. I didn't feel like a goddess, especially when she was watching me undress. Her breasts are so perfectly formed, and so soft to touch. "It felt strange at first massaging a woman," I say, "but I got over that. I loved her massaging my breasts. Although I admit I would have found it difficult to touch your breasts or Rachel's." Rachel sips her wine and continues to look thoughtful. "Where to next?" I ask her.

"I accept I've got to do something. I am running on empty. I need to put some pleasure back in my life. And, for me, that means a man in my life, a real man."

"Amen to that," says Cindy, raising her glass. "But how, my dear?"

Rachel pauses. "Dating... Not online dating. That takes too much time and energy. Too many jerks online. Speed dating."

"What's speed dating?" I ask, interested.

"I hate the idea of speed dating," Rachel goes on, "but I know I need to get past my need to save men. To meet men in a more controlled environment."

Cindy sees my confusion and explains, "It's a type of matchmaking service, Eve. Where potential partners meet for seven minutes before moving on to the next one. At the end of the night, they make a list of those they're interested in dating."

"And... because I'm only interested in people who have their shit together," says Rachel, grinning, "it will be speed dating for professionals 35+, with six figure incomes."

"Only six figures, Darling. Not enough. Seven is more my style," says Cindy, theatrically waving her hand with the large diamond ring on it.

I laugh. "Good on you, Rachel. What about you, Cindy?"

"Not quite ready for speed dating, Darlings. But I will start strutting my stuff around the wealthy philanthropists involved in the foundation. See who is at a loose end." She turns to me. "And what about you, dear Eve?"

"No dating. I'm not ready for any kind of dating, yet. Couldn't bear the thought of kissing any more frogs." Matias is still too close to the bone. "More learning and more exploring the goddess within for me. A yoni massage with Francis. But first, my new friend and I are going to get acquainted." I pull out my jade egg. "We're going to start eggsercising together." We all erupt into laughter. It has been a good day.

32. The jade egg

I'm lying on my bed, naked after having a shower, beginning my warm up. I breathe deeply, taking the time to tune into myself and how I am feeling. I begin massaging my groin, my vulva, and my inner thighs before touching my perineum lovingly. This, I learnt recently, is the delicate area between the anus and the vagina, which can stretch. I've been learning lots of new things about my body lately.

I assiduously follow the instructions for becoming intimately acquainted with my new friend, Jade. Jade is now sterilized, after being boiled in hot water for ten minutes. Not a very friendly thing to do, but nevertheless crucial to our wellbeing and continuing friendship.

I hold Jade up and look at her. "Hello. I hope we're going to be good friends." One metre of unwaxed dental floss is threaded through the hole in her body, with a knot tied at the narrow end of the egg. "Okay, dear friend, ready to begin," I say out loud as I bring the big end of the egg to the opening of my vagina.

I massage around it, making slow circles, and breathing deeply waiting for my vagina to open so I can gently sip the egg inside. Nothing happens, so I gently apply pressure, moving the egg inside, smiling as I accept it into my vagina, as per instructions. I sigh, stand up and give a little wiggle. There is a feeling of fullness. The only external evidence of the egg is the length of floss hanging down. I squeeze my PC muscle, (the pubococcygeus muscle, that makes up the floor of the abdominopelvic cavity), to give Jade a couple of friendly hugs, before heading into the dressing room.

As I put on my panties, I feel a slight, stinging sensation around my labia and inside my vagina. I shrug it off and continue getting dressed. It's probably just my body adjusting to this new presence inside me. The stinging intensifies. I pace up and down the bedroom, hoping it will stop. Faster and faster, Kiki alerted by the movement, pacing behind me. I don't know whether I'm stinging or burning. I switch to hopping — from one foot to the other and whooping. "Oooooh! What's happening, Kiki?"

I race to the ensuite and pull out the floss packet to read the fine print. I can't see it clearly. I find my glasses. "Oh, my heavens, Kiki. It's waxed floss. It's toothpaste that's causing the stinging." I pull down my panties and yank the floss hanging down. It snaps. I stare at the length of soggy floss in my hand. I fling it in the toilet bowl. "Oh, no! What now!" I'm burning up. Desperately I find some wipes and clean myself. The pain outside eases.

I lay down on the bed, trying to calm the tide of panic rising inside. I put my finger inside my vagina. I can't feel it. I push my finger further and further inside, around and over what seems like a bony corner. I realize I still don't know enough about my anatomy. I can just feel the tip of the egg. I push in further but my fingers aren't long enough to get behind it and lever it out. "Shit! Shit! What in the hell do I do now?"

Kiki, jumps on the bed and looks at me, head on one side, sensing my distress, listening for instructions. "Dr. Daniels, I'll call Dr. Daniels, Kiki. He'll get it out. Oh, God. No way!" I say holding my hands to my head. I'd be mortified. "Cindy. I'll ring Cindy. She'll know what to do."

"Calm down, Eve. Take a deep breath and tell me what's happened."

"I've swallowed my egg, Cindy. It's stuck inside me. I can't get it out," I start bawling. "And I can't tell Dr. Daniels. What am I going to do?"

"Oh, Eve, Darling," Cindy starts to giggle. "You swallowed your friend, like a whale swallowed Jonah?"

"Yes, and it's not funny," I say, my wounded pride talking.

"Sorry," she says trying to muffle her laughing. "Where are you, Eve?"

"In the bedroom, why?"

"Put the phone on speaker, then sit on the toilet. I'll talk you through this," her laughing becoming louder.

I sit on the toilet, trying to ignore the laughter, and listening for further instructions.

"Push down and squeeze your pelvic muscles like you're having a baby."

"I've not had a baby," I say, voice rising.

"Shut up, Eve. Just sit there and keep squeezing really hard."

I do, squeezing so hard, contracting my muscles back and

forward, as if my life depends on it. Bang! Crash!!! The jade egg crashes loudly into the porcelain toilet bowl.

" I've laid an egg. Cindy," I cry out in jubilation. "I've laid an egg."

"I know. I heard. Congratulations, Darling. I'll hang up now, while you check the damage and clean yourself up. Ciao!" she signs off, laughing loudly.

I stand up and look into the bowl. A hairline crack leads a trail to the jade egg sitting on the bottom. I lean in and fish it out. "You're no friend of mine," I say sternly before washing it and tucking it away safely in its green satin pouch.

33. Yoni awakening

I take a deep breath as I open the door. "Hello, Francis. Come in." I say, stepping back to let him in. He's carrying a large rolled up mat.

"Hello, Eve. Nice to meet you." His deep blue eyes look at me through rimless glasses. "Where do you want me to set up?" He flashes me a warm friendly smile that puts me at ease. I look him over. Tall, dark and good looking, he's casually dressed in jeans and black T-shirt. Italian perhaps? Late thirties, maybe. He's pencil slim and fit looking. His dark brown hair is cropped short, as is his beard.

"This way." As I lead him to the guest bedroom and ensuite upstairs, Kiki follows quietly. Francis unrolls his mattress, a traditional futon mattress, and places it on the floor. The space is too small for it to fit.

He looks up at me and asks, "Is it okay if we use the bed?"

"Sure," I say.

Francis lays out one of the towels I left for him on the dressing table. He turns to me and meets my eyes, "Where can I change and wash up? And while I'm changing, you can undress."

"Which way do you want me on the bed?" I ask, shyly.

"Face down," he replies. He is softly spoken, but there's a quiet confidence emanating from him. I point to the ensuite bathroom and turn to go into the dressing room. Kiki is there, quietly sitting in the doorway, looking at me expectantly.

"It's okay, Little Girl. We're both feeling our way here. I'll be alright," I say, closing the door. When Francis comes back into the room, I'm lying on my stomach, my face turned towards him, arms cradling the pillow, naked, breathing deeply and willing myself to relax. He's wearing a T-shirt and knee length loose cotton trousers, olive in color, with a drawstring around the waist — Thai fisherman's trousers, I find out later. He covers my legs and bottom with a second towel. I breathe deeply.

Francis presses his hands firmly either side of my back, near the shoulder blades, holding them there for a few seconds before moving downwards by degrees. He places one hand on the base of the spine and the other in the middle, near the heart, and exerts pressure. It is as if he's using his hands to listen to what my body is saying, to get a sense of who I am before he starts massaging. He removes his hands. All is quiet. An absence of feeling for a few seconds, then I feel something cold on my back. Tiny drops of oil are being slowly dripped on me, up and down my back. Francis removes the towel and continues dripping oil over my legs. My body jerks reflexively at the light, sensual touch.

Another pause, before his hands start smearing the oil over my back and legs. Strong, firm hands work with surety, massaging firmly, alternating working from either side of the bed. My back, my neck, my arms, my legs and my bottom. Pushing, pulling, pressing, and kneading deep into the muscles, my body swaying with the movement. Then he changes pace, alternating rhythms, with the lightest of touches. His fingers dancing lightly across my skin, up and down my thighs and between my cheeks, nearer and nearer to my yoni — *my sacred temple.* Teasingly they dance in and around the lips, squeezing, tapping and touching, before his fingers find their way inside, filling me, briefly. Such exquisite pleasure.

His hands alight on a sensitive spot near the base of the spine, applying the gentlest of pressure. My body jumps joyfully in response. Soft whimpers escape. Timing is as important to this maestro as touch.

"Is it alright if I take off my T-shirt?" Francis asks, his voice breaking into my thoughts. Up until now, no words have been spoken.

"Yes," I say, lifting my face from the pillow where it has been buried and taking a deep breath. He takes it off and drops it on the floor, then straddles my legs, half kneeling, half sitting on my bottom. As he starts massaging my back and neck strongly again, I feel his power and energy radiating through me.

He stops and lays his bare torso on one side of me, breathing with me, into me. The heaviness of his body contrasted by the gentle blowing in my ear. My nether regions dance and quiver, as if the two are joined. I moan with delight. His fingers gently pull my ear lobe and dance in and out of my ear before he blows into it again, sending shivers down my spine. His hands work their way powerfully down my arms, my outstretched fingers meshing with his, held there in time and space. My body trembles with anticipation as he transfers his weight to the other side and the whole delicious, erotic process starts again.

"Can you turn over now, please, Eve?" Francis says as he stands up. I'm so wedded to the bed and the pillow, I don't think it possible to move, but somehow, I do. My hair is awry. I manage to tuck it back into the scrunchie. My face is wet. My mascara has probably run, but I don't care. Francis lifts my head and straightens the pillow. I look into his face and see only tenderness and care. I trust him. I close my eyes and lie there, barely breathing, wondering how much more pleasure I can take.

I jump involuntarily and keep jumping as the oil anoints my highly aroused body, sighing and moaning at the deliciousness of the sensations. The oil stops. Another pause heightens the arousal. Francis straddles my legs again. Kneeling either side of me he massages upwards from my thighs, to my abdomen, breasts and neck and back again, alternating firmness and pressure with a delicate lightness of touch. He stops once more, strategically placing his hands on my heart and my sex at the same time sending electrical charges through me. My body keeps jumping involuntarily as if it has a mind of its own. I laugh. My mind and body soften, opening up to his sensual touch, wanting more.

Francis kneels in between my legs, my knees are slightly bent, my womanhood exposed, quivering. I'm a lady in waiting. I close my eyes again and breathe deeply and slowly, allowing the energy to flow through me. He drips oil onto my mound of Venus and down the outer lips of my yoni, surprising me, making me inhale sharply. As his fingers gently massage the mound and the outer lips I consciously relax and open up to his tender ministrations. He leans over me and blows gently on my yoni, surprising me yet again. I quiver at each breath.

His delicate fingers resume dancing, tracing patterns up and down my thighs, on my belly this time and around the entrance to my sex before alighting on my clitoris – *the crown jewel*, stroking and squeezing it, then blowing on it again. Francis' attention moves to the outer lips of my yoni, followed by the inner lips. Touching, tapping, squeezing, all the time, varying the pressure, movement and rhythm before he slowly inserts a finger inside me, gently exploring and massaging the inside of my yoni. Then there are two fingers, fluttering inside me. When he places his other hand on my belly, I cry out and start spasming. It is a symphony of sensation. I'm awash with emotion – laughing, crying and moaning. My hands reach up to hold onto his lithe body, wanting to draw him further into me. Francis stays there poised, letting me hang on to him.

I lie there for a while, blissfully at peace, feeling mellow, like fine wine. Francis, knowingly, allows me time to savor the sensations before his hands start stroking my legs, belly and breasts again. I open my eyes and look at him. He doesn't say much. He doesn't need to. His hands do the talking. He smiles at me, in that warm friendly way of his, places his hands on my heart and my yoni and presses down firmly. A small spasm in reply. I smile, knowing my yoni awakening is not yet over.

34. High Priestess

What a wonderful morning. Winter is on the wane. Soft pink streaks across the sky, warming me, warming the day. I love the sunlight. My day has lit up like my mind. As Kiki and I walk through the woodlands, my brain is racing, my heart is pounding. I can't believe what I have done. Of all the crazy things I have done in my life, this would have to rank right up there with the best of them. I have an appointment to meet Anthony next week. I'll tell Cindy and the others tonight.

Yesterday it was my Tarot card that was the catalyst for bringing my wildest idea to fruition – the third step in my sex education program. I'd been hesitating, but once I flipped over the *High Priestess*, I knew what I had to do. *The High Priestess — the Guardian of the Unconscious, who sits in front of the thin veil of awareness, all that separates us from our inner selves.*

The High Priestess knows the secret of how to access these realms. My body holds knowledge. I need to explore it, to learn from it, to know its secrets. But I need a teacher, a guide. Realization dawned. And, I know where to find one. Ten minutes later I had a conference call with the ladies who run Aphrodisiac Male Escorts.

"Eve, we have a gentleman who would be perfect for you, Anthony — the James Bond of our team," said Mary Jo.

"He's a caring soul as well as a refined Englishman," said Ruby. "Could you send us a written proposal for what you want, please?" It took me a while to work out what to write, but I got there in the end.

Dear Ruby and Mary Jo,

I am looking at several rendezvous where Anthony is the master, or perhaps teacher is a better word, and I am the pupil.

The goal: to be transformed into a goddess of love.

Anthony leads in a way that encourages, nurtures and may sometimes challenge and shock me, to allow the goddess within to emerge so I can assume greater power and control over my body and my sexuality.

His role is to introduce me to the beauty and joy of sex — the depth, breadth and subtleties of the language used to express sexuality, sensuality, romanticism, love and passion.

These are to be *lessons in loving,* culminating in the emergence of Aphrodite. They are not sex therapy. Heaven forbid!

There is to be one final rendezvous where I take the lead. I have no idea of specifics yet, and won't until I become intimately acquainted with him and what is possible.

But first, I'd like to meet Anthony, to know if we can work together. Please let me know what you think.

Warmest regards,

Eve

And the Lovely Ladies came back to me this morning. Anthony said, "YES!" Whacky doo!

∂☙

"I'm coming back over this side of the river again next week," I say to Cindy, keeping my eyes firmly fixed on the road as we make our way through the Holland Tunnel to Richard's new apartment. It's freezing cold and rain is not far away. The traffic is continuous both ways which is making me edgy. I need to tell her about Anthony, but I'm feeling more and more nervous and apprehensive about meeting him, the longer I wait. I'm no longer sure it is the right thing to do.

"Why is that?" she asks, interested.

"I've been in touch with an escort agency. It's run by women for women."

"What? Why?" she asks, shocked into silence.

"I asked if I could have some lessons in loving. I want to become a goddess."

"A goddess! For goodness sake, Eve! You do come up with the most fanciful ideas."

I gulp, but go on. "One of their gentlemen, Anthony, is willing to work with me, to help me transform into Aphrodite, the Goddess of Love, Beauty and Desire."

Cindy laughs out loud. "In your dreams. It's another one of your fantasies."

"I've wanted to become a goddess since I saw *Venus de Milo* in the Louvre."

"*Venus de Milo* is a statue, Darling Eve. She's not real. You are," she says in a softer voice. But the impact is not.

In spite of my hurt, I persist, "I'm not going back to find men online. There are too many weirdos, too many frogs, and it's not safe. It's really important to be safe, Cindy. Working with Anthony will be much safer."

"Yes, I know. But I've been worried about you lately, Eve. First the Goddess Shaney. Next a jade egg. Then a yoni massage and, this time, an escort. For heaven's sake, he's just a glorified male prostitute!" The knife cuts deeper. "Can't you do anything the conventional way?" Her words wound.

I reflect on what she's saying. I've always felt different. Creative, a thinker, a dreamer with big bold ideas, always looking for ways to bring them to life. But, oh so sensitive. That's what she usually loves about me. I glance over at Cindy. She's looking very uptight. I decide discretion is the better part of valor and say nothing, trying to concentrate on driving instead.

Dark clouds loom ominously over the heavily residential neighborhoods as we near the West Village, mostly mid-rise apartments and 19th-century row houses. People and cars are everywhere.

"Don't you dare tell anyone else about this, especially the twins. They will not understand and they will not forgive you, like I do," Cindy lectures me, believing she is saving me from myself.

I tuck my hurt away, out of sight as usual, realizing the need to go deep underground. On my own. "There's the Village Green, our turn off," I say, relieved. I am relieved also to be warned that this time, my fanciful ideas will not be well received.

ॐ

Richard opens the door, beaming. "Bonjour et bienvenue chez Richard, Mesdames," he says, mimicking a French accent." He bows and waves us into the entrance foyer, before closing the door behind us. "Ma cherie, Eve." He holds my shoulders and kisses me on both cheeks before turning to Cindy and doing the same. It's great to see him so relaxed. "Come and see who's here," his voice returning to normal as he walks us through a doorway.

Rachel is talking to a very tall man, their backs to us, looking out a large window of what is a very large living area. He looks vaguely familiar. They turn and smile.

"James, how lovely to see you again." I walk over to them. "And you too, Rachel," I say kissing her on the cheek. I hold out my hand to James.

"I think we're past that formal British stuff now," he says, his cultured English voice still sounding very formal. He leans down and kisses me on the cheek.

"Goody," says Cindy coming over, puckering up her lips.

James smiles, moves out of range and politely kisses her on the cheek, too. "Hello, Cindy. What do you think of Richard's new apartment?"

"They haven't seen it yet," says Richard. "Come and I'll give you a tour. It's part of a twenty-story post war condo with one of the best layouts. Six rooms, two bedrooms and one and a half bathrooms or a powder room plus a full-time doorman — whom you ladies have already met," he boasts proudly."

The condo is spacious and airy with lots of light. He brings us back into the living area to the window.

"And because we're near the top, great views of the Village. Washington Square Park is over there, just ten minutes' walk." The trees in the park are bare allowing a glimpse of the Arch and the hordes of people, even on a cold winter's afternoon.

"What a fabulous view, Richard," I say.

"And... entertainment options galore," chimes in Rachel, "and, lots and lots of cafes and restaurants." She looks as thrilled as Richard.

"They took me to lunch at Caffe Reggio today, home of the original cappuccino," says James. "Do you know, they still make coffee with an antique expresso machine that dates back to 1902? Amazing."

"Speaking of drinks, can I interest anyone in a glass of champagne?" asks Richard. A chorus of yeses. "Okay. James, can you help me, please?" James nods and follows him.

"Great condo," Cindy says to Rachel.

"Yes, it is. I don't think I've ever seen him so happy. It's like he belongs here," she says smiling. "He and James have signed a contract to start building the apartments in London. Mega bucks. Dad's really pleased for a change. That project will start very soon, so he'll be flying over regularly to keep an eye on things."

"You're looking happier, too, Rachel," I say. "What's happening in your life?"

She laughs. "You always have a way of knowing how I feel, Eve. But you're right. I am happier. My speed dating night produced five matches. I've been sampling, cherry picking ever since. I'm enjoying myself."

"Good on you," I say. "I'm delighted for you."

"Me, too," says Cindy, who has been uncharacteristically quiet. "It's time to get serious about finding Number Four, but first I need to get some weight off."

"Here we are, ladies," says Richard coming back into the room. James is carrying a tray with glasses full of champagne. Richard hands one to each of us, then takes the tray from James, who takes a glass. Richard puts the tray down and picks up the remaining glass. "To life. To life continuing to be good. Cheers."

"I'll drink to that," I say. I walk over to the window and gaze out. The others all start talking animatedly. I look back at them. My family, finally, is moving on. I won't have to worry about them for a while. Time for me now.

35. Farewell Frogs

I arrive half an hour early at the Empire Hotel on West 63rd Street, but still later than I'd intended. I left home early but the traffic was a nightmare. Construction work on the Lincoln Tunnel had all but closed it, causing heavy delays. Anthony and I are meeting at 7pm. As I step from the elevator into the Rooftop Bar on the twelfth floor, stunning views of the iconic Manhattan skyline greet me. I look around.

Sophisticated comfort and edgy décor. Bold leopard skin and tiger skin cushions scattered amidst plush leather stools and chairs. Rich golds, tans and browns pervade. The modern black and silver bar is softened by a wall of warm lighting. Few people are here yet, fortunately. I choose two comfortable lounge chairs in a quiet corner. I unpack my bag, placing the contents on the table. Three flower arrangements made by the local florist using my orchids – a pale pink button hole, a white orchid for the wrist, a spray of lime green orchids and my cell phone.

A waiter comes over. "What would you like to drink, Madame?" he asks, courteously, smartly dressed in black trousers, starched white shirt and black bow tie, befitting the swank elegance of this old hotel.

I look the menu over. "A glass of Black Kite Pinot Noir and some iced water, please." He returns quickly. I alternate sipping my wine and water and breathing deeply, consciously relaxing. I'm doing a lot of deep breathing lately. I look down at my clothes. I decided on a smart professional look – navy blue pant suit with a lovely lime green camisole. The heart chakra. I'm hoping Anthony and I will have a heart connection. And of course, my hair is down. Soft and feminine. I wonder what he'll think of me. Time disappears. A text alert sounds.

Anthony has arrived. He will be with you soon. Enjoy your evening.

LL (Lovely Ladies)

I reach for my wine, take another sip, place my glass down and look up to see a young man make his way through the bar towards me. As I take another deep breath, the world slows. He is gorgeous, drop dead gorgeous. Thirtyish, tall, lean, dirty blonde hair, immaculately groomed. He looks very cosmopolitan in a tapered navy-blue suit with narrow legs, open necked red and white striped shirt and tapered continental black shoes. He's chosen navy blue too! Although he's definitely not your quintessential English gentleman. We make eye contact. He smiles as he nears.

"Eve?" I smile and nod. He kisses me on the cheek, then sits down, his piercing blue eyes looking into mine. A waiter hovers.

"Anthony. Lovely to meet you. What would you like to drink?" The waiter hands him the drinks menu. My cheeks flush. I put my hands to them while his head is down. They feel hot. Oh dear.

"I'll have the Californian Pinot Noir – the Black Kite and iced water too, please." Then turning to me, "I'm a big Pinot fan." Cultured voice. English private school. Eton? No, he's too relaxed for that. Somewhere smart though. My heart is beating very fast. My fingers are drumming on my thighs again. Breathe, Evie.

"I have some orchids here, a button hole for you." Shaking, I hand it to him and he pins it to his suit coat. The pale pink orchid symbolizing a lover of beauty.

He seems genuinely surprised and pleased to receive this gift. "Thank you," he beams at me.

"And the white one for me. Could you tie it on for me, please?' I hold out my wrist while he ties the white satin ribbon expertly. White is totally reflective, awakening openness, growth and creativity. You can't hide behind it as it amplifies everything in its way.

"And one for someone special in your life." I hand him the spray of lime green orchids. "They're all from my garden."

He looks them over keenly before placing them back on the table. "They're lovely. Thank you." His wine arrives. He raises his glass. "Here's to you, Eve, and your beautiful orchids."

"Thank you." I raise my glass and touch his. As I take a sip, I look at him. He is looking at me, too, closely. I want to explain the meaning behind the orchids but the words won't come. It's too soon. The whole setting seems surreal.

Anthony places his glass down and leans in towards me. "Tell me what brings you to this point in time."

Relieved at the entrée, I tell him the story of William and the psychic, asking me to let him go. Soon I'm talking fifty to the dozen, laughing excitedly as I relive the fantastic frog tales. I pause and look at him. He is so easy to be with, so comfortable to talk to. Usually, I'm a listener who talks very little, but here I am hardly drawing breath. He listens in a way that is as disarming as it is encouraging. His eyes and smiles speak volumes. A warmth infuses me. I genuinely like him. His age is irrelevant. All I see and feel is a man I can relate to. Anthony sits there waiting for me to go on. He knows there is more. I tell him of my epiphanies in Europe – in Monet's Garden and in the Louvre, and my passion for beauty.

"You must think it strange, someone my age wanting to become a goddess."

"No, not strange at all," he says. "I understand this. I understand passion. And I understand beauty. My background is in Art History, a Ph.D. actually, so we have a few things in common already." The gentle touch on my knee is unexpected, but reassuring, suggesting he's there for me in more ways than one, creating a connection.

"Farewell frogs and hermit crabs." I want to dance and shout. "Welcome Prince Anthony and what a charming prince you are. Daniel Craig, eat your heart out!" Instead, I remain seated, the words unsaid. I sip my wine and smile. A smile that comes from deep inside.

"I'd like to start our journey in spring with our final rendezvous in summer. Spring is a few weeks away." Anthony nods, sensing more. He is very intuitive. Hesitantly, I add, "I want us to be in harmony with nature. Beauty abounds when we are in harmony with nature," wondering whether he'll think I am fanciful, like Cindy.

He smiles and touches my knee again. I inhale. "What a beautiful woman you are, Eve." A text alert sounds on his phone. Anthony checks it. "The Ladies are asking if you want to extend our rendezvous." I look at my watch, amazed. We've been talking for well over an hour.

I shake my head. "No. Could I ask one more thing of you, please, Anthony?"

"Of course."

"The night before each rendezvous, could you send me an email, please? Maybe some suggestions of what to wear, what perfume or what the lesson will be about." I sigh. "It will help. To heighten the sense of anticipation, or maybe to lessen my anxiety." A nervous laugh escapes, highlighting the point.

"My pleasure." He stands and picks up the spray of orchids. "Thank you again for the orchids." I stand. He leans forward and kisses me lightly on the lips. "See you in spring." He turns and walks away. I stand there waiting for my breathing to return to normal before sitting down. What a wonderful way to start our journey together. Who knows where it will end? What more could this woman want? Well...

36. The rites of spring

Today the air is laden with perfume. Sprays of cherry blossom and apple blossom hang heavily from their branches. Birds and bees abound. Spring is just around the corner. I head into the orchid house to check my babies. Luscious spikes are everywhere, reaching out, searching for the light, each spike vying for its own space, loving being so close, longing to let go, to open up, to flower.

My eyes alight on Persephone, the Goddess of Spring. Her eight-inch pot is crowded, bursting at the seams like my mind. This year is Persephone's crowning glory – sixteen spikes and her last year in this pot. Each spike is an individual expression of the whole plant and the beauty yet to be revealed. Each spike the repository of my hopes, dreams and desires; my belief in the future. A future that is beautiful, boundless and timeless.

There's a subtlety and variety to Persephone's nature – at times shy and retiring, closed over, in hiding. At others poised to open, on the brink of transforming. Her colors are muted, soft tints of what is to come. Persephone is waiting for spring to unleash her precious beauty on the world. It has taken years for her to reach this stage.

It will take some weeks for her splendor to fully emerge, and it will emerge slowly, from the bottom of each spike to the tip, sometimes one at a time, sometimes in concert, a dance — a sacred ritual of flowering. This beautiful lady is in waiting, waiting for Mother Nature and the warmer weather to lead her in the dance of the rites of spring.

I do a pirouette and talk to Persephone. "And this beautiful lady has only ten more days in waiting for Anthony to lead her into the rites of spring."

Dear Anthony,

Spring is here. The season of hope and new beginnings. My precious orchid, Persephone, is already stirring, trembling with anticipation. The dance has begun.

Aroused from winter hibernation by the last few warm days, Persephone quivers with excitement as the precious bounty on her spikes starts to transform. Hooded helmets hide the delicate beauty inside, but not for long. Shy smiles will give way to joyous laughter as their faces open to usher in the new season.

Being surrounded by and immersed in beauty creates a peace and harmony within, which is why I feel such an affinity with you. There will be beauty in our coming together and from it, I believe, will emerge some of the most exquisite experiences ever.

A feeling of languorous lusciousness has come over me and it is beautiful. Let's hope it stays with me until we meet in the flesh. I feel good about this journey with you as my guide. I am in safe hands. Please know that you will be safe too.

Eve x

PS My desk calendar today gave me a giggle.

I am the star in my own movie. I am also the author and director. I create wonderful roles for myself.

Dear Eve,

You seek understanding in all life's complexities, from the orchid to the blossoming woman. A warm welcome to spring. The clichéd smell of cut grass greeted me yesterday. This morning I was astounded by the beauty of a sunrise over the ocean and caught off guard during the day by the brightness of the sun's rays as I stepped outside.

I am engaging my mind on tomorrow night, predicting how things might develop. One should never predict too much though, as you leave no room for spontaneity. Your garden of delights excites me. Does that bring a smile to your lips? I hope so. I remember that smile from our first encounter, the way your eyes sparkled as you opened up about your quest. I put my hand up for this project when I heard about it, my childish sense of fun drawn to your own childlike excitement.

Until then,

Anthony

37. Lessons in loving

I wheel my overnight case into the elevator and press the button for the first floor. The day has finally come and I'm feeling calm and peaceful. Our card this morning was *Justice* — the search for truth, restoring nature's balance. This is a card through which one takes responsibility for one's actions, realizing that everything in the past has shaped them, and everything that they do in the future will continue to do so. I like that. I typed up the meaning for Anthony and will give it to him tonight.

I turn and look in the mirror. I can't keep my mind off him or tonight. Such openness. Nothing hidden about either of our roles. That is so liberating. His email last night took a while to digest, but he writes well. A romantic at heart. There was nothing suggestive or dirty which was wonderful. I have no idea what he will do or what will happen. I just know that I very much want it to and I am grateful that I've been able to arrange an extended *coming out* phase with the Lovely Ladies. The elevator door slides open.

For the first of my *lessons in loving*, and so I am starting on the first floor. I've booked five two-hour lessons with Anthony, at fortnightly intervals, here at the Empire Hotel. The sixth and final rendezvous, on the first full moon in summer, is to be at home. When I made the hotel booking a month ago, the receptionist was discreet enough not to inquire why I was requesting the second floor for the second night, working my way up to the fifth floor. I'd have explained that the spiritual meaning of five draws our attention to the wonders of life. Or that to Jung it is the symbol of creative life and erotic love. Although I doubt that would have made much sense to him or to many others.

It's just after four. Anthony will be here at seven. My suite has a largish lounge and dining area with an opening leading to an adjoining bedroom. The mahogany bed is draped in Italian linens and animal print cushions. I walk through to the bathroom. Warm wood grained panelling with white fixtures and white towels. The same earthy tones of Central Park in each room as in the lobby and the bar upstairs. Sophisticated and comfortable. Nothing discordant.

I sit down on the bed, take off my shoes and sit there rubbing a heel. What next? Wine. I need wine. Perhaps some strawberries to go with it. Maybe I should order something light to eat as well, before I shower. I pick up the phone and see my hand is shaking. Suddenly I'm nervous. Very nervous indeed. Thoughts of the evening go round and around in my head. I order sushi, a bottle of Sonoma Pinot Noir and some strawberries.

I lay out what I have chosen to wear, each piece a touchstone for the occasion. I touch them, feeling their soft silkiness. White floral bras and panties, a riot of roses trimmed with navy blue lace and straps, for spring. Silky cobalt blue pants and matching V-neck blouse, buttoned down the front. Tiny pearl buttons. My forefinger and thumb start from the top and rub each one in turn. I put my fingers to my throat and stroke it gently. Blue — the throat chakra. The spirit of truth and purpose. My fingers find my ear lobes and lovingly rub the pearl studs – the astral stone for Gemini.

I take the perfume bottle from the case, smell it and laugh. The only spontaneous decision. When my hand reached for *Sensuous Nude*, I spied *Lou Lou*, in its blue bottle, sitting next to it on the shelf. When I saw it, I laughed again and thought, that's what I am, a loo loo. A loopy loo loo. Way over the top. So, I grabbed it and threw it in the suitcase.

A quest to find the goddess within. Maybe Cindy is right, and I am being ridiculous. I shake the thought away.

38. Sensuality center stage

The text alert startles me. I've been waiting for it and yet I jump.

Anthony has arrived. He is in the lobby. He will be with you shortly.

Enjoy your evening.

LL

I check myself in the mirror and scan the room. All is okay. My heart is beating fast. The knock on the door is firm. I consciously will myself to slow down as I open the door and stand back.

"Hello, Anthony. Come in." A lovely smile as he walks toward me, bends slightly and kisses me gracefully on the cheek.

"Hello, Eve. Lovely to see you again." He enters the room and places down the tan leather satchel thrown over his shoulder. He is immaculately groomed. Tailored navy suit again, this time with a stylish white open neck shirt. They fit him perfectly.

"Lovely to see you, too. Would you like a glass of Pinot?" I show him to the couch. "I've got some strawberries, too." My throat is dry. I sit down beside him and take a sip from my glass of wine, trying hard to breathe normally.

"Yes, please," he says turning to face me with a broad smile. "What's been going on?" He seems so comfortable and confident; so urbane. My hands shake a little as I pour him a glass of wine. He hands me mine, then picks up his glass and says, "Cheers. To us."

"Cheers, to us," I respond in kind tapping his glass, taking a sip, then putting it down as my hands are still shaking. "Not a lot. I've been spending some time in the garden and with my orchids. Mostly I've been thinking about tonight." My fingers rubbing nervously on my thighs as I speak. "What about you?"

"I've been getting my camera out. I'm a bit of a photographer, for myself anyway. Not for any commercial purposes." He smiles at me, warmly. "Landscapes mostly. I share your love of nature." His blue eyes smile too, as he touches my leg. My hands still. I pick up my glass, again. As I sip, I look at him closely. He's so good looking, but so young. He reminds me of someone, I think. Oh, dear me, it's Phillip — David and Susan's son. Much the same age as Phillip and the twins. Why, I wonder, would Anthony be excited about working with someone my age?

"Thanks for your email. What was it about my quest that excited you?" I ask.

"I like challenge. And this is challenge, in big, bold letters. It's up there," he says thrusting his hands up in the air, surprising me. His voice big and bold, too. "It's not a sexual challenge. It's about self-development. It's personal growth with a real purpose. Don't get me wrong. I enjoy clients who don't know what they want. The finding out is the challenge there. But here, I guess it's the challenge of living up to expectations whilst seeing which new direction this takes both of us."

He stands up, then holds out his hand to me. "Shall we?" I stand up. Still holding my hand, his head leans into my neck. His other hand brushes aside my hair while his mouth grazes my neck. A tingle runs down my spine. He picks up his bag and walks me to the bed. I sit down and watch while he places his bag on the dressing table and opens it. He removes some silver satin ties and waves them at me, before placing them on the bedside table. He shows me a roll of black duct tape. My eyes widen.

"To bind us together." He looks at me and laughs. He's joking, thank heavens. Relieved, I swallow nervously.

"So, this is your bag of tricks?" I ask with a laugh.

"Yes," he says with a cheeky grin on his face, the ice broken. Anthony brings out three bottles of massage oils. "I have three flavors. Which one's yours? There's a sandalwood, but that's not very popular. There's a citrus and lemongrass and a floral and rose peony. See which one you prefer." He takes the caps off and puts each one to my nose, in turn. I smell each and choose the citrus fragrance. He places it on the bedside table and stands in front of me, holding out his hands to help me up. He opens his arms and I walk into them. Wrapping his arms around me, he nuzzles into my neck. I hold him tightly, swaying in his embrace. He draws back, kisses me lightly on the lips, before starting to unbutton my blouse, slowly.

"I think some clothes need to come off at this stage," he

whispers into my ear. He drops the blouse on the floor, then unzips my trousers. I step out of them, leaving them on the floor, too. Anthony holds me to his chest, nuzzling my neck again, while he expertly undoes my bra, dropping it on to the pile below, but I care not for my clothes. His fingers hook themselves into the waist band of my panties. He takes his time, pulling them gently down my legs until I slip them off.

"Come and lie here. Face down," he says, removing all but one of the pillows. He settles me tenderly, head turned to the side. As I watch him undress, everything appears as if in slow motion. His fingers undoing the buttons on his shirt, removing one arm at a time, before dropping it. He unzips his trousers and steps out of them. And does the same with his underpants. Adonis stands before me. I've never before seen such a beautiful body. Anthony lives up to his namesake. He is indeed worthy of praise. I close my eyes wondering if this is really happening.

The oil anointing my skin tells me yes. Soon his powerful hands are stroking and rubbing my neck and back, his fingers kneading into the muscles. More oil on my legs and bottom. He kneels either side of my legs, massaging the calves, then the thighs, his fingers kneading my bottom, before moving to the insides of my thighs. My brain is still in gear. I'm thinking rather than feeling, finding it hard to relax. Wondering whether this crazy idea could work. His fingers find my sex with surety. My body quivers in response. He holds them there. A warmth suffuses me. Anthony asks me to turn over.

I look into his eyes. He smiles as he anoints me with oil

again. I close my eyes and surrender to the movement, to his tender loving touch. Everything disappears. I become lost in the sensations of touching. My breasts, my belly, my face and finally my sex which quivers again in response. He kisses me, gently on the mouth; a lingering kiss. Such intimacy. It is so utterly unexpected and so beautiful. My hands reach out to stroke his beautiful body. So taut and toned. So sensuous. A pleasure toy in its own right. Anthony leans down and kisses me again. The sweetest of kisses. I hug him, holding him close, feeling connected to him.

His arousal surprises me. Somewhere deep inside, I thought being with me wouldn't arouse him. I was wrong. He reaches over to his bag of tricks and pulls out a condom. I lie back and watch as he puts it on. He pulls out some lube. He squeezes some onto his fingers which gently find their way to the entrance of my vagina before wiping the rest on his erect penis.

I feel like I'm outside of myself, watching a movie, like it's happening to someone else. But it's not. It's me and it's here and now. Anthony eases his way inside me, slowly, gently, tenderly as he has been all night, treating me with such adoration and respect. It is so long since I've had someone to touch — to touch me; to love — to really love. As his powerful body starts to move inside me, tears gather. My mind wanders back to William. And I start to dry up. I stop moving, mortified.

"Could we try the Yab Yum position?" I ask, surprising myself as well as him.

He sits back on the bed and looks at me, with a query on his

207

face. "Yab Yum? A Tantra position? I'm not sure of that one, you'll have to show me." He smiles, a knowing smile and traces a finger tenderly around my chin. I know I am safe. I ask him to sit up, legs astride. I sit on top of him, my legs either side of his body, our genitals touching, but now in repose.

I wrap my arms around his neck, kiss it gently then leave my head lying over his shoulder, clinging to him, unwilling to let go. Anthony responds by wrapping his long, lithe arms around me and leaning into my body. As I stay there locked in an embrace, peace and calm descend. Warmth suffuses me once more. I am lost in the eons of time.

After what seems hours, still draped over his neck, my hands and fingers start moving, slowly, sensuously, feeling his amazing body. Tracing patterns over his back, his neck, his shoulders, his arms, his chest, his face. Humming. Talking now and then. Of what I know not. Every now and then, my mouth grazes on his neck, his shoulders, his mouth, anywhere I can reach without letting go.

Anthony has given himself up to my touch, surrendered his body to me, sensitive to my overwhelming need to hold him, to be close to him. Such sensual delights coming after a period of such intense longing. My sexuality finally starts to stir. Still holding on to his neck, I move around on him.

He stirs, too. He moves his head back so he is looking directly at me. "Would you like me to come inside you?" I nod. Another condom on, he sits with legs astride as I lower myself onto him gently, moaning as my sex wraps around him. I lock my arms around his neck once more. We sit there, joined, barely moving, writhing with the delicious pleasure of being so closely connected.

As he starts to move inside me, I feel my sexual energy building very quickly. The kundalini is rising up our spines. Our breathing synchronizes. I feel a quivering in my belly and my whole body begins to shudder and keeps on shuddering as my head falls forward on to his shoulder once more. I stay there as the delightful quivers keep on coming, totally immersed in my first lesson in loving. As the quivering subsides, I lift up my head and kiss him on the cheek. "Thank you. That was wonderful."

"My pleasure," he says, beaming at me. I lay my head over his neck and close my eyes. A peace and harmony come over me.

Instead of starting with the base and sacral chakras we started with green, the Heart chakra and moved upward, communicating with our bodies. When Aphrodite is near perhaps red and orange, passion and fire will be more to the fore. But for now, Persephone is here. Small, fragile, pale muted colors, flowers still opening up, a gentle, formative, loving process, her delicate beauty uppermost.

For now, it seems the heart connection and the sense of touch are to the fore and need more nurturing. Sensuality center stage; eroticism in the wings, with Anthony as the director. I am in good hands.

39. Slow dancing

Red Dogwoods and red Flanders poppies in full bloom. I am looking out at them, through a veil of tears. Kiki is on the window seat beside me, cuddled up close. On the horizon is my sixtieth birthday and the eighth anniversary of Williams's passing. It's nearly a year since William asked me to let him go and this momentous journey started. The sadness is exacerbated by the loneliness and longing that besets me around this time each year. I'm in desperate need of someone to hold me, to make it all go away. I still haven't let go, as much as I've tried. I'm not sure I ever will. It's like a protective mechanism. The past is a known quantity whereas the future is a foreign country unknown, almost unknowable. There is only the present, and Anthony. I dry my tears. He'll be with me again tomorrow, but here. Here where I belong.

ॐ

Anthony has been and gone. What an exquisitely tender evening. My second *lesson in loving*. He is so sweet; I drink him in. Being with him is like sipping nectar, the nectar of the gods. Sitting here drinking the last of the Pinot, I smile thinking how right I was to move all our rendezvous back here, to my home. I feel like a goddess in this paradise I created. Anthony loved being here too. The possibilities and potential for us expands exponentially in such a lush and beautiful setting. As I gaze out at the garden in the moonlight, I relive the evening once more. Slow dancing.

Anthony and I are standing, intertwined, our arms around each other, holding each other gently, exquisitely, his fingers slowly dancing down my arms, around my neck and over my back. My fingers echo the slow, sensuous pace up and down his arms and his back in return. As his fingers run through my hair, he picks up strands and slides his way sensuously along one precious strand at a time, sending quivers rippling through me. Anthony's attention turns to my face and neck. His luscious lips move in concert with his fingers, delicately kissing my skin, light as a feather. I'm swept away by the sensation of it all.

Our bodies, still standing beside the bed, sway rhythmically like giant kelp in a sea of sensation as our fingers dance lightly across the skin. We may have been here for five minutes or fifty. Lost in space in a timeless reverie. A dance of love. This is not sex. It is making love as a total body experience. I think I've died and gone to heaven.

All this soft billowing, pillowy feeling, like floating on a cloud. The sensations are other worldly. And in my own private paradise. How much calmer and easier it feels, and how natural it is to be here. This is where I belong, this is where the essential

Eve can come into being. I feel like a child of God, loved, blessed and beautiful. Oh, so beautiful.

We move to the bed. We sit, legs intertwined, mine over his. Arms around each other. Anthony alternately gently lifts strands of hair or traces his fingers around my neck and back. I hold him close. Sitting on him is as natural as laughing. This is where I'm meant to be, close to him, face on, talking, looking into his eyes, kissing him. My fingers ceaselessly stroking his beautiful body.

He moves and eases me back, holding me until I'm lying on my back. His fingers delicately trace my nipples, giving them a flick now and then. My nether regions twitch with each delicious jolt. The tracery continues, up and down my belly, my breasts, my arms. He turns his delicious attention to my legs, the insides of the thighs, all the while coming closer and closer to my sex. The pace is slow, rhythmic, loving. My vagina is silently screaming – come closer, touch me.

Soft moans and whimpers escape me as do quivers of anticipation as the delicate tracery moves to my sex. The lips of my labia open their petals to greet his fingers, before they alight on my clitoris massaging it with a sublimely enticing sensual touch. Yet I feel no hurry, no urgency. Working up into a peak, coming back down, holding it back, relishing it. Letting the feelings come and go, not needing to explode or to finish, just wanting the endless pleasure of the slow dancing to go on and on. Such bliss. I doubt anything could top this. Or could it?

39. SLOW DANCING

Dear Eve,

To tomorrow's booking. It has been cooler but is warming. A citrus fragrance would be my preference. Along the lines of DKNY *Be Delicious*. I have a candle that I think will be suitable for the sense of smell. I've chosen some music as well. You will be stepping further out of your comfort zone, entering a new place. But that is okay, I am there to guide you. I shall take the lead but you will take over at some point. Talking and questioning is encouraged. Intuition only ever gets me so far with clients.

I don't mind what you wear. I'll relax the suit, but still be smart, as always.

Anthony x

40. Rite of passage

*T*HE WORLD: *attainment. I am born to dance on top of the world. The World represents all elements coming together in order for us to receive the fulfilment and success for which we've been striving.*

In spite of my Tarot card this morning, I don't feel like dancing. I've been like a cut cat all day, unable to sit still. I feel squeamish. My tummy is still threatening to cause havoc, but at least I smell good. The perfume Anthony suggested, *Be Delicious*, is lovely. I bought it yesterday. The mobile pings – the text I know will come before each rendezvous.

Hi Eve,

Anthony is on his way in. Enjoy your evening.

Warmest regards,

LL (Lovely Ladies)

෧෨

My heart misses a beat. I take a few deep breaths, tummy still roiling. Kiki and I go out to greet him. Anthony leans down and kisses me on the cheek.

"How are you?"

"A bit nervous." Understatement of the day. He walks to the kitchen and places his bag of tricks on a stool, seating himself on the one next to it. There is a surety about him. He seems so comfortable in his own skin.

"Why are you nervous?" He looks down. "Hello, Kiki." I see Kiki has wrapped herself around his leg and is humping him, again.

"Kiki, stop that." I smile apologetically. "She's drawn to you, too. You have that effect on the women in this household. I'll lock her in the laundry tonight so she doesn't try to bash the door down, again."

He laughs and pats her. "Yes, she gets a bit excited, doesn't she?" Kiki stops humping and starts licking his shoes instead. I move to pull her away, but Anthony puts his hand up, "Leave her, she's okay."

"She's a bit obsessive, like her mom," I explain. "Would you like a Pinot Noir?"

"Yes, please. Have you had one?"

"No, I've been drinking soda water with ice for a change." I pour us both a glass.

"Why are you nervous?" Anthony asks again.

"You're taking me into new territory. It's a bit scary. In my work in education, I was always encouraging people to change, but learning involves risk. Now the shoe is on the other foot, it doesn't seem so easy. The alternative is for me to stay in a box and pull down the shutters, but I can't do that either."

His piercing blue eyes meet mine. "I want to take you where you haven't been before, Eve," The light touch of his hand on my forearm is reassuring. "To lose yourself, not to lose control, but to disappear into another space. To let go. It will be okay. I'll be with you. And it's okay to be nervous. Nothing wrong with a few nerves every now and then."

જ

Anthony lays out his kit on the window seat in the bedroom. "If you take away the sense of sight, other senses come to the fore. I want to blindfold you with this. Is that okay?" He shows me two silver satin ties – one for him and one for me. I nod. He hangs them over the bedhead. After lighting the candle, he places it on the bedside table, its smell echoing the citrusy spring notes of my perfume. He switches on the music he's brought, then turns to me. An amazing voice fills the room. "Regina Spektor," he tells me. As he puts his arms around me, she sings to me.

It started off as a feeling,
Which then grew into a hope.

I nuzzle into his chest. A softness envelops me and I start to relax. To let go. Anthony leans down and kisses me.

"I love being kissed. It happens so rarely."

He kisses me again, then smiles. "How are you with buttons?"

I unbutton his shirt, kissing his chest softly as I work my way down. Anthony takes it off, drops it on the floor, and then undresses me slowly, before gently laying me on my back, sideways across the bed. I watch as he finishes undressing, in awe of his lithe body. He picks up a satin tie.

"We're going to take turns. Do you want to go first or me?"

"Me, please," I giggle. He ties the blindfold. Regina's voice and orchestra fill the room with a charm and grace that moves me and stirs my soul.

Anthony's magical fingers trace new neural pathways up and down my limbs, around my head and face, my eyes and my hair before dancing their way around my breasts and the insides of my thighs. I tingle all over. The sounds, the smell of the candle, the touch. My mind wanders to nowhere but here. Anthony's fingers trace delicately then press firmly into my flesh, all over my body. He gently rolls me over and repeats the same on my back. His strong fingers work deeply into my muscles and shoulder blades.

"Not much stress here. That's good." I only manage a small grunt in reply. His hands move inexorably downwards until his fingers reach round and find their way to the entrance of my sex, moist and warm and longing to be touched. Soft moans keep time as they move in and out of me and around my clitoris. I feel Anthony reach sideways. Soon, much to my surprise, there is a pleasure toy pulsing intermittently in place of his fingers. A pregnant pause when he moves off the bed, then the rustling noise I love. It lets me know he is putting on a condom and will soon be inside me.

I come quickly, but the delicious aftershocks that rock me go on and on.

"I can't stop."

"That's good," he whispers in my ear, while removing the blindfold and brushing strands of hair away from my face. His lips lightly caress my neck and the side of my face. I am in his embrace, beneath him, skin on skin, inhaling his cologne. His warm body covering my back, his fingers slowly stroking my ear, my neck, my hair, my arm. I smell delicious. I feel delicious. As the aftershocks continue on and on, I lie there, my mind reeling as the revelations wash over me. Whilst discovering my erotic fingerprint, I'm relearning the language of loving and rewriting the script for my life imbuing it with softer, subtler and more nuanced meanings. In the aftermath of our lovemaking, in the comfort and safety of his warm embrace, a sense of knowing emerges that is just as profound.

"I feel important."

"You are," he says, still lying on top of me. I turn my head to talk to him.

"I love the way you make me feel, the way you listen. You hear what I say. I am not in love with you, yet I love what you do to me. I can see there is beauty in both. Being loved for totally different reasons. Pleasure from sex just for its own sake. A new form of communication for me." I turn to him and snuggle into him.

"You don't possess me. You ask me what I want. My body belongs to me."

"That's the way it should be," he says, looking at me with understanding.

My body holds memories and the debris has accumulated over time. When territorial rights were claimed, I gave in, surrendered. My body did not belong to me. Sex was often about power, something that was done to me, using my body. I had no voice, no choice. But now I know it was my passivity, acquiescence and silence that disenfranchised me. I give Anthony a kiss on the cheek and a big squeeze. "Thank you. Thank you, so much."

"What for?" he asks smiling.

"You have a sense of knowing about me, that leads me on to higher places. There is beauty not only in what you do, but in the way you do it." Anthony returns the squeeze, pleased with me, with himself. "I'm starting to slough off the shackles of the past. I am learning that my body is a temple, that sex can be sacred," I say running my fingers over his belly. "And, I'm learning to trust. To trust me and those I entrust with me. That is so rare and so precious." I snuggle into him. A deep sense of peace comes over me as my body quietens.

Dear AA, the Adorable Anthony as you have now become, I am transforming. The next two lessons will be formative but I have entrusted this task to you. You have proved worthy of my trust and have earned pride of place in the Pantheon of my heart. This is a rite of passage.

The Aphrodite I am becoming is significantly different from what I originally imagined. As is our time together. Perhaps she will surprise me. Perhaps you will too.

Our final rendezvous will be *A Night to Remember in Aphrodite's Temple*.

Warmest regards, Eve xxx

41. Rewriting the script

Soft sunlight is streaming through the window. I'm lying in bed, Kiki nearby. Life has a surreal feel but I've surrendered and I am going with the flow. Letting the thoughts and feelings wash over me, through me, knowing that there is a spiritual and guided dimension to what is happening.

The delicious aftershocks from last Tuesday night linger on as do the memories. Tuesdays will never be the same again. I started off feeling unwell, apprehensive, and just plain scared. Seeing Anthony, being with him, evaporated all those fears. An unintended side effect is that this has become a profoundly healing process. A way of removing the toxic waste and shame choking my system, allowing me to emerge from the shadows.

It's more than sex. Much more than sex. I'm being liberated, freed from the constraints of the past. He's moving me from what was to what can be and I am willing to let him be my guide because I trust him. What goes between us could only happen because I trust him. Not only what he does to me, but the loving way he does it. He's showing me a new kind of pleasure, new ways of pleasuring, softer, subtler and more nuanced ways. My body arcs up again, at the thought. It is wonderful. I must share this with Cindy and Rachel. They'll think it's wonderful too. Perhaps I'll invite them here after I've seen Anthony again, next week. I check my horoscope. Yes. I will!

Today is all about expressing yourself. Don't hang back, waiting to be noticed. Leap out to center stage. Amaze everyone with your pep and dynamic energy. Now is your chance to blaze new trails across the landscape of your life. Others will have no problem following your footprints, even if you've got a head start. You've got good ideas now, and people know your creative perspective is worth listening to.

᪣

Eve,

For tomorrow night I want you to choose a fragrance that you feel most comfortable and beautiful in, from your current collection. I want you to wear what you feel most beautiful in, jewellery included, should you choose. A dress, perhaps. I'll leave that with you. I'd like us to sit outside for a short while to start, so that we can spend some time in the garden that is so pivotal to you.

When we move inside, I may wish to shower to freshen up. You have the choice of joining me or waiting until after. In the shower or after, we may begin to explore the two areas of interest you suggested last time. Through verbal and nonverbal communication, I intend to make it uniquely pleasurable and exciting for you, whilst exploring sexual desires that may carry some baggage for you.

Until tomorrow, Eve.

Anthony

వ

Anthony's car pulls up in the driveway. Who is this young man I've entrusted myself to, have opened up my whole being to? My life is starting to read as a fantasy and yet it isn't. It is real. I am grounded in the here and now. The involuntary whimpers and the soft spasms that have confounded me ever since I read his email yesterday are testament to this. I breathe deeply and surrender to the beauty of the feelings that rise up from the depths within me.

I look, feel and smell lovely. The elegant black Helmut Lang dress that hugs my body is set alight by strappy black heeled sandals and Argyle diamond pendant earrings and stud neck-lace. Underneath is sexy black and cream underwear. My hair is up. Bouncy curls frame a newly made-up face. I've spent some time working out how to look beautiful this evening. This is something I rarely do. I accept that I am beautiful on the inside, but the outside never seems to measure up. So, unlike Cindy, I don't bother much. Again, it is typical of Anthony and his sense of knowing that he chooses differing ways to push me out of my comfort zone and expand my horizons. I open the door to greet him.

"You look lovely." He reaches down and kisses me on the cheek.

"Thank you. So do you."

He is immaculately groomed as always, clean shaven, hair swept back with not one hair out of place. He is in more casual attire again tonight, as promised wearing a fitted, crisp white shirt with 1920s Italian collar. The intricate detail on his patterned, tight-fitting trousers in muted colors is very European as is the stitch work on his dark cream Italian leather shoes. Fortunately, Kiki is in the laundry so she can't cover them in saliva. I pour each of us a glass of Pinot Noir — Sonoma again and lead us out into the garden.

Spring has worked its magic in the garden and around the new pond. The air is filled with soft fragrances. There is color for as far as the eye can see. The bamboo is a lush, bright green with many new shoots. Rainbow-colored Japanese koi dart amongst the islands of leaves of the dark green water lily pads. It is too early yet for the water lilies to bloom. But blossoms abound. Pale pink cherry blossom, white apple blossom, red and white Dogwoods, lilacs and irises, plus an array of wildflowers and perennials. Drifts of bulbs wend their way through the garden, spilling over rocky outcrops – daffodils, snow drops, bluebells, tulips and crocus. A profusion of flowers growing as freely and naturally as in Monet's Garden.

I lead Anthony over the bridge and stop in the centre, listening to the sound of water trickling across the rocks and falling into the level below.

Anthony looks around. "This is magnificent, Eve. Well done. It's a testament to you, to your hard work and passion. I have a lot of respect for people who listen to their hearts and do what brings them pleasure, even if it does entail hard work. Maybe especially when it means hard work."

"Thank you, Anthony. You're a true gentleman. Look at these wisterias. I love them." I finger the long pendant mauve racemes cascading from the vines. "Wisterias are fast growers, but these have surprised even me." I stand there admiring the way the wisteria vines have threaded their way from either side of the bridge to almost touch each other. Anthony raises his glass. I raise mine to meet his.

"To your garden of delights," he says, wrapping an arm around my back.

"To the garden of my delights." I tap his glass and take a sip. Twilight is nearing.

"Let's sit down and drink in the garden and the wine." I take his hand and lead him across the bridge to the granite seat, in an arbor surrounded by silver birch trees and New Jersey tea shrubs brimming with white flowers. We sit down.

Anthony raises his glass and says, "Cheers." We tap glasses and take a sip, then Anthony entwines our arms. "Cheers again."

I smile. In the embrace of the garden, and in the company of this delightful young man, peace and harmony descend. Talking with him about anything and everything, whether about others or the intimacy of us and what we are about to embark on is easy; as natural as breathing.

He leans towards me, "Are you comfortable about tonight?"

"Yes, I trust you. I've found being with you very healing."

"I'm not a trained therapist."

"I know that. I've had extensive counselling. They can't do what you do. Theirs is a strictly hands-off approach. They own the process; they are the ones in control." There is no need for artifice. I am rewriting the script for my life and, in so doing, exorcising the baggage. "You make it easy. With you, I feel in control which makes it easy for me to be me."

Anthony appears almost shy, at the compliment. He smiles at me and ducks his head a little. "Why, thank you. I'm no gigolo, Eve. Well, I am, but I'm not. Just me, with nicer clothes and neater hair." I laugh. "Shall we go inside now for lesson number four?" Anthony asks.

42. Places beyond imagining

Anthony comes to me and wraps his arms around me. I snuggle into his chest and sigh deeply.

"A peace comes over me when I am with you." He kisses me tenderly.

"That's good."

"I'm wearing *Sensuous Noir*."

"I like it. It's very subtle."

I snuggle into him again. "You smell good too. What are you wearing?"

"*Issey Miyake*. I love it."

Anthony starts to unbutton his shirt, but I take over, exposing his beautiful chest. Not an ounce of fat, and just the right amount of hair. He drops his shirt on the floor, unzips my dress and drops it too before positioning me crossways, face up on the bed. My body quivers with anticipation yet I am mentally relaxed.

I trust this man with me and love the slow and easy sensual caressing that begins each *lesson in loving*. I love that I can look into his eyes and feel validated. He surprises me today, as he rubs his penis, still encased in his underpants, sensually up and down and around my belly before removing our underwear. I hold my breath, wondering what will happen next.

A gasp of surprise escapes as his lubricated fingers find my clitoris and their way inside me. My body responds knowingly, eager for his touch. Soon I'm writhing, arching up from the bed, moaning. Then his mouth and tongue enter the fray. His touch is exquisite. I am blown away, my inhibitions gone as I climax. As the spasms go on and on, I capture his magic fingers by drawing my knees up. My inner goddess temporarily overwhelmed, unable to cope with the pleasure being heaped on it.

Anthony strokes me gently until I quieten then positions himself so that his erect penis is close to my face. Another surprise. He is offering himself to me. I take him in my mouth. There is no force, no implied threat. His hands are on my head, pulling strands of my hair gently as my head moves up and down. I'm unsure if what I'm doing is giving him pleasure. I find my voice.

"Is this okay?"

"Yes. It feels good, too if you use your tongue around the tip." He shows me where. I lick the top of his penis like a lollipop. He tastes warm and wonderful.

He stills me, then turns me over, face down. "I'm going to come inside you first." A whimper escapes as he enters my vagina from behind. We move together in unison as we have been here before. Suddenly his magical fingers find their way into my behind and start moving in tandem. I am full of him. He fills my very being. His breathing becomes heavier. I groan with delight and explode. He feels this, stops moving and lies me down, still on top of me, behind me. Lying there beneath him, sated beyond measure, I start laughing.

"I'm not supposed to laugh."

"That's totally fine. You go right ahead. Why not?" He kisses me on the cheek and I realize I have journeyed to a place beyond imagining but in this place, fear no longer holds sway. The bogey man has gone. I laugh again. What a delight this man is. He has just shown me anal sex can be pleasurable too. I turn to face him.

"I want you inside me."

When he enters me again, I arch up to meet him and wrap my legs tightly around his back. It feels like coming home. I greedily gather him up, wanting all of him in me and he gives himself to me. I ride the wave with him until I come again, loudly this time. I leave my legs wrapped around him, not wanting to let him go as the aftershocks rack my body. All too soon that luscious languidness overcomes me.

Tonight, I am replete. I visited places beyond imagining and it was as natural as breathing. As we lay back on the pillows, my body draped over him, snuggling into him as he wraps one arm around me and strokes me. I'm in the process of flowering and, although a late bloomer, I am loving it and I will be beautiful.

I pat him fondly on the chest. "Thank you."

"My pleasure."

"You do realize you have spoilt the possibility of me finding anything approximating an ordinary, normal kind of relationship," I say, patting him again.

"Why on earth would you want to settle for anything

ordinary?" he says turning to me, the expression on his face deadly serious. We laugh in unison.

We drink some more wine. I cuddle into him as we talk. My cup runneth over.

43. Cindy and Rachel

I open the door. "Thanks for coming. It's so good to catch up. It seems ages since I've seen you both," I say to Cindy and Rachel as they walk in. Kiki sits there smiling her doggy smile, her tail wagging, much happier to greet guests than being locked in the laundry.

"It is, Darling. Mwah! Mwah!" Cindy's lips brush my cheeks. "I've been very busy," she says, sashaying into the hallway looking a million dollars in another designer jump suit. Dark blue this time. She looks like she has lost weight.

"Not since we went to Richard's new apartment," says Rachel, brandishing a bottle of bubbly. As she gives me a kiss on cheek, a big smile flashes across her face. "Evening, Eve. Evening, Kiki." She is looking fabulous, as if she has a new lease on life. In a jumpsuit, too. Dark green. I close the door and follow their swaying bottoms into the kitchen thinking, maybe I should buy a jumpsuit, too.

"You open the fizz, Rachel." I place some champagne glasses on the bench in front of her. She pops the cork and pours a little in each glass, allowing it to fizz to the top, then going back to top them up. Rachel hands Cindy and me a glass and picks up her own. Her eyes are sparkling. She raises her glass.

"A toast, Ladies — to pleasure."

Cindy and I echo her toast and tap glasses. "To pleasure." As we all sip our wine, I look at them both. There are big smiles on their faces. They're happy. Just like me. Life must be good for them, too.

"You look both look fabulous," I say. "Time to 'fess up the secrets.'"

"You, too, Eve. What's your secret? Do tell," says Cindy, eyeing me off.

"I will, but first tell me about these jumpsuits. Where do they come from?" Cindy stands up, spins around like a model, and then stands with her hands on her hips, smiling. Her face lights up as she speaks.

"On-line. Halston Heritage, in storm blue crepe, with slit length sleeves and elasticized waist, designed to go with metallic accessories, like this crisscross snake-belly mesh-rhinestone chain-belt," she says swaying her hips, then lifting the leg of her jumpsuit, "and matching sandals." We laugh at her, loving her exuberant display.

"I love your bangle," says Rachel. "Where did you buy it?"

"Oh, now that would be telling, Darling," she says, feigning shyness. "But I know you two can keep a secret." She moves in close, putting a forefinger to her mouth. "From Fernando. We've been working out, regularly. In more ways than one," she says, winking. "I've lost a stone. I feel wonderful. And..." she says waving her hand with her silver bangle, "Don't you think I look wonderful, too?"

"Yes." Rachel and I affirm for her. It's good to see her so happy again.

"What about you, Rachel? You look wonderful, too."

"No secrets with me. I've been refilling my pleasure tank. Buying some fabulous clothes. Like this Lagerfeld number." She hooks her thumb into the tan leather tie belt around her tiny waist. "Richard brought it as a present for me from Germany, as well as these shoes. He has good taste, no? He says Mom helped him choose them, but he's pretty stylish himself."

"Ah, but I can see there's more than clothes in your pleasure tank, Darling. Do tell."

"Mmmmmmm..." Rachel says teasingly, taking another sip of her wine. "Massages and Men, with a capital M. Lots of them. And it's..." her eyes dancing with delight, "Marvellous and Much Overdue."

"And, what else, you wicked woman? What else have you been indulging in?"

"The greatest pleasure of all, Cindy, as you well know," says Rachel throwing her hands in the air, "Sex. Sex with a capital S and lots of it. It's wonderful. He's wonderful. Nothing serious right now. Just great sex." she says, hugging herself. She looks at me. "What about you, Eve? Are you getting any? You look as if you are."

Thankful for the entrée, I dive in, head first. "Yes, I am. And it is beautiful."

Cindy and Rachel scream and punch the air. "Woo hoo!!! Go, Girl!!!"

"More. More, please, Eve," begs Rachel going down on her knees.

"I'm having lessons. *Lessons in loving.* Learning that there is beauty in sex."

"Oh. Oh!" says Cindy, her face starting to cloud over. She shakes her head at me. Rachel looks at her, wondering. Then at me. I shrug my shoulders and go on.

"Learning that you have to find your own erotic fingerprint for your sexual potential to be unleashed. For the goddess within to emerge." Cindy's eyes are boring into me. I take a deep breath and continue. "Being with him is like therapy, but like no therapy I've previously experienced. And so, healing. I'm throwing off the shackles of the past."

"Who is this demigod you are dating, Eve?" asks Rachel, doubtfully.

"I'm not dating. I'm working with a young male escort called Anthony."

Rachel spits some of her bubbly over her lovely Lagerfeld jumpsuit. She holds her glass away from her, incredulous. "An escort? You're paying for sex?" Her voice is starting to rise ominously. "How young?"

Nervously, I say, "Thirty-three. He's wonderful. He..."

Rachel stands up. "That's my age!" Holding her palm up in front of my face, her eyes flash. "Stop. No more. I don't want to know," she says, angrily. "How would you feel if I was dating someone your age?" It wouldn't worry me, I think, but I know now is not the time to say so. "That's spitting on the memory of

Uncle William. How could you do that to him, Eve?" screwing up her face. Disgust is written all over it.

She slams her glass down on the bench sending shards of glass and champagne flying everywhere. Kiki whimpers and ducks away. Rachel is surprised by the broken glass but something holds her from reacting. "I don't want to know. And I don't want to know you, Eve. I don't know who you are, anymore," she yells, picking up her bag and storming out. Her words hit me like a body blow, doubling me up. I clutch at my belly.

"Rachel, wait," I call weakly.

She opens the door and turns to me, livid. "Just wait until I tell Richard. He won't want to know you, either, Eve." She slams the door. The glass rattles ominously. Kiki whimpers, again. I turn around and see Cindy with her bag under her arm, looking gobsmacked.

"I can't believe you did that, Eve," she says, astounded, but still with the wherewithal to scold me like a schoolgirl. "I told you not to say anything to her. You know how volatile Rachel is and how much she loved William. There'll be hell to pay for this. You reap what you sow. I'll go and see if she's alright," she says pushing past me. "I'll let myself out, thank you. Good night!" she says, opening the door. She stalks out, closing it with a bang. The glass rattles again. Kiki howls this time. A sinking feeling in my stomach as my insides hollow out. I sit down on the step, shattered. Kiki sits beside me, looking up at me. I start to shake. What have I done?

44. Loss and longing

The cell rings. I don't want to talk to anyone ever again. I stand up, walk shakily back into the kitchen and check. It's Susan. I can't ignore her.

I sit on a stool as my legs threaten to buckle underneath me. "Hello Susan, how are you?" I ask, struggling to make my voice sound normal.

"Hello, Eve. Good to hear your voice. You've been on my mind. On both our minds, really. We're so looking forward to seeing you this weekend." I feel bad. I've hardly given them a thought. Anthony and my *lessons in loving* have taken precedence over my life, recently. And they are such dear friends. I silently beat myself up for being so self-absorbed, and forgetting I was visiting them in Spokane this weekend.

"I wonder why," I say, teasing her a little.

"Well, it's been nearly a year since we've seen you. When you got us together then decided not to spread William's ashes, again," she laughs softly. "Men don't understand these emotional responses, do they?" The empathy and understanding in her voice gentles me.

They moved to Spokane soon after William died which was

a double blow. David was offered a job at Washington State University. Our catch ups are few and far between now. "And… someone has a very big birthday coming up which is cause for celebration."

A wry laugh erupts. "It certainly is a *big* birthday. Sixty for heaven's sake. I'm not sure it's cause for celebration, Susan." Gloominess overtakes me.

"Of course, it is, Eve. It's the beginning of a whole new era in your life."

I don't think so. Not anymore. It's another milestone like menopause, a glimpse of a slow, lingering decline. The feeling that I am shrinking in the eyes of the world around me. No longer vital or important or noticeable to others. Shrivelling up inside. No longer a woman, no longer attractive and no longer desirable.

Susan continues unabated, "We'll be a few days early, but that won't matter."

I don't feel like celebrating anything but I can't tell her that. "Sure, Susan. It will be lovely to see you. I can't wait."

❧

Freezing rain sounds innocent enough, until it becomes a layer of ice, enveloping every single thing in its path in a heavy, unwelcome embrace. As David drives from the airport his eyes are firmly fixed on the road ahead, squinting through the rain. The sky is dark and ominous. It's only three o'clock, but it looks like midnight. The temperature is plummeting. The road is slushy and hazardous as the snow turns to freezing rain and sleet.

I shiver as I look out, and draw my coat tighter. It feels like a deep dark winter evening, not spring. Nature's cold shoulder has turned on Spokane, as it often does. When I dropped Kiki at the kennels, her tail was tucked between her legs. She looked at me like I was punishing her, that I'd turned the cold shoulder on her. She hates it there, but what else could I do? Cindy's on the west coast catching up with friends and family. And the twins... Susan breaks into my gloomy thoughts.

"Let's hope it's just a late spring shower, that there's not another ice storm on its way," she says worriedly looking over her shoulder at me.

"Not too long, now," David says. Relief in his voice.

"Thank heavens," I say. "What a dreadful day."

"The fridge and pantry are stacked with food. David's wine cellar is still well stocked. There's plenty of wood for the fire," says Susan smiling ruefully. "We'll just stay indoors. Besides, we have plenty to talk about."

ॐ

After a fabulous dinner of hickory smoked baby back ribs in barbecue sauce, fried green tomatoes, baby potatoes and watercress salad, coleslaw and honey corn muffins, we're sitting in comfortable lounge chairs circling the fire, drinking a fine Bordeaux. I'm drinking quickly. Too quickly. Susan is a fabulous cook. David is a wine buff. He tops up my glass again, then sits down.

"It's good to have you here, Eve," says David. "We miss you. We miss William, too." So, do I. It used to be the four of us sitting together. "Remember this wine? We first tasted it when we were travelling around South West France. St Emilion Chateau. They still produce the ripest red wines in Bordeaux today."

I nod. I remember. I take another sip. Good food and good wine and marvellous company. Just the four of us. We all got on so well. We travelled all over the US and Europe together for two decades. A tidal wave of loss and longing washes over me, threatening to engulf me. I take another sip and surface. In the past, again.

"My favorite holiday of all time was when we were on the canal boat travelling from England to Wales. Five days of absolute bliss." I close my eyes and I am back on the boat. Sitting companionably in silence in the bow, beside Susan, soaking up the scenery and serenity as the canal unfolds in front of us. Soft sunlight makes the canal water glisten and lightens the trees and vines overlapping the banks. It is hauntingly beautiful, particularly with the autumn tones. Birds are everywhere. There is a sense of timelessness as we glide slowly through this wilderness.

"I loved that one, too," says Susan excited by the memory, bringing me out of my reverie. "Heavens. That was ten years ago. You and I sat up the front and jumped out at the locks. Twenty-three of them, if I remember right. We could walk faster than the boat. It was wonderful."

"Sixty foot long, five and a half feet wide, with a top speed of four miles an hour and a hundred foot turning circle," joins in David, smiling at me. "With William and me steering at the back. We made a formidable team."

"We sure did." We did, just like William and me.

"How about being able to walk to a pub for a pint and some dinner after we moored each afternoon." David smiles at the recollection.

"Ooh, Eve. Remember the time David and I jumped off to do the lock for a change?"

I frown at the memory. "Do I ever? I was scared to death." I can see the lock looming. William is steering. We negotiate the lock successfully but the boat is swept up without warning by fast flowing water leaving us stuck on a concrete causeway. I look with horror. David and Susan are stranded on the either side of the bank unable to clamber back on board. Fortunately, with David shouting directions, we pole off the concrete and get the boat moving again.

"It was the only time I'd ever seen William rattled," says David. "That was a great holiday." He raises his glass. "Here's to great holidays, Eve."

"Our last holiday together," I say, voice breaking, as a wave of sadness engulfs me once more. I love them dearly, but being with them always reminds me of William and the good times we had. The sense of loss, magnified. There's no way I can talk to them about Anthony or what I'm doing. They wouldn't understand. Rachel and Cindy don't understand. Sometimes I don't even understand it myself. It'd be much simpler and safer to stay numb and live in the past.

སྡ

"I'm here to pick up Kiki," I say to the receptionist at Welcome Kennels. "Kiki. Kiki Jardine." It is early Monday morning. The kennels aren't open on Sunday, so she's had an extra night's stay. "How was she?" I ask, worried.

She smiles at me. "Just a moment, I'll check her notes." She reads, "Kiki didn't touch her food the first day, barely ate Saturday. Nothing yesterday." She looks up.

"Anything else?" I ask, feeling sick to the stomach.

"She didn't seem well or happy. It's been a long time since she stayed here."

"I know. She hates being in kennels. I had no one to look after her," I say apologetically. I feel so guilty. I pay the bill.

"I'll go and get her. Wait out there," she says pointing to a courtyard. I pace up and down, waiting. "Here she is," says the receptionist bringing in Kiki. She just stands there looking at me, accusingly. No signs of animation. Her tail nowhere in sight. She has lost weight. Her coat and eyes are dull. I take one look at her and burst into tears. I bend down and pick her up, cradling her in my arms.

"I'm sorry, Little Girl. Let's go home." I want to be home. I need to be home. Anthony emails me late afternoon, early evening. Tomorrow is his final lesson. I'm so looking forward to it. It's been a bad week. I'm out of synch with everyone else in my life, except him, an irony and a bitter pill to swallow.

సా

I drain the last of my wine. I'm feeling a little light-headed. A little squeamish. I've had too much. Much too much. It's been a bad day. Kiki still hasn't eaten. She went straight to her basket in the laundry when we got home and stayed there. If I go near her, she turns her head. It's my turn for the cold shoulder. I anxiously check my watch. I've been checking it on and off all day, to no avail. It's after 11 pm. Nothing from Anthony. That familiar sinking feeling in my stomach again. He doesn't want to have anything to do with me either. Fuck him! Fuck everybody! I rip open my iPad.

Dear Anthony,

You have let me down, forgotten to email me. Fuck you. I trusted you with me and to play along with my weird and wonderful ideas. I believed in you and you let me down.

Fuck you. Fuck you. Fuck you.

Eve

Two seconds later. Ping! I feel sick.

Dear Eve,

Apologies for being so late. I hope your weekend away was enjoyable and you have returned to gardening with vigor. Over the weekend I've thought what Tuesday shall bring out, rather, what I shall bring to Tuesday. It will be hot it seems so a shower straight away would be appreciated, so that I can cool down. Please return to the D&G apple fragrance that I suggested a few weeks ago. Wear cool clothing. Tomorrow we'll explore a few more sensory focuses and, if you choose, advance our oral sex and anal sex play.

Sleep well. I shall see you tomorrow evening.

Regards,

Anthony

45. Falling apart

I wake and try to open my eyes. My eyelids are stuck down, caked with dried tears. I've been crying most of the night. Great whooping cries as if my heart was breaking. It is. Pain is uppermost. Kiki is lying on the bed, her head over my shoulder. She's been there all night, waking every now and then to lick the tears from my cheeks. Since she heard me crying, upstairs alone, she hasn't left my side. My whole world is falling apart.

The weekend reunion with David and Susan brought back everything I'd loved and lost. I feel so utterly bereft and alone, desperately clinging to anything that will bring meaning to my world. And now I've pushed away the one person who was showing me I was capable of feeling; of being a woman again. To punish myself. To sabotage my ridiculous quest. Me transforming into a goddess. How pathetic! And yet I know it isn't. In spite of all the humiliation and heartache, deep down I know what I'm doing is right for me. Being with Anthony has been one of the most liberating experiences of my life. And now I've messed that up, too.

Another thought crosses my mind. I sit bolt upright. Kiki jumps up startled. "It's my birthday, Kiki." The tears start falling again. I reach forward and draw her towards me. My arms around her neck, I nuzzle my head against hers. "I love you, Little Girl. I'm sorry for leaving you." She licks my face with gusto, her tongue raspy on my cheek licking away my tears.

"Okay, okay Little Girl. Enough licking. I won't have any skin left. I know you love me. Now, off the bed. Let's check the damage to your Mom's face. And then I'll check in with the spirits to see if there's any more shit going to rain down on us before we go for our walk." The word *walk* is the only one to elicit the desired reaction. Kiki wags her tail hopefully and spins around. I hop out of bed and head to the bathroom.

What a sight! My eyelids are swollen. My eyes red rimmed and wet. The sides of my cheeks are sore, raw in places where the tissues wiped. My hair is all matted. I brush the knots out of it and tie it up. I splash cold water onto my face, then dry it before putting moisturiser on. I'm dried up inside, too, but it doesn't matter. Anthony won't be coming tonight. I'm certain of that.

I head into the dressing room. It's warm already. It's going to be a hot day. Shorts and a T-shirt and my track shoes. Summer is only a week away and the first full moon in summer, two weeks away. There will be no night to remember in Aphrodite's Temple. No Aphrodite either. As I bend down to tie my laces, the tears gather again. "No, Eve. We're not going to go there." I walk to the study. Yesterday's desk calendar is still up.

It is healing to express my emotions. It is safe for me to be vulnerable.

Ha! I don't think so. I tear it off, screw it up, throw it in the waste paper basket and read today's. I read it again. And again, letting it sink in.

To let go is not to regret the past, but to grow and live for the future.

❧

Cold water is dribbling down my chin and trickling between my breasts. I'm drinking too quickly. Sweat is pouring off me. We walked for over an hour, and at a cracking pace. Every time my mind kicked in, I upped the pace. Kiki's tongue was hanging out by the time we got home. Poor thing. She's much kinder to me than I've been to her. The phone rings.

"Hello. Eve Jardine, here."

"Hello, Eve. It's Ruby from Aphrodisiac Male Escorts. Is this a good time to talk?"

My heart is in my mouth. "Yes, it's fine, Ruby." I take a deep breath. "Apologies for being so rude. It's so unlike me. And to Anthony of all people. I'm mortified by my behaviour. He didn't deserve that."

"Mary Jo and I were saying it's so unlike you, too. Is anything wrong, Eve?"

"Yes." I sigh. "A crisis of confidence caused by an attack of the sads. My family doesn't want to know me because of Anthony. I've spent the weekend with close friends, whom I'm too scared to tell about Anthony. And when Anthony was so late emailing, I thought he'd forgotten me." I pause. "But that's no excuse for behaving so badly," I finish lamely.

"Oh, Eve. He hadn't forgotten you." Mary Jo explains. "He had a booking that was extended. He asked us to apologize on his behalf. The last thing he'd want to do is upset you."

"There's no need for an apology. Anthony has nothing to apologize for."

"Ruby and I just wanted to check you are alright. Now that we know you are, we want to know what you'd like to happen from here on."

"Happen?" I scoff. "I didn't think you or Anthony would want anything more to do with me. No one else does." I chastize myself. Stop it, Eve. That's enough. Enough wallowing in your own misery.

"Perhaps write to Anthony. Let him know what you want. Okay?"

"Okay. Thanks. I'll think about it. And thanks for your forbearance."

I put the phone down and turn to Kiki who is sitting there, ready to counsel me. "What do you think, Little Girl?" She sits staring up at me, her tongue poking in and out, licking the air. She is so fiercely loyal. She loves me. She loves me unconditionally, just like William. The words on my desk calendar spring to mind again.

To let go is not to regret the past, but to grow and live for the future.

"I know what I must do, Kiki." I say out loud. She tilts her head to one side, listening. It doesn't matter what anyone else thinks. I have to be true to myself.

Dear Anthony,

Apologies for my intemperance.

If forgiveness is part of your amazing repertoire, then I would love to see you this evening. It is just for me, to bring me back into the real world, the here and now, to show me I am capable of feeling, of loving, of being loved again.

I just want to lose myself or maybe to find the me who remains. To find a way forward to a future with meaning, with purpose for me. I am sick of being sad and lonely. Would that you could introduce me to an uncle. I am much in need of a good man to hold me, to keep the world at bay.

For the time being, dear Anthony, you will have to do.

Warmest regards,

Eve

46. Coming out

Kiki races to the door, and stands there, tail wagging. She knows who is there without them ringing the bell. I follow, wondering who could be here at ten o'clock in the morning. I open the door to find Richard grinning widely and holding a magnificent multi-spiked pale pink cymbidium orchid in his hands.

"Happy birthday, Eve," he says, walking through with a kiss on the cheek as he points the orchid at me. "Where do you want this?" I nod in the direction of the kitchen, overwhelmed to see him.

"It's beautiful, Richard."

"Six spikes. One for every decade," he says proudly.

"Oh God, I'm going to cry again." I put both hands to my face and follow him, shakily into the kitchen. He places the orchid on the kitchen bench and turns to me.

"Come here. I didn't know you were that sensitive about your age. No wonder you didn't want to have a party." He opens his arms and I walk into them, burying my face in his chest, body heaving. I don't even come up to his armpits. The real reason is I couldn't bear being shunned again. He rubs my back soothingly until I stop heaving. I step back and grab a couple of tissues from the box on the bench.

"It's not that. Oh, I'm sorry Richard. I'm so sorry for upsetting you and Rachel. I didn't mean to offend you," I say sniffing. "I just go about things differently from most people."

"You didn't offend me, Eve." Richard pats me on the shoulder, reassuringly. "I wish I'd had the courage to explore my sexuality much earlier. And..." he says with a shy smile.

I look up at him, this gentle giant of a man. My tears have stopped. I'm feeling calmer now. "Let's sit on the stools, so I can see your eyes, without getting a stiff neck." I sense this is going to be something special. We sit and face each other.

Richard takes a deep breath, pauses, then he finally speaks, "I'm gay." He looks me over, examining my face and bodily reactions to guard against any outburst of anger or sorrow that I might direct his way, unsure of my response.

It doesn't make any difference to me. I love him, irrespective. He is a beautiful man. And my nephew. But in a way, I think I've always known.

"Are you happy?" He nods. "Then that's all I care about. If you're happy. I'm happy. I love you no matter what your sexual orientation is." I can see emotion rising and falling in him. I think this is the validation he needed.

"Does Rachel know?" I ask, worried about her reaction.

He nods emphatically. "I told her first. Do you know what she said?" I shake my head. "'About time! How funny. She is right though. She said she thinks she knew before I did but was never sure because I had a few girlfriends in my late teens. Then she threw her arms around me and hugged me to death. Hugging seems to be a thing with us, a family disease." I see his relief as he talks about his sister. It wasn't only his dad that he was worried about.

"And what about your dad?"

"I think he's always suspected too. Maybe that's why he always tried to man me up with the work, getting me into weights and with the tough love. Look, he didn't say very much. I'm not sure he even said anything. Just told me there was a beer in the fridge and I could do what I want."

"Anyone special in your life yet, Richard?" I ask, tentatively.

"Not at the moment. Well, maybe. You know James, who you met in London? It's not easy when you live on different continents. But we're in touch. He may come and visit after Christmas." I pat his knee fondly. I love this boy.

"There's no hurry, Eve. It's taken me this long to come out. For the time being, it just feels good not to have to hide who I am." I know the feeling. A wry smile crosses my lips. "What's that for?"

"Oh, nothing. Not you, anyway. Just a sixty-year-old woman choosing not to hide who she is and getting into trouble for it."

"Give Rachel time. I've told her she should be happy for you, too. She'll come around. She loves you. She just has a funny way of showing it sometimes, especially where Uncle William is concerned. The age gap was hard for her to handle as well, but I met a wonderful man who was fifty-six and, well..." Richard stops himself from divulging anymore. I don't think he's quite ready to share any more details about his new found sexual liberation. Although I get the feeling he's been exploring his sexuality for some time now.

The phone rings. I pick it up and look. "It's Cindy," I say to Richard.

"I've got to go, Eve." He comes over and kisses me. "Happy Birthday, Eve. Have a good day. I'll let myself out." I pat him on the arm and mouth a thanks.

"Hello, Cindy. How's life on the West Coast?" I ask with a gaiety I don't feel.

"Deeelightful, Darling! Now that I've finished all the foundation business, I'm having a ball. And what about you? It's your 60th birthday. How wonderful. What are you up to today?"

"Richard has just left. He gave me a magnificent pink orchid," I say avoiding the question.

"How is he, Darling boy?"

"Richard came to tell me he was gay."

"Aha. I suspected as much when I last saw him with James. Good luck to him. Each to his own is what I say. Is that gorgeous man James still over here?"

"No, he's gone back home. Richard says they're just good friends now."

"Pity. I rather liked him, but when he avoided my clutches, I was suspicious." I laugh in spite of myself. She is so confident of her drawing power to men. "Have you heard from Rachel?"

"No, I haven't Cindy. Richard says she'll come around. I'm not so sure."

"Well, you know now not to mention *you know who* ever again. Think of it as an aberration, Darling." Yes, it's much easier for them to cope with the idea of Anthony as an aberration of mine. More's the pity, I think.

"I doubt I'll be seeing him again." Why would he want to?

"That's probably for the best. Not everyone is as understanding as I am. Must go now, Birthday Girl. Mwah. Mwah. Have a wonderful day."

Not likely, I think.

47. Stripped bare

"I didn't believe I would see you again, Anthony." He's here and we are talking. We're close, but not too close, on the comfy chairs in the conservatory. My knees are tucked up on the chair with my arms holding them. My chin leaning on my knees, looking into those piercing blue eyes trying to see through me. The tears are not far away.

"Tell me what's been happening," he says gently.

I take a sip of my Pinot. "The intimacy of us, what's happening, what I want to happen, is becoming harder and harder to come to terms with. It's like being stripped bare, not only in front of you, but with the people I care most about in the world watching on, waiting with bated breath, and I get scared."

I take another sip. "Scared they won't approve. Scared they won't love me anymore. Scared I'm doing the wrong thing. Scared I'll never find anyone to love me again." I dab at the tears forming. "All the ugly demons of the past are raging at me, threatening to undermine me, overwhelm me. I feel like a pariah," I say hugging my knees even tighter. Anthony touches me reassuringly on the arm, encouraging me to go on.

"In my day, women were either Madonnas or whores. And

this mentality still prevails, particularly for women my age." Anthony nods knowingly, content just to listen. "The idea of me exploring my sexuality and becoming a goddess makes sense when there's just you and me. But to the outside world it doesn't. Rachel is angry with me. Cindy thinks I'm in cloud cuckoo land and I didn't dare tell David and Susan. I spent the weekend feeling isolated and alone, pining for William. When I'm with them I feel like part of me is missing."

I take another sip of my wine. "The funny thing is I know William would approve. The only person with the remotest understanding is Richard. Bless his soul. He came to visit today, to give me an orchid, and to tell me he's gay. It's taken him all this time to come out. He's been scared, too." I smile, remembering. I let go of my knees and put my feet on the floor.

Anthony leans forward. "What do you want to happen tonight, Eve?"

"More than anything else, I need to be held." Anthony puts his glass down, stands up and holds out a hand. I take hold of it and stand up. He puts his arms around me and holds me close, gently. Ever so gently. As my head nestles into his chest, relief floods through me. I sigh, softly. He leads me upstairs to the bedroom.

৵

Anthony undresses me with exquisite tenderness and care. I sit on the bed watching as he undresses. He lies on his side with his arm outstretched, the warmth of his smile inviting me to lie down beside him. I snuggle into his body, my head tucked under his neck. He wraps his powerful arms around me and holds me tight. As I lie there, basking in his proximity and warmth, the sadness disappears. All the bad things go away. Being held, helps to put my world to rights. The certainty that what I am doing is not only right, but right for me, returns.

I move my head out and reach up to kiss him. "Make love to me, please."

As he enters me, I look out the bedroom window, to the sky and the moon beyond. "Could we move to the window seat? But please don't let go of me." Somehow, Anthony's powerful arms and legs manage to move us from the bed to the window seat still locked together. There, under the new moon above, I let go. I feel Anthony's energy pulsating inside me as he lets go, too. Our lovemaking becomes more urgent, more elemental.

Afterwards, still holding me close, he says, "You're quivering. Your whole body is quivering."

"I know. It's lovely. Being with you touches deep chords, sometimes chords I don't even know are there." Anthony squeezes me.

"And I could feel you this time. I was aware of you."

"Good," he says, kissing me tenderly.

"In many ways you treat me like an exotic orchid. One day soon, I will flower because of your work with me."

"Thank you. You know, this is what it is all about. Intimacy, connection. I love this part of it. Humans are connection junkies. We just choose the wrong connections sometimes," he says, kissing me again.

"What a lovely birthday present you are." I cuddle into him.

"Is it your birthday today?" he asks. I nod. "Really?"

"Yup. And we've christened the window seat, too."

"Really? Oh, I like that. I always like christening places. My favorite was a broom cupboard, just because."

"And next time we meet we are going to leave memory trails all through the house and garden. I want you to make love to me in the garden, please. In the moonlight."

"Easy," he says and kisses me tenderly on the neck. How can something so intimate, so beautiful, and gives so much pleasure, be wrong?

౭৯

Dear Anthony,

Last night was precious. Thank you for being there for me.

Without you the goddess quest would have been abandoned and the garden become a seared wasteland again. You inspire me.

The learning from my fifth and final lesson in loving — Clarity. I was blind, but now I see.

X Eve

౭৯

PS My horoscope for this week. Just as profound.

Lead us not into temptation, and deliver us from evil, is a request that Christians make of God when they say the Lord's Prayer. If we define temptation as an attraction to things that feel good even though they're bad for you, this part of the prayer is perfectly reasonable. But what if temptation is given a different interpretation? What if it means an attraction to something that feels pleasurable and will ultimately be healthy for you even though it initially causes disruptions? I suggest you consider experimenting with this alternative definition, Gemini. For now, whatever leads you into temptation could possibly deliver you from evil.

48. Summer

Summer is here. The sun is higher in the sky, more intense, the sky a brilliant blue. The garden is alive with color, sound and smell. There is a richness to the greeny hues. Ripe berries, fruit and flowers abound, as do birds and bees feasting on summer's bounty. The water lilies are finally open, their yellow, pink, white and blue petals pay homage to the welcoming sun. Rebirth and regeneration.

My journey with Anthony is coming to an end. When we meet again it will be our seventh occasion. Our journey began a few months ago, yet the impact of him will remain with me forever. The past year, since William asked me to let him go, have been ones of transition and momentous changes in my life. These have been echoed in the garden. I was angry with him at first. How dare he ask such a thing? He was all I had. But deep down I knew, more than anything else, William would want me to be happy, not to waste my life waiting to be with him. And that means moving on, starting over. Awakening to life and living again.

And so, I started over in concert with the garden. I imagined what my garden could be, and then lovingly tended it to bring it into a reality. I also imagined what I could be, but I did not know how to bring myself into being. Anthony did. He's an artist too, who not only envisaged what I could be, but lovingly tended and helped shape me. I'm starting to bear the fruits of his labor and I like the way I am shaping up. Being with him, has been one of the most creative times in my life.

Dear Anthony,

I have been working on making our last rendezvous a night to remember for both of us. If magic happens, Aphrodite will be here, too. If all augurs well, the weather warm and sunny, but not windy. Comfortable enough to move in and out and around the house and garden. The full moon will be ever present.

I am planning a shared feast for the senses — giving and receiving. The night will just unfold, with pleasure to the fore. I am hoping you will be able to relax and let go, but your *Lessons in loving* are not yet complete.

There is still more of you and more in your bag of tricks that needs to be revealed, as indeed, there is more of me wanting to be revealed. Anthony, could I please ask you to take me for a walk on the wild side, to finally unleash the Wild Woman within?

I will be wearing red and *Passion*, and I want to be in your arms watching the sunrise, as a new, and even more magical era, in my life dawns.

Warmest regards,

Eve x

PS. From Pablo Picasso: *Everything you can imagine is real.*

Eve,

Tomorrow night sounds intriguing. I normally plan these things myself so it is unusual to have them planned for me. You call me an artist. I prefer muse. The energy is always with the woman. I am there to reveal, unleash what is within. I cannot create. As King Lear said,

Nothing will come from nothing.

Please wear what you feel is appropriate. I will bring myself, my bag of tricks and my desire to make this a truly memorable evening for you. I always hope that the memory and changes in a woman live on and help them in their future endeavour; often relationships, but sometimes other things — like with you, the garden.

Dawn will be beautiful. To be at my best in the morning, it would be better to set an early alarm to give us both a few hours of sleep. I hope that is okay with you.

Until tomorrow.

Anthony x

49. Aphrodite's temple

I'm waiting near the glass front door as Anthony's car pulls into the driveway. No Kiki to alert me. She's with Richard. A sigh of relief escapes involuntarily as he steps out of the car. I open the door to greet him for our last night together, the culmination of our journey, the final *lesson in loving* and, ultimately, the realisation of my quest to emerge as a goddess. Our Tarot card is *The Lovers*. The spirits are with us.

"Hello," I say, smiling. He smiles in return, walks over to me, and opens his arms for a change. I open mine and we hug, then share a kiss.

"You look great," he says, admiring my stunning red jersey jumpsuit.

"Thank you. So do you." Tonight, he is more casually dressed, but still smart in jeans, jacket and white T-shirt with logo partially obscured. "Does that say Bitch?"

"No!" With a cheeky grin on his face, he opens his jacket to reveal *FITCH* in bold letters across his chest. He could surely have been a model in earlier years. He's too sophisticated for that now. "A girlfriend gone by queued for over an hour to buy this for me. I thought I'd go for a relaxed but not slouchy look tonight. Hence the hair is less than perfect, but secretly I've placed every hair exactly where I want it."

I laugh. He may actually be telling the truth about his hair. He collects his bags from the boot of his little sports car. Three today — his bag of tricks, an overnight bag and a third bag from the Lovely Ladies which he hands to me. I thank him warmly and open it at the kitchen bench. A stunning ceramic tile depicting a voluptuous naked woman looking at the moon. A goddess if ever there was one.

I laugh again and kiss him on the cheek. "Thank you. Thank you so much. A perfect gift for the occasion. How has your week been?"

"Busy. Wrapping things up for the summer break."

I hold out my hand. "Come, I'll show you around. I want you to see the settings for this evening."

I walk him in and out of every room. Every room is adorned with candles, flowers and rose petals. At each door entrance, Anthony pauses and wows. He seems genuinely impressed. Red and white orchids, roses and rose petals scattered. Ethereal heart-shaped red anthuriums with their protruding phallic like spikes, have been used to create a spectacular heart shaped dinner table setting in the conservatory. This impresses him the most until we head out into the garden.

I show him an even more spectacular five foot tall, heart-shaped arrangement woven with sword grass, anthuriums and Monstera deliciosa — the leaves of the fruit salad plant. It is hung between two silver birch trees; a backdrop to the granite seat – the love seat, tonight an altar.

He smiles. "You've really put a lot of thought into this. I'm incredibly impressed. Well done, you. I mean, wow!"

"It was fun. I have a fantastic florist. We talked through what I wanted and she went away and did it."

"You got her over here? Gosh. You have thought of everything." We walk behind the seat, near the rear of the property.

"This is your tree. An oak tree. I planted it for you. It is a symbol of courage and power. Of standing strong and tall through all things."

"I don't know what to say. Thank you, Eve. This is amazing. I feel honored."

"One more thing," I say leading him into the orchid house, a little giddy with excitement. There are a few orchids still flowering, but it is late in the season. As we enter, "I want you to meet Persephone again, but in a new incarnation," I say, pointing to three lush pots of green leaves lined up on the bench. I pick one up. "This one is for you. It's up to you to make Persephone flower again." I kiss him and hand him the pot.

"Thank you, Eve. I'll take very good care of her."

"I may have the garden open next spring. Perhaps you'll come back to see it."

"Yes, for sure. Of course." Our eyes meet. I squeeze his hand and he smiles.

I lead us back into the kitchen. Anthony seats himself at the kitchen bench. I look at him with wonder. My fellow journeyman along a road less travelled.

"Tonight, it's my turn to treat you." A thank you to the one who not only understood the quest, but believed in it and was willing to work with me, to show me the way to realize my dream. Tonight, fantasy will become reality. "But first, what would you like to drink?" I ask.

"Water, please, Eve. It's a warm day. I'll start with a sparkling water before moving onto anything more potent. We've a long evening ahead of us. I've a few ideas for this evening, but I can see you have planned thoroughly, so I'll leave much of it to you."

I pour us both a glass, then pull a bottle of Mumm Rosé champagne from the fridge and hand it to him.

"Lovely," he says, between large sips of water.

"Would you open it, please?"

He pops the cork subtly. No big flourish, no need for a big sound or an ego boost from this gentleman and also a gentle man. He pours two glasses. I sit on the stool next to him and we toast.

"Cheers."

He places his glass on the counter and stands up, arms out towards me. I put down my glass and walk into them, relaxing into him as he holds me close then kisses me. Whereupon I enter a magical kingdom, the *Land of Feel Good*, where everything is alright, everything makes sense and anything is possible. I linger there for a while, swaying in time with the soul music that embraces me in this beautiful man's presence, before releasing him.

We chat companionably while eating pork rice paper rolls

and sipping champagne. When the rolls are finished, Anthony places his hand on my leg. His blue eyes look directly into mine.

"What do you want to happen tonight?"

Momentarily overcome by shyness, I hesitate before saying, "I want you to leave your best work behind here. I've planned a series of treats, things I want to happen, but I want the evening to flow naturally, to leave room for other things that may happen, that you may want to do." I pause. "I want to leave memory trails all around the house and garden that will linger long after you have gone." I look into his eyes. "I wanted to have our appetizers in the bedroom but thought it might have been too messy."

Anthony stands up, kisses me lightly on the lips, and then leads me to the bedroom. He starts to undress. I sit on the bed watching, waiting, wondering what is going to happen. One by one he removes his clothes and shoes and, unusually, places them in a neat pile by the dressing table. Naked, he climbs on the bed and lies down beside me, watching, waiting for me. Tonight, his gift, is his confidence that I can take the lead. I undress and lie down beside him. I snuggle into him and kiss him, falling comfortably into the sanctuary of his arms.

I take heart from the statue of Aphrodite and her reflection in the dressing table mirror and smile at the tiny red orchid flowers I used to adorn her hair. Beside her is a tall, dark red vase. Lush spikes of red orchids hang pendulously over the edge, the centrepiece, a heart made of sword grass with spikes shooting into the air from the centre of the heart. Red rose petals, the Passion rose, are strewn across the dressing table and bedside tables.

I inhale deeply and my perfume, *Passion* wafts up. *Evie, you can do this!* Anthony lies still, silently offering up his body. I accept the gift and begin to stroke his chest lovingly for a few minutes before moving to his genitals, gently encasing his penis with one hand. It is still flaccid. As the fingers of my other hand dance lightly up and down and in and around the tip, his penis awakens and starts to flex its muscles delighting me. I lick and kiss the tip, my tongue flicking in and out of the hole at the top, paying attention to the sensitive area under the head. Slowly I move downwards, gently kissing and licking the shaft and his scrotum before moving back up to the tip.

His penis stiffens. I take him in my mouth, moving up and down, swallowing him ever deeper, stopping now and then to suck him firmly like a mango, a succulent, sweet, juicy mango. I alternate kissing and licking the shaft and the tip with eating him, all the while treating his *wand of light* as if it were precious. I love hearing the changes in his breathing, the small groans of pleasure and the slight shifts in his body.

It's an intensely intimate connection, and this time my pleasure is in the pleasuring. Loving is about giving and receiving, the woman feeling as comfortable initiating sexual pleasure as the man. At this moment it is my turn to give, to give back, by seducing him, making him feel desired. I continue pleasuring him until he groans loudly. His body tenses momentarily, then he comes. As I watch him lying there, the semen spilling out over his taut tummy, I smile.

"*La petite mort.*" He smiles back, a grateful smile. I stroke his cheek fondly. "If you are back in the land of the living, would you like to have dinner now?"

He grins. "Yes, please. A shower first, though."

"Good. Then you can grill the shrimp while I make a mango and avocado salad. There's a lovely bottle of Napa Valley Riesling there, too. I'll put some music on, your music. I burned a disk. I'd never heard of most of the artists before, but I like them."

The sky has darkened. I move around the house lighting candles and into the conservatory where we'll be dining. As we succumb to the amazing voices of Florence and the Machine, Regina Spektor, James Blake and London Grammar, the beauty of our surroundings and the flickering lights of the candles, the mood becomes more intimate. We savor our entrée, then share a lobster tail, dauphinoise potatoes and green salad.

After dinner, I leave Anthony to relax awhile in the conservatory while I ready the next offering in Aphrodite's Temple.

50. Adonis and Aphrodite

I turn the taps off and test the water temperature. Perfect. The bathroom is filled with the flowery, sweet and erotic scent of Ylang Ylang essential oil. Beauty and sensuality were uppermost in my mind when creating this encounter.

The earthy toned ceramic tiles around the edge of the deep white spa bath are scattered with white rose petals. On the white Caesar stone vanity top sits a tall vase with long, luscious sprays of white Singapore orchids. More white rose petals wind their way across the vanity.

The stunning visual effect is magnified by the flickering lights of the candles and our reflections in the mirror as we stand naked facing each other. A beautiful young man, a mortal, and his lover — Adonis and Aphrodite.

Anthony smiles, and looks at me expectantly, waiting for my lead.

I kiss him on the lips, lightly, tenderly. "Hop in. I will sit behind you." He does and I slip down into the bath allowing my legs to stretch out either side of him. As Anthony leans back and relaxes into me, I enfold my arms around him and rest my head against his back, drinking him in.

I liberally soap his back and arms before massaging them, stopping now and then to kiss his neck. The smoothness of the soap on his smooth tanned skin is tantalizing. Touch, touch, glorious touch. I am hooked on it, can no longer live without it. A small tremor from my nether regions signals my arousal.

"I want to soap your front now." Anthony leans back into me. I kiss his neck and lather the soap on his chest and the front of his arms. My hands glide easily over his body, rubbing and kneading, every now and then dipping lower to tease and tantalize before heading back above water. Soon his penis appears above water like the conning tower of a submarine.

He turns to me. "Do you want to make love?"

"Yes, please." Making love in the bath wasn't part of the original script but it is now. A condom appears from Anthony's clothes on the floor. He positions me at the wide end of the bath, I hold my breath and moan as he enters me. Heaven. I'm in heaven. I lift my legs to rest over the top of the bath opening myself up even further, whimpering with need as he buries himself inside me.

Water splashes everywhere as we let go and surrender to the urgency of our lovemaking. I hold on tight, drawing him closer, unable to get enough of him as he thrusts harder and harder and faster and faster, riding the wave with him. Suddenly, magically, I cry out and we crest it together. I draw him to me and hug him, moaning as each successive tremor rocks my body.

"That was wonderful," I say, holding on to him. When my body stills, Anthony stands up, tracing a finger across my torso as he does so, sending little shockwaves through me again. He tentatively steps out of the bath, avoiding the water that splashed on the tiled floor. He holds out a hand to help me out then wraps a towel around my back. We towel ourselves dry, Anthony wrapping his around his waist. He looks at me grinning with youthful exuberance.

"What now, Goddess?"

"I want to give you a sensual massage."

෮

We adjourn to the guest bedroom. A tall narrow vase holds two long stemmed roses, one red and one white and a heart made out of sword grass. White rose petals are strewn across the dressing table and the bedside tables. The large candle flickers, the changing patterns of light adding to atmosphere. The mirror magnifies the effect when lying on the bed; the doona cover is a riot of white, pink and red roses, testament to spring and our *lessons in loving*.

"I'm going to blindfold you." Anthony hands me the satin tie and turns his head so I can tie it. "I want you face down, first. Do you need the pillows?"

"No," he says. I remove the pillows while he lies down on the towel I have placed there. His body is so long his feet hang over the edge. What a beautiful body it is — tanned, toned and taut, tapered to the waist, then flaring out into the cutest cheeks. As I rub in the massage oil, I pay homage to the value of his investment in a healthy lifestyle. I give his butt a fond slap to finish off.

Standing at the end of the bed, I begin massaging his feet and toes followed by his legs experimenting with different touches – rubbing, pulling, stroking, gathering the skin together and firmly kneading, alternating the use of hands, fingers, fingernails raking downward or fingertips lightly dancing across the skin, the lightest touch of all on his inner thighs. The soft moans letting me know I'm pleasing him.

I hop on the bed and kneel astride him, massaging his arms before kneading deeply into his upper back, shoulder blades and neck stopping every now and then to lean forward and kiss him on the side of his neck. I brush my breasts up and down a few times before turning my attention to his lower back and his cheeky butt, my fingers moving more deftly now, massaging playfully around his cheeks and crack, flickering around his inner thighs again, loving the soft moans my attention is eliciting. I pick up a silky blue scarf. Holding each end, I trail it down his back a few times. Finally, I pick up a large feather and trace delicate circular patterns across his arms, back, bottom and inner thighs, the reaction to which signals it is time to turn him over.

"I'm going to sit on the bed with my legs under yours." Anthony lifts his legs while I slide on the bed, my legs outstretched, before positioning them on top of mine and around my hips. I cannot reach the massage oil.

"Could you reach over and pass me the oil, please? It's on the bedside table to your left." Still blindfolded, he stretches his hand out.

"A little higher." His fingers find the bottle and hands it to me.

I dribble some oil to his legs, arms, torso and genital area before placing it back. Starting with the legs first, both at the same time, I massage the full length at a time, straying closer and closer to his penis on the upstrokes, which does a little jump each time I touch it. To draw out the pleasure, I move to his arms and chest, massaging them, alternating touches once again, before the scarf and feather add the finishing touches.

Finally, my fingers and hands give their wholehearted attention to his penis, his *wand of light*, waiting in readiness. Here my Tantra readings come to the fore as I experiment with the differing types of massage to see what he likes – rock around the clock, pop the cork, rubbing like a firestick, ups and downs, twist and shout – until his penis is very erect, standing at attention.

"Can I sit on you, now?" I ask.

"Yes. You'll have to fetch a condom from next door."

"Okay. Wait here."

I place it in his hands. Even with the blindfold on, he deftly tears open the packet.

"Do you want to put it on?" he asks.

"Yes, please." He hands it to me right side up and I slide it on, enjoying the sensation, squeezing the tip to release the air bubble and lubricant.

I rise from my seated position to kneel either side of him and lower myself onto him, gasping as I feel him move to meet me. I am home. I pause for a while, revelling in the feeling. Then I ride him, taking him deeper and deeper inside me each time I come down on him.

I want to treat this special young man, to sweep him up and take him along for a ride, with me leading for a change. Our movements are in harmony. I feel him quicken, hear his breathing change as does mine which almost stops before I cry out and fall over on top of him. I release his blindfold and kiss him and hug him for the bountiful gifts he has brought to my life while the quivering goes on and on. We finally stand up.

Anthony asks with a big grin on his face, "Where to now?"

"To the window seat in the living room, my favorite place in the house."

❧

Anthony, now wearing lounge pants, swings his legs up, leans against the cushion and pats the seat in front of him. Wearing a red slip dress, I slide in between his legs, easing my back into his chest and waiting arms. I lean back into him drinking in this precious intimacy. Inside the flickering lights of the candles highlight large palms, peace lilies, bright red poinsettias and a red Singapore orchid and maple leaf table arrangement.

Outside the trees and plants are black silhouettes illuminated by the full moon. Tonight, the clouds and mist form a halo around it. As we look up above the trees, the clouds move and the moon shines down onto the window seat where we sit. Here, surrounded by nature and the beauty of the moment, we sway gently as Beethoven's *Moonlight Sonata* echoes through the room. A peace comes over me. We savor it in silence for a while longer but there are still more memory trails to leave behind.

I pat his thigh and move off. "Time for dessert." I return with a raspberry cheesecake and freshly whipped cream. It's delicious, but too rich for both of us. I clear two half-finished plates.

51. Aphrodite's altar

"And now it's time to adjourn to the garden. Midnight in the garden of my delights." I am having such fun. So, too is Anthony. He was the perfect choice for this and is the perfect gentleman. I gather up the sheepskin rug and the lighter. We head out through the conservatory and over the bridge to the granite seat that sits in the center of the back garden. The garden has been transformed over the past year and is now, Aphrodite's Altar, where my transformation is to be consummated. I lay the sheepskin rug over the granite seat, while Anthony lights the candles.

In their ethereal light, a new kind of beauty surrounds us. Rocks and plants are intertwined, looking as if they had grown there naturally. Bluestone paths and dry-stone rock walls with their cascading greenery and flowers wind their way around the pond and across the garden to the love seat. Weeping silver birches form an honor guard, silent sentinels to this sacred rite of passage, as is the newly planted oak tree, the memory tree whose memories will linger on.

The heart shaped centrepiece with heart shaped anthuriums suspended from the branches of two birch trees provides a beautiful backdrop. The silence is broken by the splashing sound of water cascading over the rock spillway into the pond below. As the moon breaks through a cloud, we look upwards and silvery moonlight washes over us, highlighting us on the altar. Anthony removes my slip followed by his pants.

Our naked bodies look surreal in the moonlight. He holds out his hand. I take it and we move to the seat where he gently lays me down, positioning my head comfortably. As he moves towards me, the world stills, I am in awe of what is happening. As he enters me, I look up. The moon is obscured.

"Could we sit up please, do Yab Yum?" Still entwined, handling me with care, his strong arms raise my back to a seated position, until we are locked together, me sitting on top of him, legs straddled, arms around each other, looking into each other's eyes with knowing smiles. I writhe with the pleasure of having him so deep inside me. I love feeling his powerful energy course through me and the passion it generates.

Our bodies talk to each other in a language that is heaven sent and we keep on talking, I feel alive, truly alive. As momentum builds, time slows, a hollow roaring sound as if in a pipeline. I look up to the moon and cry out as wave after wave envelops me in exquisite agony. I hold him close as the waves continue to wash over me and the tears flow.

When I am stilled, Anthony releases me, then lays me down gently on the love seat again, cushioning my head. I whimper with delight as I realize he is going to make love to me again. I feel blessed – the beauty of the setting, the wonder of this man and the lengths to which he will go to help me realize my dreams and make this a night to remember.

My heart expands as my vagina opens up like the petals on the water lilies, to welcome him once more. His exquisite touch excites me, igniting a hungry fire in my belly as I seek to devour him. The wildness of our passion claims our bodies, transporting me to a place beyond imagining. Under the light of the full moon and embraced by the garden, we reach a shuddering climax together. Anthony falls forward resting his body on mine, our minds and bodies spent as the aftershocks continue to rack us. He levers himself up to look into my eyes, delicately traces his finger around my forehead to remove the hair from my eyes, then kisses me. The sweetest kiss imaginable.

"Thank you. Thank you for everything," he says.

"My pleasure," I say, kissing him on the lips. "Time for bed." We slip our night attire back on. Anthony extinguishes the candles while I gather up the sheepskin rug. As we walk back, Anthony pauses and looks at me.

"I liken my role in your life to a bridge. From what was to what can be. From sexual shackles to sexual liberation." He puts an arm around my back. He leans over and kisses me. "Welcome, Aphrodite." I hug him tightly. We walk inside.

I move around the house extinguishing all the candles. When I return to the bedroom, Anthony is lying down under the covers. I smile. The ultimate intimacy, to share my bed and wake with this man beside me to usher in the dawn. As I hop into bed, Anthony blows out the remaining candle. I snuggle up close and lovingly run my fingers across his chest, then squeeze him tight. This goddess is replete.

Sleep soon claims us.

52. Wild woman unleashed

I wake and look over at the clock, 5.00 am. Fifteen minutes
before the alarm. Sunrise is 5.25 am. I go to the bathroom
to have a pee. When I return to bed, Anthony is awake.

"Did you sleep well?" I ask.

"Yes. And you?"

"No. I kept waking to touch you, see if you were still there or
if it was all a dream."

"It's good to wake up with someone in the bed beside you, isn't
it?" he asks rhetorically.

"Yes. But it is so rare, I miss it. I long for it." I slip my arm
under his back as he stretches out his arm to welcome me into
him, then folds it around me. My legs wrap around him, too as
we turn to face the window wondering what sunrise will bring.

"The last two days I set the alarm to see the sunrise, but there's
been absolutely no color."

"Look, there." Anthony points to a faint wash of apricot high
in the sky. More apricot appears on the horizon. Then the soft
wash spreads across the sky, faint at first, but deepening. Soon
the whole sky is apricot. I am hoping for a big, bold sunrise full
of color. Instead, it is a sublimely soft, subtle, sensual sunrise,

the color of a lush ripe fruit. Eos, the Goddess of Dawn has presented us with the perfect lead in to a sublimely sensual final *lesson in loving* and the end of our journey. Hopefully as sublimely sensual and subtle as the experience of holding on to his beautiful body watching the day unfold. Thoughtful communication is the meaning of the color apricot. How appropriate. We snuggle up and catch another couple of hours sleep.

જી

"Tea or coffee?" I ask when we wake again.

"Coffee, please. Always start with coffee. White with no sugar." I bring the drinks back to bed. We sit close together, bodies touching, sipping in silence.

"Lesson, shower, breakfast. What order would you like them in?" Anthony asks, taking the lead.

"I think that order sounds right. The final lesson?"

"Yes. First I want to show you my bag of tricks." He slips out of bed and delves into his bag.

"A friend gave me this book." He hands me a copy of *100 Hot Sex Positions*. I leaf through it and make a note of the title and author.

"This is my tool kit." He unwraps a pink cloth to reveal a pretty, pink and white vibrator, a glass dildo and something I don't recognize with a small handle on it.

"I've been introduced to these two before," I say, pointing to the vibrator and the dildo."

"This is a butt plug. We won't be going there today, though." He wraps up the tools carefully and puts them away. What looks like a small black whip with a leather flag at the end emerges from his bag of tricks and another from his overnight bag. A longer whip with pink and black stripes along the handle. He places them on the bed. He picks up the large one and taps it on his palm.

"These are riding crops. This is my own personal one. It's too big to fit in my bag of tricks," he says, as he returns the smaller one to the bag.

"I'm going to use this one on you. I want you face down on the bed, on your tummy, facing this way and over this side." He masterfully positions me and positions the cheval mirror so I can see myself in it. "You can watch if you like." A silent prayer ensues.

First, he anoints my back with oil. Soon his strong hands and fingers are working their way deeply into the muscles around my shoulder blades, my neck and down my spine. I slowly relax and succumb to the sensuousness of the movement. All too soon, he stops and places my arms behind my back, one wrist over the other. His naked body fills the mirror as he shows me the grey satin tie.

"I'm going to tie your arms together. You can use the safe word *red* if you feel uncomfortable." I close my eyes and take a deep breath. Power, control, submission. A new viewpoint of lovemaking. Anthony has my trust, built over many weeks and sessions. I sense him standing beside me and surrender, allowing him to bind my arms.

I give a start as the edge of the crop trails sensuously down my back with the lightest of touches, followed by a sharp crack as the leather slaps against my flesh. It does not hurt. This pattern continues rhythmically, the delicate tracery followed by the crop slapping every few seconds up and down my back, my arms, my legs. He grabs a handful of hair pulling it firmly so my face is lifted from the bed while slapping the crop with the other hand. The contrasting sensations are exquisite. When the crop strays to my inner thighs and the lips of my sex, my nether regions contract in concert adding to the deliciousness. The garden of my delights is soon writhing, crying out to be watered. And then he stops.

"Oh God, no. I want more," but the words are unspoken. Anthony unties me.

"Stretch your hands out in front and cross them over again." He ties them again and climbs on the bed, legs astride me, laying his body across mine for a few precious moments. Now it's his penis he uses to trace patterns up and down my legs, around my bottom and in between my cheeks. Shivers run up and down my spine and into the deepest part of my soul. I'm suspended in time, writhing in an exquisite agony of wanting that takes my breath away. And he stops again.

"Oh God, please don't stop," but only I can hear. A pregnant pause. I look in the mirror and see the crop in his hands. I close my eyes and say a silent thank you as the ritualistic rhythm of the delicate tracery and alternating slaps claim me once more. A willing hostage, but not for long. As the escalating lightning bolts rack my body, I'm in an agony of wanting, my loins on fire, my sense of touch denied me. I'm desperate for him to be inside me. He stops once more, unties my hands and instructs me,

"Kneel at the foot of the bed, on the side here. Lean over and stretch your arms out again." I do as I am told, letting him position my body as he wants, putty in his hands. He reties my wrists.

"So, you can see." As he repositions the cheval mirror, I see his erection and say another silent prayer. I look at myself and see a supplicant begging for mercy. Tremors erupt every few seconds. My body has developed a mind of its own, no longer under my control. I close my eyes and wait and want. I feel him kneel behind me and gasp as his fingers find the luscious lips of my labia and move in and out of me. I'm wet beyond belief. My body starts to buck backwards and forwards in concert with his fingers. It is not enough. My insides are screaming. I want to grab him and put him inside me but my hands are bound.

"Mercy. Have mercy on me." I mouth wordlessly. Another silent scream as his penis finally finds my sex. Holding onto my sides, he rides me hard, holding great swathes of my hair and pulling back to tilt my head and remind me with every thrust who is in control. I respond wildly, moaning and groaning, all inhibitions gone, lost in the depths of submission.

Pleasure and pain collide as he thrusts deeper and deeper inside me, but I cannot stop until I reach the top. I keep climbing, climbing. Sound stops. The world slows, then stills. I scream. The Wild Woman is unleashed. As the waves crash over me, I explode into little pieces and fall face forward on the bed.

Anthony wraps his body over mine enfolding me while the tremors rock me. He leans over and unties my hands. They swing down limply to rest by the side of my legs, unable to do anything more. I look in the mirror and see me lying there, prostrate. My bottom swaying slowly from side to side to an ancient rhythm, unable to speak, beyond words. I am aware of Anthony moving around but I continue to lie there, while the aftershocks continue.

His gentle fingers alight on my face, removing the hair from my mouth and eyes which start to fill with the tenderness of his touch. He strokes my arms and back and smiles knowingly as yet another of the slowly subsiding tremors rocks me. He knows he has left his best work behind here.

"You took me for a walk on the wild side."

"I did, and it was my pleasure." He leaves the room to fetch himself and me a glass of water. Every movement, every statement is assured and confident. He returns with the water, pushing my hair back so I can take a sip. He helps me up. As I stand and look him in the eye, I feel strength in my submission to him. "You are a beautiful woman, Eve. With a true heart." He kisses me.

"Thank you," I say, returning the kiss and the glass.

We shower together, my hands now returned to me, content just to caress his chest. We dress, then move to the kitchen where Anthony cooks breakfast, as confident in the kitchen as he is everywhere else in my home, and always with an eye for detail. This time it's the basil leaves he tears to top the artfully arranged bacon, tomatoes, hash browns and eggs on our plates.

"A work of art," I say.

"That's me. It's never enough to cook food. It has to look good, too. Presentation is just as important."

After we eat, Anthony asks, "Can we go out into the garden once more before I leave? I'd like to take some more photos."

"Sure." What better place to end our night to remember?

I love my garden with a passion and I have learned to make love with a passion, a kind of passion I have not experienced before. I have done great work here, but my best is yet to come. A bridge to the future that I must yet cross with a man I am yet to meet. I trust the Universe will place him in my path soon.

PART 3:

THE HARVEST

Do not be satisfied with the stories that come before you.
Unfold your own myth.
Rumi

53. Summer's largesse

It may be past eleven o'clock but I'm treating myself, still snuggled up in my new satin sheets, luxuriating in my nakedness and ruminating. The scene outside catches my eye; birds feasting on summer's largesse, but the sounds are drowned out by Vivaldi's *Four Seasons* playing on my surround sound system. The fast-slow-fast summer movement, with violins, violas and cellos playing their heart out, reverberates around the room,

Creating a garden is like conducting a symphony — a symphony of the seasons. You can't be a gardener without being in harmony with nature or inspired by the beauty of what could be.

Summer is a busy time in the garden –harvesting fruit and vegetables, watering, weeding, repotting and feeding orchids, and readying the vegetable garden for fall planting. In between times I'm cultivating the fertile ground that is my life. I'm in search of a happy ending, an ending with passion, befitting a woman in full bloom, no longer inhibited by her sexuality, but loving it, loving the new ways of expressing it and the freedom she feels.

I reach into my bedside drawer for my Tarot cards, eyeing them fondly, my spiritual guides along the way. I wonder what is in store.

The Sun: Rebirth. A wondrous event is about to occur.

The doorbell rings. Kiki barks and races downstairs. Cindy's early for a change. She wanted to come over and discuss Strategy with a capital S. Apparently, we're going speed dating. She's getting very serious about finding me a man and is determined to find herself one as well. She's back to holding my hand, keeping me out of trouble. Or more likely, trying to curb my tendency to fanciful thinking. I doubt she'll ever appreciate how important Anthony was in the grand scheme of things. My grand scheme of things. I smile again at the thought of him.

My hand goes to grab my dressing gown off the hook but it isn't there so I run down in my birthday suit. Nothing Cindy hasn't seen before.

"Hello, Eve. Do you greet all your callers this way?"

"Sven!" I am stunned, frozen like a deer in headlights. It takes me a few seconds to process and then I wrap my arms around myself. To preserve any dignity I may still have remaining.

He laughs aloud, amused that he has both embarrassed me and seen me naked. "These are for you." He bows his head like a gentleman as he hands me a gorgeous bunch of dancing ladies, kissing me on the cheek. I take them and use them to protect a little extra modesty. "By way of an apology, Eve. I didn't behave in a gentlemanly fashion the first time we met. I want to make it up to you." He kisses me again, on the other cheek.

I pause to consider my options. "Give me two minutes. Here, hold these." I hand him the flowers and close the door. I quickly shower, throw on a summer dress and brush my hair. Nearly ten minutes may have passed but he's still waiting at the door. I think I was testing him. He passed.

"Come on in, Sven. I hide behind the door as he walks past me. Like more of a gentleman, he keeps his gaze averted, but I can tell he's smiling. Kiki follows at a safe distance.

"You look wonderful, Eve. Although, I didn't mind the first dress, either." I remember those beautiful eyes of his. The animal magnetism that drew me in. I look at Kiki. She is definitely not amused. Sven hands me the orchids, again.

"The orchids are beautiful, Sven, thank you." I kiss him on the cheek and throw him a genuine smile.

"How could I forget?" he says, bowing his head again. His smile widens. Such an enticing smile. There's a card attached to the orchids but I need my glasses and I'm too vain to put them on.

"Could you read it for me, please, Sven?"

He lowers his voice and quotes.

Our bodies are our gardens to which our wills are gardeners.

"Shakespeare again." He nods and reads from the card.

"It is summer again. A year since we were together. The first act in your garden was delightful. Would you care to join me for *le deuxième acte?*" Sven then gazes into my eyes seductively.

"Tempting. Very tempting," I say wryly. "How long are you in town for this time?" He shifts on his stool. "The truth, please, this time."

"Three weeks."

"Three weeks?" A flash in the pan. No, I don't think so.

"Thanks, Sven, but no thanks." It's just a dalliance, a delightful one maybe, but a dalliance nonetheless. I want more. Disappointment flashes briefly across his face, then disappears just as quickly. A rare rebuff for this sexy man, I think. No matter. There'll be plenty of other moths to his flame. It burns brightly. He pats my hands briefly, then draws back, sitting upright on the stool. The seduction is over.

"Would you like a cup of coffee?" I ask.

"No, thanks, Eve. I have to go." We walk to the door.

"Thank you for the orchids."

"Lovely to see you again, Eve," he says with a cheeky grin as he leans down and kisses me on the cheek. I smile and watch as he walks away with a swagger. I'm still smiling as I close the door. I look at Kiki. She's sitting there smiling, too.

54. Stepping out

Our driver pulls up outside three drab grey doors in a back street punctually at seven o'clock, a rare feat when going out with Cindy, which is why she hired a private driver. The only clue to the Soho venue, the name Jimmy above the middle one. As we ride the elevator to the bar eighteen stories up atop the James Hotel, she eyes me over again, approvingly for a change.

"You look lovely, Eve." I do. I'm wearing a figure hugging burnt orange chiffon creation. An optimistic and uplifting color that's as warm and inviting as the dress. The warmth echoed in the cognac diamond studs, visible because, under orders, my hair is up, albeit with soft curls escaping.

"You look lovely, too Cindy." Stunning in fact. In a darkly romantic black Dolce & Gabbana macramé lace dress with matching Crystine lace ankle boots, she expounded on the way here.

"Have you got your spiel ready, Darling?"

I nod to her and giggle. "Yes, mom." My spiel to lure my man. Only Cindy could come up with something like that. She's managed to insinuate us into an elite group of executives and professionals. An attractive twenty something woman is waiting at the door. "Hi, I'm Kelsey." A bright, breezy voice and winning smile. "I'm your host tonight." On her name badge, the firm's motto – Live, Laugh, Love! I peer into the room behind her at the other guests chatting, supposedly a dozen of each gender, nearly all here I see.

"Hi Kelsey. I'm Cindy and this is Eve." Cindy's voice brings me back.

Kelsey sifts through the box. "Here is your personal 'match card' where you write down the names of the men you meet," she says, handing us the match cards. Have either of you been before?"

"I have," pipes up Cindy, "and I've explained to Eve how it all works."

"Good. Go grab a glass of wine then introduce yourself to the other guests and have a lovely evening, ladies." We walk into the room to where the drinks are.

Cindy hands me a glass of champagne. "Go, strut your stuff, Eve. Make them notice you, before we all have to sit down."

"Okay," I say, smiling back at her as she sashays over to a group of men. She'll knock their socks off. There's no way I can compete with her. I don't want to. I'd prefer not to be here. Where men are concerned, we're on different wavelengths. I gaze out of the wall of windows at the panoramic views of Midtown and take a sip.

"Eve?" A voice from behind me. I've heard it before. I turn.

"Adam! What are you doing here?"

"And I was about to ask you the same thing!"

Adam was my guardian angel – our guardian angel – who helped get William onto a clinical trial in the melanoma research program that he was running. He was wonderful and kind, and did such a lot to help William and me get through. He may be a doctor, but he spent time with us, got to know us. Working against overwhelming odds, he lessened William's suffering and prolonged his living. I loved this man.

"Eve, it's lovely to see you again. How long has it been? It must be seven years."

"Just over eight," I reply, feeling a little shaky. So many thoughts flood back. The last time I saw him was in hospital just after William had passed away.

His blue eyes smile at me, yet with a hint of sadness behind them. Oh my. This is too much. He looks around the room briefly, then back at me. He leans in and whispers,

"Want to get out of here and find a quiet place to talk?"

"Wait here a moment." I walk over to where Cindy is holding court to tell her.

"Where is he?" she asks. I point him out. Standing there, wearing a well fitted black suit and open necked white shirt that highlight his tall, slim build, he turns to us. I notice the small tuft of dark brown hair falling across the forehead. He waves at us.

"So cute, Darling." Cindy gives me the all clear. We agree to catch up in the morning.

Adam and I escape around the corner to the Soho Grand Bar. He raises his glass of Shiraz and I raise my champagne. "Cheers, Eve. To escapades."

"To escapades and old friends, Adam." We clink glasses then we both look away, reminiscing about William. Well, I am. Adam brings me back.

"Tell me what's happened since I saw you last, Eve," he asks quietly.

"Not a lot. I've become quite a solitary soul since William died. I only maintain contact with close family, really. The twins, Rachel and Richard, whom you met in the hospital. They're now thirty-three, believe it or not. And Cindy, my cousin, who recently came over from LA."

"What else?"

"My garden has become the love of my life and my best buddy is Kiki, a ten-year-old Welsh terrier." I look up and see him listening attentively. "Until earlier this year, I hadn't been overseas since William died. My life is very simple." And sometimes lonely, but I don't say that.

Adam leans in and begins to tell me about the past eight years for him. It turns out he divorced a year after William died. "I was married to the job. I neglected my wife. She left, then found someone else. Or the other way round. I'm not sure, but it doesn't matter really. If I'd been there for her... well." He changes the subject, bringing it back to me. "How long have you been stepping out?"

Stepping out. An interesting turn of phrase. "Just over a

year. Last summer I tried online dating but I only lasted a few months." I wonder how to phrase the next part of my life. "Then I went into research mode for the rest of the year. Tonight, is the first time I've put my head out since last fall. What about you?" I ask deflecting the conversation away from me.

He takes a sip of his wine and looks pensive. He shuffles in his chair and sits up like he's made a decision. He smiles and leans in, again. "Unlike you, I've dated a fair bit. I've travelled a lot but I haven't put down roots." He leans closer, as if disclosing. "And I haven't wanted to. Work has been my mistress. Over the past seven years, I've slept around a lot." He has a twinkle in his eye. "Working in cancer centers around the world – Oxford, Tubingen, Stockholm, Guangzhou, even Melbourne, Australia. I'm now back at Memorial Sloan Kettering where you came with William."

Our eyes meet and we share a moment. No words exchanged, just an acknowledgement to William and a look that says, 'he'd want this.' That's what I hope, anyway. "What are you doing tomorrow?" Adam asks abruptly, a grin on his face.

"Nothing, really. Just pottering in the garden. Why?" I am warming to this wonderful man, but in a new way.

"Well, the weather says it's going to be bright and breezy which is perfect for a drive down the coast with the top down. I was wondering if you'd care to join me."

"I'd love to." My spontaneity has taken me to many interesting places, but this feels safe and easy.

"Great! What time shall I pick you up?"

"Ten o'clock? I'm usually an early bird but, new sheets. I like to lie in."

"Ten o'clock it is!" He pulls out his cell and punches in my number and address. I get mine out as well. There is a voice message waiting from Richard. Adam and I part company a little too formally outside the bar. He wasn't my doctor but a little of that reticence remains.

❧

I call Richard up on the way home. "Tell me about your wonderful man, Richie."

"That's what he calls me. How did you know that?" He laughs down the phone. "What a silly question. Well, he's an architect. He has his own practice and specializes in landscape architecture."

"That's not what I mean. Tell me about the kind of person he is." Men are so practical sometimes.

"Okay, okay," he says, his voice softening, "His name's Jeremy. He's funny, witty, and comfortable in his own skin. He came out as a teenager. He's a few years older than me, shorter and slimmer, hates working out and loves to cook."

"He sounds wonderful, Love. How long have you known him?"

"A few months now. I'd like you to meet him." I can hear the happiness in his voice. "Can we meet up for dinner next week? Friday night, perhaps."

"Love to. Just tell me where and when. I'm happy for you,

Richie." And I am, so happy.

I look up to the sky. The moon appears cut in half. It's a last quarter moon. A time to let go, release and forgive anything and anyone who has hurt you. A time to allow the universe to take over. One twin is happy. Rachel's happiness is a more challenging beast to tame. I sigh, wistfully. A text alert sounds on my cell.

Three matches: A heart surgeon, a stockbroker and a banker. All as rich as Croesus!!!

Talk soon, Darling. Doubt I'll have much time to catch up for a while.

xxx Cindy

PS Have you found your man?

55. Adam

Adam is wandering down the path with his back turned to me when I open the door. He's wearing jeans, checked shirt and loafers. It's the first time I've seen him without a suit I realize. As I come closer, he turns to face me with a broad smile.

"Good morning, Bright Eyes. I was just admiring your garden. A real labor of love out here! Kind of reminds me of my career."

"Good morning to you, too. Yes, it has been and still is. It's my passion just like your career is yours, I guess."

"Indeed, indeed. It really is a beautiful part of the world, Eve. You're very lucky."

"Ah, Adam. You've just admired my hard work, not my luck. My successes are usually the result of my own hard work. Unlike yours, of course," I say tongue in cheek. His quizzical frown softens into a grin when he sees my cheeky smile. Kiki interrupts our little moment by sitting hard up against his leg and looking up, adoringly. "Hello to you, too. Kiki, is it?" he asks, bending down to tickle her under the chin then looking up at me. "Is she always this friendly?"

"Yes, this is Kiki and no, she's not always this friendly. She's got an inbuilt crap detector for people, but you seem to have snuck under her radar. It mustn't be tuned in, today."

He laughs and gives Kiki's head a playful scratch. "You're just jealous that I'm paying more attention to her than you," he retorts, grinning. "Are you ready to go? Great day to hit the road."

I laugh. "I'll just put Kiki inside and fetch my sweater." What a charming man. Far more relaxed than I expected and he passed muster with Kiki.

ॐ

We hit the road and hit each other up for questioning. I lead to begin with, as he got so much out of me last night. "My grandparents on my mother's side were English," he says, eyes firmly on the winding road that heads towards the coast. "We'd come down here on our summer vacations, as it would remind mom of England." We're making our way down to Cape May on the Garden State Parkway with the top down in his SLK.

He's a great driver, as confident and capable as in his medical guise. I'm sitting back feeling relaxed, very comfortable in the car and in his presence. He is cheery and breezy, but in a charismatic way, so different from the serious doctor side I was used to seeing. As we near the end of the toll parkway, Adam glances over at me, "I used to love coming down here."

"How long since you've been here?"

"Nearly thirty years. Before I went to college."

"Heavens." We get off the parkway and work our way towards the seafront.

"The good thing is it hardly changes. It's a city in another time." We both look around, as we pass by, taking in the historic houses, the gentility and elegance of another era.

"An era that you loved?"

"More so that mom loved. But she died when I was at college so we never came back here." Instinctively I rub his arm, soothingly, leaving my hand there.

" I'm sorry. What did you love about coming here?" I stop and pause, "Adam, you haven't been back here since your mom died? Oh my..."

"I did come back once, briefly, to scatter her ashes. Is that weird? That I decided to bring you here?" He places his hand over mine.

"No, no, I mean, it's a little sad. But why here, today?"

He squeezes my hand gently. "It'll be twenty-nine years since she passed away next week. She was all the family I had. This time of the year always brings that up." He throws a quick glance at me. "It's not so sad these days, but I was thinking of making a pilgrimage here next year. Then when I saw you I thought, why not come here and show someone else what my mom thought was so great about it. I knew you would understand."

I squeeze his arm, softly. "Well, she had every reason to love it. It is beautiful."

Even from the side I see his face light up. "The beach, the natural beauty of it. It is the southernmost beach in the state. It's wild at times. Here we are. Cove Beach." He parks the car and clambers out quickly. "Come on." I follow his excited frame up the sandy track, past the fences holding in the remnant grasses onto the beach. My sandals sink into the soft sand.

Adam turns around and sees me struggling. "Here, give me your hand." I hold it out. He pulls me along, eager to be on the beach. We move to the crest of the sand and stop to look.

My eyes move from one vista to another taking in the miles and miles of unobstructed beach and the breathtaking view of the ocean meeting the sky. I turn to Adam. His eyes are alive. He puts his arm around my shoulder, hugs me, then leaves his arm there.

"Isn't it beautiful? Can you see why I loved it here?"

"Yes, I can. It's a beautiful part of the world." I lean into him.

"I even started painting here."

"Really? It's easy to see why." The panorama of a deep blue sky, the expanse of grey sand and the gentle surf rolling onto the wide, gradual shore is one of serene oceanic beauty.

After sharing a moment looking out, we walk along the beach.

"Hold on." I remove my sandals and slip them over my fingers. We walk in companionable silence, hand in hand, soaking in the beauty of this idyllic coastal setting. Adam appears deep in thought. I'm content to leave him be for a while. A peace descends upon me and I disappear into the ether, too.

"I'm interested in hearing about your research." Adam's voice shatters the peace, calling me back. My heart starts beating faster. "Any clinical trials?" he asks, grinning at me. Heavens above. How to tell him? What can I tell him? I look up at the sky hoping for guidance, but none is forthcoming.

"Quite a few trials. I doubt they're as clinical as yours, though. Perhaps the findings first," I say turning to him with a shy smile. "The greatest thing to come out of this year is that I finally own my body and the sexuality that has been repressed most of my life." I pause, trying to read his face for fear. He seems to be making no moves to run...yet. "I'm reclaiming my birthright." I breathe in deeply, hesitating.

"Go on, Eve. I can hear this. I'm a big boy."

"I had some *lessons in loving* with a young male escort called Anthony. While the formal *lessons in loving* are over, I imagine it will remain a lifelong interest." I turn to look at him, searching his face. There is no censure, just an encouraging nod and a thoughtful expression. "I've learned that my body is a temple. No forced entry permitted."

"You were abused?" His fingers touch my arm gently.

I nod. "I have found my voice. I've learned that touch is integral to my being," I pause again. Adam squeezes my hand, signalling me to go on. "I'm no longer naïve. I've left behind that which no longer serves me, and...." I turn to face him, grinning, "and I'm definitely no longer tame."

Adam guffaws. "I've been warned."

I laugh. I feel my body start to loosen up. "I feel reborn, Adam, free. Finally free to be me. And..." I draw it out longer by kissing him on the cheek. "I sincerely believe the best is yet to come." His eyes smile, deep and wide.

"You got me. I'm hooked. A little flabbergasted, but I'm not running away if that's what you're thinking." Oh, he's good. How did he know what I was thinking?

"Tell me about Master Anthony and the lessons. If that's okay?" he asks, his hand stroking mine. We sit down on the sand, facing out to sea. With his gentle prodding, I open up to him, holding nothing back, including the heartache of my alienation from Rachel.

He turns me around to face him. "Few people have the courage to explore themselves the way you have, Eve. I doff my hat off to you." He mimes the action, playing with me, trying to help me relax. "Most Western cultures have Victorian attitudes to sexuality. It's good you've finally escaped that." He draws me to him and kisses me on the lips. He pauses, leaving his lips there. "Good for me, too." He kisses me again. Such lovely soft lips.

"Now it's your turn," I say pulling back a little. "Tell me about your painting."

"I'll go one better, Madame. I'll show you. Tomorrow. Darken my doorstop at eighteen hundred hours and I'll show you my etchings." His voice changes to the authoritative Doctor Adam. "I'll even cook dinner for you." A wide grin splits his face. "Perhaps we might conduct some research of our own." He kisses me again, a lingering kiss, before offering a hand to help me up. "Now, how about some lunch at the Lobster House before we head home?"

"Wonderful." I feel relieved. I opened my life up to scrutiny and I survived. Not only survived, but found someone who understands, and even applauds the quest.

After a long, lazy lunch of crab fingers, hot and spicy shrimp, barbecued clams and oysters, washed down with a glass of Californian Chardonnay, we head north on the Garden State Parkway, Van Morrison ringing in our ears. I pat Adam's leg fondly.

These are the days of the endless summer
These are the days, the time is now
There is no past, there's only future
There's only here, there's only now

56. Magical kingdom of feel good

Honey locust trees line the street, which is just steps from Central Park, in the most desirable section of the Upper East Side. It's a classy part of town, and walking distance to the hospital. His apartment block is a red brick building, four storeys high, with arched mullion windows.

"Come in, Eve. Welcome," Adam opens the door wide. He leans forward and kisses me on the lips before drawing me inside and closing the door. He wraps his arms around me and kisses me, again, a lovely lingering kiss, before releasing me. "Mmmmm," He smacks his lips then shakes his limbs loosely, as if limbering up. "Enough, Adam. Behave." I laugh and hand him the wine, a Sangiovese. "Thank you. Would you like to see the apartment, first?"

"Yes, please."

"I've been renting here since I came back to New York six months ago. It's been renovated recently." I look around the large living, dining and sitting room we are in. A high-end renovation by the look of it.

"You have a window seat, too," I exclaim. "I love window seats."

"Yes, and it doubles as a day bed."

"Mine, too."

"And the terrace. Perfect for entertaining. I hardly ever use it, but tonight we'll be dining al fresco." The canopy of a large London plane tree overhangs the end, shading the outdoor setting.

"It's lovely, Adam." He shows me through the rest of the apartment. A marble kitchen with maple cabinets and state of the art appliances. A luxuriously renovated marble bathroom with a deep Jacuzzi tub and a large walk-in closet.

"This where I keep most of my paintings. I'll show you some later. Let's have a drink first."

"Where's the bedroom?" I ask puzzled.

He looks at me and smiles, then picks up a remote control. "Da. Da! The pièce de résistance." A bed slowly comes down from the wall.

"Amazing. What a fabulous apartment. I've never seen anything like it."

"The truth is I'm hardly ever here. I spend most of my time at work and when I finally come home, I pass out on the day bed. I rarely cook and never entertain." He turns to face me. "And, if more truth be told, I need more in my life. He cups my face in his hands. "You are beautiful, Eve."

He kisses me slowly, suckling my lips, then kissing me again. He keeps hold of my head while moving his face back, looking at me intently, then he kisses me again, before sitting me down on the couch. I shift my legs to face him and my skirt rides up. He looks down. "You have great legs." He lifts my legs up over his lap and pats them.

"I know." I laugh at my immodesty. But I do. "My best feature, I think."

He laughs and starts running his hands over my legs, stroking my knees, moving his hands up my skirt a little, before wandering back. He leaves one hand resting on my knee while the other picks up my right foot. He twists and kneads the heel and the toe, then massages one toe at a time. He looks deep into my eyes. "You are so sexy." I give him a disbelieving look. "You don't know that you are sexy?" he asks with a surprised look on his face. "How amazing. You are so naïve, Eve. That makes it even better."

He cups my face and kisses me, eating my lips, savoring me. Then he cups my breasts and leans down to kiss them one at a time, holding his mouth there for a few seconds. I can feel his heat even through my blouse and bra. He leaves my breasts be, then nuzzles into my neck. His mouth even hotter against my skin. "I want to devour you. I could eat every part of you." I laugh, a little self-consciously. I don't know what else to do with such a display of affection.

He lays my legs down and stands up abruptly. "If I don't stop this there'll be no dinner, but a drink first." Adam opens the Sangiovese and pours. "Your wine, Madame." His face breaks out into a grin. "Or is it Maîtresse?"

I tap his glass and smile. "To mistresses."

"To mistresses," he echoes. He takes a quick sip, puts his glass down and starts pulling food out of the refrigerator.

I sit there sipping wine, watching him unobtrusively, for a few minutes. He definitely knows his way about a kitchen. He looks up at me and smiles briefly before turning his attention back to the food. I look out the window at the fading sunlight on the townhouse gardens, hoping to find some tranquility. My mind is racing. Doors are opening, some new, some wider than ever before. This old soul is on the cusp of something new and exciting, yet with a childhood wonder and dreamlike quality about it, as when one enters the magical Kingdom of Feel Good.

ॐ

"More?" My plate is empty but my belly is not. Adam is pointing to the bowl of pasta carbonara. I shake my head. He points to the salad. I shake my head. "Bread?"

"No, thank you, Adam. That was delicious but I can't eat any more. I'm full," I say patting my tummy.

"More wine?" He waves the wine bottle at me.

"No, thanks. I'm driving." I stand and go to clear the plates.

"No, leave them." Adam stands, picks up my hand and leads me to the bed. I stand at the foot of the bed and look into his face. I feel like his eyes are examining me. There's a seriousness about him now.

"Lie with me, Eve." He turns on a lamp and turns off all the lights. He slips off his shoes and lies down on the bed. I follow suit, nestling into the crook of his arm. Our bodies touching, our fingers intertwined. We lay there quietly, the warmth of his body permeating mine. The sounds of our synchronized breathing rhythmically rising and falling is all that can be heard. How sweet it is. I close my eyes.

Adam lifts his head, waking me. He nuzzles into my neck and sniffs. "Lovely. I love your perfume." He sniffs again, then lays his head back against the pillow. I lift my head to look at him and see a smile wrapped around his face. I stroke his lips.

"It's a classic — *Chanel No. 5*." I kiss him tenderly, then draw back to look at him. I look beyond the enticing blue eyes and see deep into his soul. I like this man. I like him a lot. I always have. I run my fingers over his forehead, and tug the stray lock of hair that always seems to fall down. "Cute." I look over at the clock. It's past eleven. I pat Adam on the chest. "I have to go." He looks disappointed. "And you have to work in the morning."

"Stay the night." I look at him and think there is nothing I would like more than to stay and spend the night with this man, but I can't. I stroke his lips again. Soft lips.

"I can't. Kiki calls. I don't like to leave her on her own for too long. And my horticulturalist will be there very early in the morning. He comes once a month to help out in the garden." He sits up and cups my face, looking at me with longing, before kissing me. Another tender, lingering kiss. And another.

"Will you come back on the weekend and stay over? And bring Kiki?"

I smile. "I'd love to." There is no hurry, this man is not going to go away.

57. New moon

A week later, a worried looking Adam, is checking the stairs behind me. "You've lost Kiki."

"It's okay. I sent her away for the weekend with Richard and Jeremy."

"Why?" He takes my overnight bag and closes the door.

"I want your undivided attention. I don't want to be competing with another female for your affections." I turn to him and pout. "One woman at a time."

"Come here, you." He wraps his arms around me and hugs me, swaying from one foot to the other. "It's good to have you here." He kisses me, long and slow, then starts swaying again.

"It's good to be here." And it is.

"I'll leave your bag here by the bed." The bed is tucked away out of sight.

"There's a bottle of wine in there that needs to be chilled." He zips open the bag, takes the wine out. "Nice. *Saint Chinian Blanc*. I'm very fond of French wines."

"Me, too. I'm very fond of France," I say, hearing the nostalgia in my voice. "Living in Paris is a dream of mine."

"Interesting. Mine, too," he says, smiling at me, while placing the bottle in the refrigerator and taking another one out. He opens one of his elegant birds-eye maple cabinets and removes two wine glasses. "Getting back to Kiki, Richard and Jeremy?"

"Richard invited me to dinner to meet his new partner last night. I asked if he'd mind Kiki this weekend. He said they were going to Jeremy's beach shack for the weekend and would be delighted to take Kiki with them."

"What's Jeremy like? Adam asks as he opens the wine.

"He's nice, an interesting guy. I like him. His work sounds really interesting, too. I'd like to learn more about landscape architecture. The main thing is Richard looks really happy. That's all I care about." Adam pours the wine while I talk.

"Here. How about great minds thinking alike." Adam leans over the bench and shows me the label — *Bordeaux Rosé*.

I smile. "Amazing." Synchronicity, again. That magical movement of spirit.

"A la santé."

"A la santé." I reply tapping his glass, then sipping the wine. It is crisp and very dry. "Très bon."

"And I..." Adam starts off, looking very pleased with himself, "have the rest of the weekend free. I worked till two." He checks his watch. "Drinking at four in the afternoon. How decadent. How very French." I laugh. He walks around the bench to where I am standing, kisses me on both cheeks then leads me over to the window seat. We sit. I turn to look at him. His eyes are smiling. He's as happy and relaxed as I've ever seen him. He puts his glass down, takes mine and puts it down on the coffee table, too. He leans over and pulls my legs up over his lap. He kisses me long and slow, before pulling back to look me in the eyes, to check my reaction. Such luscious lips.

He leans in again and kisses me hard, his tongue moving in and out, exploring my mouth. His teeth biting, too. I kiss him back, trying to grab hold of his tongue and suck it. My nether regions contract. Adam keeps kissing me, passionately, his head moving from side to side, his teeth grazing my lips, his hands working their way up my skirt. I pull away to draw breath.

He picks up my left foot and starts slowly, sensuously sucking one toe at a time, his eyes looking straight through me, as if he can see into my soul. As tiny thunderbolts shoot through my nether regions, he smiles knowingly then picks up the other foot and works his way from the small toe to the big toe, sucking all the time. His eyes never leave me. Watching him watching me is highly erotic. I feel his hardness rising under me. Suddenly, surprisingly, he shakes himself.

"Brrrrrrrrr... Woman. What are you doing to me?"

I throw my arms around his neck. "You are one very sexy man." Adam leans over, with me draped around his neck, picks up my glass and hands it to me.

"Unhand me, Woman." I laugh, remove my arms and take the proffered glass. Adam leans over and picks up his. Still sitting with my legs over his lap, now fully exposed as my skirt is pushed right up, he pats my legs. "Great legs," he says again, raising his glass. I lean over and kiss him on the mouth, gently, tenderly, suckling on his soft, soft lips. My head nuzzles into his neck and I sigh.

We sit there for a while, talking about anything and everything, holding hands, fingers intertwined, bodies touching, kissing, holding and gentling each other. There's a seriousness that overtakes him at times when he looks deep into my eyes, a question without words. This is not a fling. I know it is something much more. I stroke his face with my fingers. I love the softness of his skin, the blue eyes that always have a smile wrapped around them. They gather me in. Smiling is a natural consequence of being with him.

"I love the way your eyes smile."

"And I love the way your eyes talk," he says patting my legs, then laying them down. "Time to cook dinner. We'll eat and then I'll show you my paintings."

෪

A dozen canvases are lined up against the walls. Impressionist in style, mostly landscapes and seascapes. Good. Very good.

"I haven't seen them for years until I unearthed them a few days ago."

"Are these seascapes from Cape May?"

"Yes. I was quite young when I painted those. En plein-air painting. It's the only true way to paint."

"You're very talented. I love the texture and colors."

"Sometimes an image builds up inside you and an

overwhelming desire to create something of beauty overtakes you. Unleashing that energy, letting it out, becomes an obsession." He looks at me. I nod understandingly.

"Brushes can be too slow, when I'm in that kind of mood. Then I'll mix the colors on the canvas using my fingers or the sides of my hands. Sometimes my arms. Building up the texture can be like a sculpture." I can see the energy pulsing through him as he talks. I squeeze his arm.

"The best paintings are done very quickly. There's a freshness and vitality to them." I point to a couple of blank canvases. His eyes light up. "The urge is with me, again. And..." He shows me a box containing his old tubes of paints and paintbrushes. "I have everything I need." He puts his arm around me and draws me close.

"I love that you're thinking about painting, again."

"Me, too." Adam smiles.

ॐ

I look around the terrace in the candlelight, while Adam clears up in the kitchen. Rachmaninov's *Piano Concerto Number Two* plays in the background. Such a romantic setting. The London plane tree dances lightly in the summer night air. Above the moon — a new moon, is just a ghostly apparition; its lighted half facing entirely away from earth. A fresh start. A blank canvas.

I sit back and put my legs up on his chair, leaning back into the night. I'm having a lovely time, very slow and easy, body succumbing to the slower rhythms and the mind imagining possibilities for the coming year. Talking with Adam the past few days has brought an amazing clarity and coherence to my life. There is a simplicity and candor about him that is as refreshing as it is endearing. No artifice at all. He's very easy to be with and best of all, he makes me laugh.

Suddenly the music changes. *The King and I.* Adam swirls around back out on the terrace, then puts his hands up in a dance hold, "Care to dance, Madame." I laugh and walk into his arms. He swirls me around once, then holds me tightly and dances me expertly around the terrace. We sway in time to the music.

Getting to know you,
Getting to know all about you.
Getting to like you,
Getting to hope you like me

As the song finishes, Adam dances me back inside, giving me one last swirl before sitting me down on the couch. The room is darkened, with only a lamp near the bed, which is now down. Adam lies down with his head on my lap. The mood quietens. Me staying over gives us freedom, time to explore, to relax into each other.

I shiver with delight as his fingers trace the inside of my thighs. Then his mouth and tongue take over. His fingers ease their way around the edge of my panties, tickling, teasing my clit. The tonguing over, he places his mouth over my panties. His hot breath makes me gasp.

"Make love to me, please," I ask.

He leads me over to the bed and undresses me slowly before undressing himself. He takes his time. I come back down again. There is no hurry. He sets the pace, slow, easy and sensuous. Kissing, long deep kisses, then moving back to look at me, always those eyes on me, savoring my pleasure. When he finally enters me, slowly, gently, I moan softly, at the delicious shock of our union. I hold him there, my body softly swaying like the plane tree in the breeze. He touches my very soul. He draws back and looks at me. I smile at him.

"Your pleasure is my pleasure," he says, returning the smile. I draw him to me. We are locked in an embrace, bodies barely moving, writhing with the pleasure of being so close, so intimately connected. I flex my love muscles a few times. I hear his breathing change. I squeeze harder and faster until my muscles contract. I start to shudder as the waves of pleasure roll over me. Adam follows suit, shudders running through his body like his love juice. I hold him until our shuddering subsides. He kisses my nose.

"Thank you," he says with a contented smile on his face.

"Your pleasure is my pleasure," I say giving him a squeeze. We lie in each other's arms, suspended in time, waiting for our bodies to uncouple. When we finally do, Adam slides out of bed. I lie there, smiling. I can still feel him inside me. My body echoes with his loving and his gentle caring ways. He returns to the side of the bed.

Wordlessly, he places one hand on my stomach which quivers

at his touch. I jump as something warm and wet is laid over my sex — a hand towel. He starts wiping me, cleaning me up. The sensation of a warm towel being guided in and around me is delightful. I pat his hand with the towel in it and look deep into his eyes. I laugh.

"Thank you. My pussy is purring nicely."

He grins at me. "At your service, Madame." He bows, pats my pussy fondly and hops back into bed. "Time to sleep. Let's spoon." I turn over. He cuddles into me. I nestle back into him. His strong arms a safe haven. His warmth is all pervading.

58. Adam and Eve

I wake early. Jolts have been rocking me on and off while I was half asleep. Adam stirs. I wrap my sex around his legs and snuggle into him.

He wakens and smiles at me. "Do you want a cup of tea?"

"No, let's just lie here." He strokes my arm and neck, then presses the bridge of my nose. Tenderness, such tenderness, and such knowing as the corresponding nerve ending in my nether regions responds with a jolt. Adam turns me on my side, facing away from him, spooning again. His fingers find my sex gently, never hurriedly and I know I can take my time responding to the intimacy and tenderness of his touch.

He fingers my anus, setting it quivering, then the entrance to my vagina. His penis rubs up and down across my butt and between my butt cheeks. I love this, the thrill that it promises. He starts to enter me from behind. Being so close takes a little more time for me to relax and open up, but he is patient and solicitous. He fills my very being.

Adam then lifts my legs over his shoulders and enters me, again. I open up and welcome him inside. I love looking at him, love the way he looks at me, looking down to see him disappear inside me. He pauses, bringing us both down, allowing us to extend the pleasure, but I can't wait any longer. I come. He waits until the aftershocks subside.

Still locked inside me, he turns me on my side, to spoon again. He thrusts inside me, then pauses, before moving in and out again, like a rhythmic heartbeat. I meet him, I greet him. I touch myself. I touch him. I touch myself again. I come again and again, until finally Adam cries out and falls against my back, spent. I grab his arms and hold them tight around me.

"How sweet it is to be loved by you," I say patting his arms.

Adam squeezes me. "You are very easy to love." He kisses my back, then pulls back the bedcover. "A shower before breakfast." He runs the shower and we both hop in. The warm water is soothing. So too the sensuous way Adam soaps my back, my arms, my butt, between my butt cheeks and down my legs. He turns me around and starts on my neck and my breasts before kneeling down and giving his wholehearted attention to cleaning my sex with his tongue.

I hold onto his head with my hands, quivering in the wake of his exuberant, over-the-top display. He stands, grabs my hands, intertwines our fingers and raises my arms above my head, pressing his body against mine. We kiss while the water streams down over our faces. Adam turns off the taps, then towels me dry, paying particular attention to my erogenous zones which dance in delight. He hands me his robe. After drying himself, he ties an apron over his nakedness.

He grins at me, his eyes alive. "No need to get dressed yet.

Sit on the window seat while I make breakfast. There's a book on the table for you to read, a book of erotic verse." I read in between watching him closely without trying to appear as if I'm doing so. He is so at home in the kitchen, efficient, capable, sparing in his movements. Bacon, eggs, hash browns, mushrooms and cheese on toast. He's very ordered, used to looking after himself. Very clean and tidy for a man, cleaning up after himself as he goes. Even cleaning me up. I love that he loves being so intimate with me.

My gaze turns to the window. It's cool outside today, too cool to stand outside on the terrace for long. The bird's eye view from the fourth floor makes the small apartment seem bigger, exposed to the elements. Open to the sky. I realize that my wings have taken flight too. I've come off my training wheels and now entered a new land, not a magical make-believe kingdom, but one in the here and now.

This is not a fantasy. There is someone real, in my real life. And what an amazing man he is. Over the top, full of life. It would be so easy to be swept away by the pleasure he wreaks on my body. I trust the Universe and us that this is the end of life as I have known it and the beginning of what has not yet been imagined.

59. Seduction

"Hello, Eve. How are you?" Cindy's voice is trilling excitedly.

"Good. Very good in fact and so are you by the sound of it, Cindy."

"You first, Darling. Do tell."

"I spent a lovely weekend with Adam. He's such a sweetie. He cooks, he cleans, and he dances. And... he's the most amazing lover."

"Is there anything he can't do, Eve?" she asks, sardonically.

"Don't be like that. His entry into my life has helped sweep most of the residual shit aside."

"He sounds wonderful. Really wonderful," a touch of nostalgia in her voice.

I continue to wax lyrical over my wonderful man. "I'm ready for him, Cindy, ready for the next step, wherever that leads. Big, bold steps." And, I think to myself, I no longer feel alone.

"Well, that's wonderful, Darling. Truly wonderful. When are you seeing him again?"

"This coming weekend. He's coming to my place. I was wondering whether to ring Rachel and ask her to come and meet him. What do you think?"

"Adam as a peace offering? Mmmmm. He is linked to William. Maybe it would work." She pauses, "Ask him to bake something for her."

"What a great idea!"

"Do you think your man is up to that?" she asks archly.

"If he's not, I'm sure he'll get up to speed. Thanks for that, Cuz."

"Don't call me, Cuz. It's as bad as Richie," she scolds. "It doesn't suit me."

"Alright, *Cindy*. What's been happening in your world? What about *your* men?"

"Well, I've narrowed it down to two. Harold, the heart surgeon is off the list."   "Why is that?"

"Well, I have some criteria I use, initially."

"Criteria for selecting a man?"

"Yes, of course," she says, as if I'm a novice. "It's important to know a man's background first before getting involved. Like which college he attended, which clubs he belongs to, whether his money is old money or not. Looks, love and whether or not he's going to drop off the perch come later." She laughs. "Come to think of it, it hasn't worked too well up to now, has it? Still, a woman can't lower her standards."

I laugh. "You're incorrigible, Cindy. Men don't stand a chance with you."

"But, *the* most important criteria is that he doesn't know any of my friends."

"Why?" I ask puzzled.

"There's no way I'm going to be seen as second choice," she says haughtily. "That's why Harold was ruled out. He'd dated Annabel, one of my college friends. He just had to go, Darling."

"So, who's left?"

"Dylan, the banker whom I'm having dinner with on Friday and Miles, the stockbroker, who I'm having lunch with on Sunday at his country club."

I chuckle. "Great. Let me know what happens."

"I will, Darling. Must be off. Ciao!"

"Oh, by the way, Anthony sent me a photo album of the garden, of the shots he took here. Beautiful compositions." I wax lyrical again. "Hints of sunlight filtering through trees, reflections on the pond, of the water lilies opening and closing. Lots of close ups of bees and insects on flowers, of poppies blowing in the breeze. Of shadows across the garden. It's fabulous photography, Cindy. Absolutely stunning. I'll show it to you when you're next here."

"Well, don't show it to Rachel. Or you'll offend her again."

I laugh, a wry laugh. "Okay, I hear you, Cindy. Bye."

ॐ

I take a deep breath. Her cell is ringing.

"Hello."

"Hello, Rachel." I hear her inhale sharply. "Please don't hang up. I wanted to speak with you." I can hear her breathing heavily.

"I'm sorry Rachel, very sorry. I'm sorry you're upset. I didn't mean to offend you."

"Well, you did. It was a shock."

"I understand that," I say soothingly.

"I felt it was a betrayal of Uncle William. The age gap freaked me out as well."

"I understand that, too. But I'm a woman with needs, just like you, Rach."

"You're like a mother to me, Eve. Kids don't like to think of their parents having sex. Yuk!" I can still hear anger and disgust in her voice. "But a parent having sex with someone that young, and paying for it, is really gross."

"I get that, but it was never my intention to hurt or offend you. I love you," I say still trying to mollify her. "Rachel there's someone I want you to meet."

"Have you paid for him as well?"

I laugh. Only in kind, I think, but I don't dare say so out loud. "You've met him before, a long time ago. You liked him and he would like to meet you again."

"Who is he?" she asks, showing some interest at last.

"Adam Jordan, William's oncologist."

"You're dating *the* Adam Jordan, Professor Adam Jordan, the eminent research scientist?" impressed in spite of herself.

"Yes," I laugh. "I'll ask him to bake something for you if you agree to come. This coming Sunday at my place."

"You've got to be kidding. He bakes too?"

"Yes, he's a great cook, Rach."

"What a man. I'll be there with bells on." I smile at the first hint of levity in her voice.

"Great. Three o'clock. I look forward to seeing you, Rach. Take care."

"You, too." She rings off.

&

I ring Adam. "Is it okay to talk?"

"Hello, Beautiful. What can I do for you?"

"I want you to seduce my niece."

He laughs out loud. "Anything to oblige, Madame. Just think of me like those around-the-clock drive-in churches: my body is available for 24/7 worship."

I giggle. "Not with your body, with your cooking. Although I'm sure anyone would love to be seduced by you."

He laughs. "My cooking? What would I cook to seduce your niece?"

"You'll think of something. Let me remind you, men who can cook are very sexy, especially when all they're wearing is an apron."

"What a mischievous she-devil tease you are. You'll be interested to know I've taken a leaf out of the wonderful Anthony's book and started filling a bag of tricks with *instruments de l'extase...*"

"Oh, Adam." I giggle some more.

"And, of course, I'm looking forward to your reactions. Seeing your pleasure is so wonderfully erotic."

"You are a beautiful man. I'm very fond of you. And so is my body."

"Oh, oh! My pulse rate just shot up. I must keep calm when thinking of your body, a hopeless addiction if ever I saw one. *Ne plus ultra.*"

"Latin, this time, Adam. *Ne plus ultra* – nothing more beyond. What riches you bring to my world, to my life, to my body, to my earthly delights. You are a treasure."

"I'd be happy to be buried in your garden any time, Madame." I laugh, then a thought crosses my mind. William is still in our garden, waiting.

"Sunday at my place. I have some shrimp and rainbow trout which will make a delicious dinner, either before or after my seduction, or maybe both. Who knows? Who cares? I'm just delighted to have you in my life, for as long as this madness lasts."

"See you Sunday, you smart, sassy, beautiful woman." He hangs up. A text alert sounds. I laugh, again. A belly laugh. Laughing is *de rigueur* with this wonderful man.

PS You ought to revise your business card to read:

Goddess, Muse, Horticulturalista & Bombe Sexuelle

That's quite a moniker you have given me, Adam, I think. Following the fourth *lesson in loving* with Anthony, having visited a place beyond imagining, I said that after working with him, I'd spoilt the possibility of finding anything approximating an ordinary, normal kind of relationship. And the redoubtable young man replied,

"Why on earth would you want to settle for anything ordinary?"

And then you came along.

۶ی

"They're delicious, Adam," Rachel says, her mouth half full of pumpkin scone. They're so moist. What do you put in them?"

"The secret is the buttermilk, buttermilk in the mixture and the basting," says Adam, smiling at her. "My mom's recipe, believe it or not? Which filling do you prefer? Butter, ricotta or cream cheese?"

"The cream cheese, I think. Wicked."

"Here, have another one, Mademoiselle." He offers her the plate.

"Oh, I've already had two. I have to watch my waistline."

"From where I'm standing, there's not a lot to worry about," he says flattering her again. "Just one more. Go on. I'm a doctor. You can trust me."

"Okay, then. If you insist." Rachel takes another scone, smiling coyly.

"And what about you, Kiki? Do you like scones?" Kiki wags her tail at Adam. "And you, Madame?" Adam offers me the plate, bringing me back into the conversation. I shake my head. "We can work it off after Rachel's gone," he says, patting my knee affectionately, before withdrawing his hand abruptly. "Oops! Sorry, Rachel. Put your hands over your ears. You're too young to know about such things." She laughs.

I've been watching the seduction from the sidelines, taking a back seat. Adam's wholehearted attention has been directed at bringing Rachel back into the fold. She is entranced with him. So am I. What a wonder he is. He changes tack.

"Pray tell about your work. You specialize in relationship counselling?"

"Yes, trying to repair couples' relationships and fractured families."

"Your work would be fraught with emotion, like mine. How do you manage it?"

Rachel's professional persona comes to the fore. "I step warily. Relationship breakdowns are minefields." She takes a breath. "When people are under threat, they can become defensive, angry. Angry people's vision becomes blinkered, full of shoulds and shouldn'ts, unable to see beyond their own fields of reference. They expect others to change to fit in with their world view."

"It's like cancer in a way, too, isn't it, Rachel? Something that eats away at the fabric of one's confidence and wellbeing. How do you counteract it?"

"That's a good analogy, Adam." She smiles at him. "The treatment I use, my chemo, if you like, are concepts. Concepts which are often alien to warring sides – tolerance, compassion, listening to one another, acceptance, understanding and respect for other people's choices and values. Ultimately, it's trying to defuse situations, not assigning blame when people don't behave as you expect or want."

Adam smiles warmly at her. "Getting that across must be very difficult."

"It is. Very. And exasperating at times."

"Cultural norms can become straitjackets. They can impede people thinking for themselves and prevent them from realizing their unique potential. Thinking outside the square is a fundamental premise in the world of research which I inhabit."

"So true."

"I've noticed people become more judgmental as they age. I hope I never get that disease." Adam reaches over, grabs my hand and kisses it. "Live and let live is my creed." Our fingers intertwine. Rachel watches, mulling over his words.

"More tea anyone?" I ask. Rachel and Adam shake their heads.

"No, thanks, Eve," says Rachel, giving me a warm smile.

She stands up. "I've got to go. I arranged to meet Richard and Jeremy for dinner, although I don't know where I will fit it in." Adam stands. She turns to him, her green eyes shining. "Lovely to meet you, Adam. I've really enjoyed talking with you. I do hope we'll meet again soon."

"Lovely to meet you, too, Rachel." He kisses her on both cheeks.

She turns to me and gives me a kiss on the cheek. "Thank you for inviting me, Eve. I've had the loveliest time."

"My pleasure, Rach. It was good to see you again." I pat her fondly on the arm. "I hope I see you again, soon." Her eyes smile at me and she kisses me again.

I close the door and lean against it, sighing with relief. "Come here, you," Adam says, reaching over and putting his arms around me. I wrap my arms around his neck, nuzzle my head into it and sway in time with him.

"Thank you for that. She was putty in your hands."

"Now it's your turn, tu belle femme. He grabs my hand and leads me upstairs. I smile. Kiki starts to follow us. Adam turns to her. "Stay, Kiki. Adults only. Your turn will come." Kiki sits, quivering and smiling. A knowing smile.

60. Seasons of my soul

Sitting on my window seat, sipping coffee, I lovingly look at the Dogwood trees and the living canvas on display before me. Spring's burgundy foliage and showy red blossoms have given way to summer's deep green leaves and clusters of shiny red berries. A host of winged creatures hover about, birds, bees and butterflies, queuing up to feed on nature's largesse.

A female eastern bluebird alights on a nearby branch and sits, patiently waiting. Her mate, a brilliant blue male, flies in, sits opposite and feeds her an insect. The summer breeding season has begun. Another brood will soon be on its way. My heart expands. Nature, in all its wisdom, is showing me that not only does life go on, it is ever-changing; and that the seasons of nature resonate with the seasons of my soul.

My eyes drift slowly downwards to the urn containing William's ashes sitting at the base of the tree. When I placed it there over eight years ago, I believed my life was over, too. I sat here and watched each season go by, longing for William, yearning to hold him once more. I didn't believe in a future for me. I believed my future was to be irrevocably melded in the past with William, that ours was a once in a lifetime love. Joined at the hip until death us do part. I never believed I would find love again. Perhaps I was just too scared to find out. Then William, in all his wisdom, asked me to let him go. Sometimes he knows me better than I do.

"And I did let go, Sweetheart." I look at the urn and smile. "Well not fully, yet, but I did open up my world and awaken to life and living again. I surprised myself, surprised you, too with some of my exploits, I imagine."

I have learned to listen to my inner voice and spiritual guidance, even if it did challenge conventional thinking about age and being a woman. I reconnected with the beauty of life and, in so doing, I found a sexual self I didn't know existed. But, more than that, much more than that, I found the possibility that love could still be there.

"I'm not scared anymore, Sweetheart. I don't know what the future holds but I do know that to be truly open to the possibility of creating a new life with Adam, I have to let go my vice like grip of the past and you as my safe harbor; and that means letting go of your ashes." I know now that it doesn't mean I stop loving William. I will always love William.

Love is eternal. Nothing is ever lost. He is part of me. I don't think you ever get over losing someone you love, but I have learned to live with it. You don't think you will stop hurting, but you do. Time does heal. Pain diminishes with time. I have also learned my heart is capable of loving more than one person. Starting over with someone else won't negate what William and I had. Just as paradise ducks start over again when their mate has died.

And what William and I had won't negate the new possibilities I have with Adam. I am not the same woman. I have grown. Although I yearned for a sexual reawakening, I have found much more than that. This past year has allowed me to understand how much of my sexuality had been repressed. Now, for the first time in my life, I feel the real me and my sexual self is unfolding. No artifice, nothing hidden. I no longer have to hide. I have found a man who understands and accepts me unconditionally, all of me — who I have been, who I am, and I know that will extend to the me who is yet to come. That is a gift beyond imagining. One I've been longing for and one worth pursuing and celebrating.

But first, I have to let go of William. Tomorrow.

61. Moving on

I wake early. The color of the pre-dawn sky is sublime. Pale blues and greens, silvery in intensity. The first splashes of color are apricot and cream, then deeper stronger pinks and purples gradually spread across the sky. Different, but still beautiful. Dawn colors delight and often surprise me. I love surprises.

As I reach into the bedside drawer for my set of Tarot cards, Kiki stirs and wags her tail good morning. Sometimes I think she's clairvoyant too. She understands me and my quirkiness. I shuffle the deck and turn one up for William – *The Fool*. I shuffle again, for me. *The Fool: the beginning of a new journey. Innocent adventurers taking a leap of faith into the unknown.* I smile. Together as ever, leaving our limbos behind.

Sunlight streams through the bedroom window. I look out on a clear blue sky. Time to meet the day.

"Walkies," I call. I slip on my track gear and head down the stairs, my loyal Welshie a couple of steps in front, tail wagging, knowing the routine. She heads to the laundry where her lead is, then waits patiently while I fasten it. I open the door and Mother Nature greets me once more.

The garden is sighing, sated after the overnight rain. Fresh aromas fill the chill morning air. As we start heading to the woodlands behind the house, all I can hear are the sounds of my breathing, my runners and Kiki's paws squelching in the damp grass. A slight movement near the pond catches my eye. Two red-throated loons are floating on the water. My heart skips a beat. William is here again. As Kiki and I continue on our walk, the loons wail in unison. It is a magical sound.

Later, wearing my ruby-red sweater – ruby for passion, love and precious memories — I walk around to the front of the house, where we married twenty-three years ago. The sun is overhead, shining down on the red Dogwoods and their dense green summer foliage and red fruits. A butterfly alights gently on a leaf.

"Just you and me today, Sweetheart. I know you are here. It's time to say goodbye. Thanks for staying around so long. I felt safer exploring with you around. I wanted to be sure. But, then again, so did you. Now it's time for both of us to move on into our brave new worlds. Hopefully happiness awaits."

I push up the sleeves of my sweater, revealing one slender arm after another, the deceptive fragility of the milky white skin, belying the inner strength gathered there. I pick up the urn, twist off the top and shake it. As the ashes spill out, a cloud of dust rises up then settles at the foot of the tree. Tears fill my eyes.

"Goodbye, Sweetheart. I love you. I'll always love you." As I let go of his ashes, I am letting go of William and, finally, finally, moving on. I sit down on a nearby rock and press play on my cell. As Lonestar's *Amazed*, the song William asked me to play at his funeral, wafts through the garden, I hear him singing to me once more.

I don't know how you do what you do
I'm so in love with you, it just keeps getting better
I want to spend the rest of my life with you by my side
Forever and ever
Everything little thing you do
Baby I'm amazed by you

I pick up the urn and check inside. "Oh, no. Please, no," I cry out. A clump of ashes is stuck to the bottom. I sit there, hugging the urn, tears streaming down my face wondering what on earth William is trying to tell me now. My eyes are inexorably drawn upwards as a plane flies low overhead.

"Europe? You want me to scatter the remaining ashes in Europe? No. No way. It's taken me eight years to pluck up this courage. Today, Sweetheart. It has to be today. We both have to let go and move on." I thump the urn on the ground a couple of times then shake it vigorously, dislodging the clump. I upend the urn and scatter the remaining ashes, singing to myself *Baby I'm amazed by you*. And I am.

The future now beckons. A future worth dreaming about.

62. Follow your bliss

I awake refreshed after only a few hours' sleep. Adam is still asleep. As I lie here, beside him, a peace envelops me. My body is in harmony with my mind and soul. When I am with him, I stop thinking in words, I relax and enter another zone where feelings are foremost, allowing the sensations of him to wash over me like waves. Sometimes the waves just lap gently around my feet moving in and out of the crevices between my toes, soothing, searching, seeking, then withdrawing. At others, they buffet me before moving back.

Now and again, they rise up threatening to roll over me, retreating just before I crash to the seafloor below. Everything else ceases to exist and it is just me. I can let go and exist purely in the moment, in the ecstasy of the moment, but each successive moment is part of a movement which in turn becomes a symphony where the crescendo slowly builds.

My primary sense of him is touch and I am revelling in it, all of it, from the soothing comfort of the cuddles, the hugs, snuggling up to him in bed with my legs wrapped around him, my sex pressed hard up against him, to the ritualistic mutual stroking of our bodies and fingers, the exquisite pressure on the bridge of my nose and the delicate tracery of my face and hair. His mouth and tongue gently suckling on my nipples send ripples to my inner core. I shiver just thinking about it.

I love the way he gently turns or positions my body when we start out, his fingers making tender incursions in and around the heart of my sex, into each and every orifice, his penis rubbing nearby, the promise of what is to come almost unbearable. When he finally decides on an entry point, I sigh and gather him deep inside me, riding his fingers or his penis, or both, softly, gently, slowly savoring it for as long as I can or as fast and hard as the moment or movement dictates, but always with a heat at my core. All the way down to the raw power of the animalistic and erotic anal sex with my hands on the violin playing my heart out, the final movement in our symphony of sex.

I look over at the man lying beside me. I love this man. I always have, but in a different way now. I love what he does to me and the way that he does it. He is so considerate and caring of me and so passionate. And I love being with him. I think back to last night. By the time we finish making love, I am sated beyond moving. Adam leans over and presses his fingers between my eyebrows. I look at him, loving it, wanting more, more of him.

"What does this woman want?" He asks, searching my eyes, searching for answers. His fingers run over my lips. My body quivers. I lie there, looking up at him, a face I've come to love. We talk. We eat and then we make love again and again. This is more than sex. Much more. I want him with a passion and I want him to want me with a passion, but a passion that will linger long after the lovemaking has finished. But we'd both have to let go of so much in our past to discover it. Are we ready for that?

"Over a year ago, someone asked me what this woman wanted and I could only think in terms of what I didn't want. I certainly wasn't looking for a lover, heaven forbid. Now? What does this woman want?" My finger traces his lips and I answer. "Someone to make my heart sing, my spirit soar, my body quiver and my garden grow." I draw his face to mine. "Someone like you. Being with you, making love with you, is sheer bliss." I kiss him tenderly. "I love having you in my life."

"Good," he responds, his eyes smiling warmly. "Then follow your bliss."

"The Hero's Journey," I say smiling in return, "Joseph Campbell."

He nods. *"Follow your bliss and don't be afraid, and doors will open where you didn't know they were going to be."*

The alarm rouses me from my reverie. Adam sits up, already alert. He leans over and gives me a squeeze. "I have to go. Early start."

"It's a full moon on Saturday night. How about dinner at my place?"

"I'd love to." He kisses me on each cheek then slides back the bedcovers. I reach for my iPad to check my horoscope.

GEMINI: You have an inventive, dynamic mind; now even more than ever. Celebrate that part of yourself! It makes you an exciting, creative person, someone other people can't get enough of -- especially today. In many ways, you're on top of the world at the moment. Here's a good exercise for you:

Stretch your mind to believe in at least three impossible things — and do it before breakfast. This could become one of your regular habits.

Three impossible things. I smile and hug myself. I know what they are.

63. Full moon

"**F**abulous, Eve. You can cook almost as well as I can," says Adam, teasingly, forking the last of his Boeuf Bourguignon into his mouth. "A Bastille Day dinner. I haven't celebrated Bastille Day for many a long year. Nor in such a fabulous setting and…" he adds thoughtfully, "never in France." He picks up his champagne, takes a sip and looks around, deep in thought. We're in the conservatory, surrounded by the moonlit night outside, the room adorned with sprays of orchids and flickering candlelight, Edith Piaf's hauntingly beautiful voice playing in the background. I sip my champagne looking over the rim of the glass at him. *Non, Je ne regrette rien* fills the room. Our eyes meet.

I lean over and reach for his hand and mouth the words, "No, I regret nothing." Our fingers intertwine, stretching out and pressing against one another. Adam squeezes my hand. "I've made Tarte tatin for dessert. Do you want to wait a while?"

"Yes, please," he says, patting his stomach and grinning. "I'd like to storm the Bastille, but I'll have to wait a while to do that, too." He stands up and holds out his hand. "Let's sit for a while. I've something important I want to run by you." We move over to the window seat. Adam sits with his back against one side with legs outstretched. He pats in between his legs. I slide in between them, easing my back into his chest and my head into his neck. As he wraps his arms around me, *La Vie En Rose* starts to play. He places his cheek against mine and holds me close. I close my eyes and translate in my mind as Piaf's soulful voice melts my heart.

Hold me close and hold me fast
The magic spell you cast
This is la vie en rose
When you kiss me heaven sighs
And though I close my eyes
I see la vie en rose.

"Beautiful," Adam whispers in my ear, then blows in it. His hot breath sends tingles all through me. He mouths my ear, then kisses it. I shiver at the touch of his warm, inviting mouth. Slowly and gently, he blows another hot breath into my ear, before kissing it again. My nether regions quiver with anticipation.

"Yes, beautiful. Her voice is heaven sent," I manage to say.

"Not her, you."

"Thank you." I give him a squeeze. "What did you want to talk to me about?"

"Later," he says, his fingers now dancing deliciously in and out and around my ear. "It's time to storm the Bastille." He lays me down and kisses me, passionately. As I kiss him back my body starts arcing up. His fingers find my panties and he pulls them off. His mouth all hot and wet on mine, he devours me.

He initiates a three-pronged attack – one finger in my behind, another in my vagina and the third on my clit. I moan with delight, not sure which way to move.

"Wait," I call out.

"Wait?" he stops, pulling back, looking at me puzzled. "What for, Woman? The barricades are nearly down."

"I want you to make love to me in the moonlight. It's a full moon tonight." I look at him, grinning wildly.

"Your wish is my command," he says kissing me hard, and pulling my bottom lip with his teeth, before standing up, bowing and offering his hand. "Madame."

ॐ

We are on Aphrodite's Altar. Adam's legs are stretched out in front of him, me behind, my legs astride him. I dribble the massage oil over his upright back. The oil slick shines in the moonlight, highlighting his beautiful body. My hands smear the oil over his back, neck and arms before beginning to massage his back deeply, fingers pressing, kneading into his muscles, finding their way around his buttocks and into his butt crack now and then. He groans, rocking backwards and forwards with the movement of my hands. I kiss his ear, blow in it, mouth it and kiss it again. He moans.

"Lean back into me." He does, his head against my neck. He kisses me on the neck, then nibbles at me. When I pour oil on his chest, he jumps. I massage it in, spreading it over his chest and his arms. I reach over and pour more on his thighs, then massage it in again. My hand is straying nearer and nearer to his *wand of light.*

Adam lies there with my arms around him, eyes closed, body rocking in time to the movement of my hands stroking him, soothing him. Then my fingers start delicately tracing pathways down his arms, his chest, and tantalizingly up and down his thighs, before finally touching his penis. It jumps and jumps again when I pour more oil on it. I start massaging it gently, encasing it with my hands, stroking it then tickling and teasing it with my fingers. I massage it up and down using both hands. His breathing changes. I stop, cupping his hardness in my hands. I blow in his ear then place my warm mouth over it, kissing it. He shivers and sits up.

"My turn," he says, turning to kiss me. As I stand up, Adam slides back in the seat and opens his legs. "Sit here, facing the moon." As I sit in between his legs, the moon bathes me in silvery light. He pushes me forward slightly then sensuously trails oil down my back. I moan as his hands start kneading my neck and back, swaying backwards and forwards like a puppet on his string. As his mouth turns his attention to my ear, lightning bolts shoot through me.

"Alright, now lean back into me." I do, and he tips oil over my front, dribbling it over each breast then down between them, and some over each thigh. He massages my breasts, then his hands find my sex, both hands working together, stroking either side. I moan some more. I want more. He senses it and his fingers find their way in and out of me, rhythmically in and out. I lean back into him and allow him to pleasure me. I'm tingling all over, squirming with delight.

Another three-pronged attack brings me undone. I cry out as the waves wash over me, up my spine, through my muscles, down my stomach and deep into the very core of my being. My body trembles as he wraps his arms around me, his cheek pressed to mine. He holds me until the trembling subsides.

Adam returns with a bottle of Mumm Rosé and champagne flutes. We sit there on the love seat in the garden of my delights, drinking, suspended in time and stark naked. Our bodies, still moist from our lovemaking, lean comfortably into one another. The silence is broken by the sound of water bubbling across rocks and cascading gently into the water lily-filled pond.

It is midnight. After a hellishly hot summer's day, the air is warm and eerily still; the sky an ethereal purple color. As the moon emerges from a behind a dark cloud, we look up to the night sky. Tonight, is a full moon. The full moon signals completion, completion of one cycle and the beginning of another. I quiver.

"To us," Adam says, his eyes smiling.

"To us," I respond, kissing him gently on the lips.

"Talk about taking a giant leap for Womankind. Most people in our demographic populate their gardens with gnomes of various kinds. However, you, Eve, have clearly upped the neighbourhood ante by collecting naked men in yours." He raises his glass to toast again. "And in this garden of men, oh my, how you grow well. Take a bow." I laugh, a wry laugh. Naked at our age. Revelling in my sexuality at sixty. It wasn't always thus.

As I take a sip of champagne, I look into his eyes and smile. Déjà vu. A dream come true. The man of my dreams. I seat myself upon him, legs astride – Yab Yum style, then wrap my arms around his neck and inhale deeply. "I cannot imagine my world without you in it."

"Neither can I," he says, enfolding me with his arms.

"You do realize that we were meant to be."

"I do, indeed."

"That the Universe put you in my path."

"I understand the sentiment, Eve. Although the scientist in me doesn't fully understand the science. Fortunately, the same revelation came to me through my own research." He pauses, then whispers in my ear. "Which is why I propose that we live together, marry preferably."

I draw back in surprise. Is he mocking me, playing with me? I look deep into his eyes. Such softness there, but a seriousness, too. He draws me back to him and kisses me tenderly.

"I realize this is all rather sudden, Eve, but I do love you." He kisses me again, suckling my lips. "Very much indeed. Unfortunately, there is a condition to the proposal," he says, smiling at me, tantalizingly. "One I do hope you will be able to meet." His body starts to move powerfully beneath me.

I laugh, wondering what the hell is coming next. "A condition? Pray tell what is it?" I move around on him, teasing him, connecting with him, wanting him with a passion again. I am gloriously wet.

"That we live in Paris for the first two years."

"Paris! Live in Paris?" I scream with delight. "You're kidding!"

"No, I'm deadly serious. That's what I was going to ask you earlier." His eyes are smiling again. "I applied for a research position at L'Hôpital Saint-Louis just before we met. A two-year posting. I've just received confirmation of my appointment today. I start in two weeks' time." He looks at me, his eyes talking, now. "Will you come to Paris with me? And will you marry me?"

"Yes, and yes; I'd love to!" Our mouths move into each other and we meld. Still holding onto his neck, our mouths locked together, in perpetual motion, I lift myself up a fraction so he can enter me. My petals opening to welcome him as I ease myself back down. I whimper with delight as I feel him inside me. I hold him there, savoring him, and our blessed union. Savoring the idea of a life with this wonderful man. And, in Paris.

Two impossible things in one night. I can't believe it. Maybe, one day soon... the third. But first things first. I start to move.

64. Brave new worlds

"See you in four weeks," he says, his luscious mouth devouring mine. "I'll be back. Next time you're coming with me. As my wife."

"How will I live without you?" I say grabbing hold of his beautiful butt, and bringing him closer to me. I sigh and nestle into his chest. Such goodness and such sanctuary there. I squeeze him tighter. I look up into his blue eyes, such loving eyes. Tears start to gather.

His finger traces under my eyes. "No tears. I'll be back. Don't worry. You won't have much free time. I've left everything in your capable hands. There's a lot to do." I nod. There is. "We have the marriage license, a date — in the fall, on the occasion of the new moon, as my precious Little Flower requested," he kisses me on the nose affectionately, "a celebrant, and..." Adam's eyes start to twinkle, "a photographer." I smile. "I'm looking forward to meeting the redoubtable young man." I stroke his arm, lovingly. Such understanding. "Heaven help Rachel if you are any guide." I laugh. I'm playing matchmaker, trying to engineer another happy ending. I squeeze him tightly. Anthony and Rachel together? Maybe?

"Thank you. I love you, you wonderful man."

"And I love you, too, Little Flower," he says kissing me once more, before patting me on the bum. "Time to go." I hop in the car, blow him one last kiss, then drive home. Little Flower, how lovely.

I check my list of to do's – invitations first, quarantine regulations for Kiki, check passport expiry, visa requirements and realtors. Then my orchids, they're spiking again. My precious babies need feeding and tending. Who will look after them while I'm away? Who will look after the house? I wonder if Richard and Jeremy will come and live here while we're away to look after my precious beauties. We'll see.

I put the four invitations in the mail box and hold up the fifth. I kiss it then squeeze it to my heart. "The third impossible thing, Kiki." I place it on top of the others and turn up the red flag. "I trust in the Universe to make it happen." Kiki wags her tail, agreeing with me, as ever. She's missing Adam, as am I. We've decided to just to have my nearest and dearest come to the wedding.

ॐ

Susan is on the phone the next day. "Oh, Eve, what wonderful news. David and I are delighted for you. Of course, we'll come."

"Come and visit us in Paris, too. Although, Adam hasn't found an apartment yet. He's been too busy settling in at the hospital and the university."

"Of course, we will Eve. William will be happy for you, too," she says warmly.

"I know. See you soon, Susan." Just as I put the cell down, it rings again. "Hello, Cindy."

"Eve, Darling," her voice is trilling. "I was just going to ring you and give you my news when I opened your invitation. How exciting."

"It is, isn't it, Cindy?"

"When did you decide all this?"

"Two weeks ago. When Adam was offered the posting," I say smiling.

"I can hear you smiling, you Darling girl. And I've got something else that will make you smile..."

"Oooooh, don't tell me you've found husband number four," I say excitedly.

"Yes, Darling. I have. Dylan. Dear Dylan. He..."

"That's wonderful news, Cindy. When are you getting married?"

"Not for a while, yet. Lots of legal stuff to attend to first. But he's Divine, with a capital D. I think I'd marry him even if he weren't rich."

"Fabulous. Bring the Divine Dylan to the party so I can check him out."

"That's why I was ringing, Darling girl. I will."

"Bye, Cindy."

"Ciao!" I put the cell down again and a text alert sounds. Rachel.

Go Girl! The best news. I'll be there with bells on. Uncle William is pleased. :)

I laugh. So am I. The cell rings again. Richard. I can't believe it. Such synchronicity. "Hello, Richard," I say laughing.

"What's funny?"

"It's like a hot line here."

"Got your invitation, Eve. Great news. Can I bring Jeremy?"

"Of course, you can Richie."

"We're living together, now," his voice softens, happiness wafting out.

Such synchronicity. The Universe is falling into place. "I'm so pleased for you, Richie. Actually, I must be psychic. I was thinking of asking you two to live here while we're away. I must have known."

"We'd love to."

I laugh. "Better talk it over with Jeremy first. I don't want to cause any trouble between you. Perhaps come here for dinner so he can see what you're letting him in for."

"Okay. Talk soon. Bye, Eve."

"Bye, Richie." I'm excited for him and for me. We are letting go, letting go of the past and creating our own brave new worlds. I smile, as has become my wont, a smile that wraps around me and holds me tight.

65. A goddess

Little Flower,

Just to let you know I've finally found us an apartment — a lovely two-bedroom apartment in Canal St Martin, with a loft and a courtyard where you can grow herbs and veg. It's within walking distance of the hospital. Close to Gare du Nord and Gare de L'Est. A great area. You and Kiki will love it. Really hanging out to be with you again.

All my love,

Adam xxx

🐦

Dearest Adam,

I have been in a waking-dreaming state all night, conscious of my body moving, writhing about on the sheets, slowly, sensuously, sexually but softer like the whimpers and moans that are the accompaniment. There is a languor to the movement, a lusciousness about my body, the desire to be with you on a slow burn. Knowing you will be with me allows me to savor the sensations, to drink deep of the pleasure, letting it slide its way down my throat and into my belly. And I hold it there.

I can still feel you, echoes of your skin on my skin, your hands guided by their magnetic compass finding new sources of pleasure, you deep inside me thrusting with a raw power that unleashes my soul and calls me to abandon everything previously known, to go where I have never dared before. My body is creating new memories where pleasure is paramount, ecstasy a given, freedom is at the forefront and love is all around.

When I finally wake, I slide my hands over my body, my fingers find my sex, the resulting small jolts my reward. I moisten my fingers with saliva and touch myself, gently, lovingly. My clit lights up at the touch but I leave it wanting. I insert a couple of fingers inside but not deeply before withdrawing them and fondly patting my mound of Venus. It is an acknowledgement of the desire, the ripeness and readiness of my body, the fire that will burn, and the passion and pleasure I know will surely come when you are with me again tomorrow, my love.

Eve xxx

&

I lean up, one elbow on the pillow, and look at my man, my tall, dark and handsome man, soon be my husband and then at my wedding present. I drift back to yesterday.

"I hope you like it," Adam had said as he handed me a huge package. I tore open the wrapping and gasped when I saw it. My

355

eyes kept going from Adam to the present and back again. Tears starting to spill over.

"I love it. She's beautiful."

"You're beautiful, Eve. A goddess."

I look at the evocative nude painting again. Of me with an orchid in my hair, resting against a tree in a bed of flowers. I smile, a smile that warms me heart and soul. I am her. A goddess. A goddess in the garden of my delights, the culmination of a sacred rite of passage from widow to woman to goddess.

I turn back to Adam and smile again. I run my fingers through his hair and tug that cute lock of hair. "Today's the day," I say bending over and kissing him on each eye, each cheek, his nose and finally his mouth. I pat his chest. "Any second thoughts?"

"Yes," he says, abruptly rolling me on my back and kneeling astride me. He grabs hold of my hands and pushes my arms above my head, arms outstretched, fingers entwined. His head leans down, his blue eyes gentling me. He trails his penis across my belly and breasts. "I want to make love to you, again." He kisses me deeply. "And again." An aftershock racks my body. They've been confounding me all night. And another. And another.

"There, my wonderful man, you have your answer."

❧

"Eve, Darling." Cindy comes over and kisses me on each cheek. "Mwah, mwah." She stands back looking at me admiringly. "You look wonderful, Eve."

"Thank you, Cindy. So do you." I look at her appreciatively. It must have taken her hours to look so glamorous. I turn to the handsome grey-haired man looking admiringly at her, too. "Welcome, Dylan?" I offer my hand. He places my hand to his lips and kisses it lightly.

"Sorry we're late. Traffic." I nod at him and smile. A gallant gentleman. A perfect match for Cindy.

"That's probably what's holding up Rachel," I say. "Come over and meet the others. Everyone else is here." As we pass by the pond, the rainbow koi dart in and among the islands of lily pads, seeking sanctuary from the loons who returned two days ago. The few remaining water lilies bask in the autumn sunshine. Warm fall colors are everywhere. The garden of my delights is at its best.

Adam is deep in conversation with David and Susan. Richard and Jeremy are talking animatedly with Anthony, who has his camera slung around his neck. I hand Cindy and Dylan a glass of champagne each and take them over to Adam.

"Adam, Darling. How lovely to see you again." Cindy kisses him on the cheek. "Mwah. And Paris, how fabulous. I'm positively green with envy." She turns to Dylan, touching him on the arm, "We'll have to go over and visit, Darling." Dylan beams at her. "Oh, excuse my manners, this is Dylan." Dylan, this is Susan, David and Adam," pointing a perfectly manicured deep red fingernail to each one in turn.

"Eve!" Rachel calls out, her face hidden by a huge bouquet of orchids. Rich autumn tonings with matching highlights on her red hair. I go over to greet her.

"Sorry I'm late, Eve. The flowers weren't ready," she says, poking her face to one side to kiss me. "Getting married and living in Paris. I'm so excited for you."

"Me, too," I say beaming.

"Can I come and stay with you?"

"Of course, you can, Rachel."

Richard walks over to greet her. "Hey, Sis." He reaches down and kisses her fondly on the cheek. "Here, give them to me. I'll take the flowers inside for you?"

"No, let me take her photo first," yells Anthony, opening his camera. Rachel turns to him in surprise. "Hold it there. He points his camera at her. Their eyes meet. He beams at her and she smiles back. He takes a few snaps, while she looks straight at him. "Perfection."

"Here, Eve," says Rachel, thrusting the flowers at me, her eyes sparkling. She quickly turns back to Anthony. I smile. Adam wanders up and puts his arm around me. As he does the loons call to each other. We look at them then at each other, and grin.

"Everybody's here and everyone seems happy," he says, hugging me to him. I nuzzle into his neck.

"Yes, very. What a relief."

"Ready?"

"Yes." I kiss him tenderly on the neck. "See you soon."

Ready for the next phase of my life. I walk inside.

66. Love beckons once more

"Everyone ready?" Wolf, the celebrant asks as we gather in the conservatory. Kiki wags her tail, a doggy smile on her face and a big yellow bow around her neck. I grab hold of the beautiful blonde-haired woman beside me and hug her.

"Thank you for coming. It means so much to have you here again." She kisses me on the cheek, grabs both hands then stands back to look at me adoringly. At the soft crepe dress in fall colors, at the gold orchid in my hair, at a face that can't stop smiling.

"You look divine, Eve. Absolutely divine." I kiss her and nod to Wolf.

Vivaldi's *Autumn* fills the air. As a flurry of violins celebrates with song and dance that the harvest is safely gathered in, we line up at the conservatory door. I watch as Wolf goes first, walking over to the center of the bridge where Adam is waiting. Kiki next. Then the third impossible thing walks out into the soft autumn sunshine.

Two seconds later, Rachel screams, "Mom," and bursts into tears. Ella walks over the bridge to Rachel and Richard, puts one arm around each of them and hugs them to her. They turn to face me, tears streaming down their faces. I wait a few more seconds then walk out.

The violins are quieter as the leaves fall softly from the trees in this, the mellowest and most beautiful of seasons. All I can see is Adam, the man I am going to live them with. His eyes never leave me as I walk to the center of the Japanese bridge. Our hands and hearts reach out for one another and take hold.

Love beckons once more.

Acknowledgements

To Leslie, Anthony and Michael, my marvellous muses,
for inspiring this tale and showing me another side of life.

To Shaney Marie, a wise and beautiful goddess,
for teaching me about sacred sexuality.

To Cousin Carolyn, for loving me, believing in me
and being there for me.

To the Goddess Kimmy, my divine friend, for her editing,
encouragement, support, and above all, her belief in me.

About the author

In this chapter of life, I have morphed into a wise woman, an elder, an old soul and a goddess in many guises. Using moon goddess symbolism, which echoes the rhythms of nature, I am in the winter of my life and the new moon phase. A time of new beginnings and rebirth.

A warm, nurturing and sensitive soul, I live in a beautiful bush garden setting in outer suburban Melbourne, with my precious poodle, Bella. I am a passionate nature lover, gardener and orchid grower with a deep commitment to health and well-being, sustainability and spirituality.

After a long and successful career in education, time to allow my creativity to flourish felt like freedom personified. Now, I am variously, a mentor, speaker, writer, cum editor and publisher, with a penchant for collecting inspirational quotes and creating beautiful books – books which delight, inspire and touch hearts, minds and souls.

I also write under the pen name, Chrissie Anthony. Chrissie is an incurable romantic, hopelessly addicted to fantasy, fairy tales, love, romance and happy endings.

Christine's first book was *The Hidden Journey – Melanoma up Close and Personal.* The second book an illustrated children's book, *Tahlia, You Can Do It!* The third, *In the Garden of my Delights – Inspiration and Quotes for the Heart and Soul.*

As Chrissie Anthony, another quote book, *How Do I Love Thee?* Then *Phantoms,* written with Michael Leon. Both books are published under the Australian Inspiration imprint.

Christine's latest book, *Goddesses in You – Discovering the myths and archetypes that are your reality* will be released late in 2022 by Exisle Publishing.

www.christinelister.com.au

Christine in the garden of her delights.